A STUDY IN TREASON

A DAUGHTER OF SHERLOCK HOLMES MYSTERY

ALSO BY LEONARD GOLDBERG

A STUDY IN TREASON

A DAUGHTER OF SHERLOCK HOLMES MYSTERY

Leonard Goldberg

MINOTAUR BOOKS

NEW YORK

A STUDY IN TREASON. Copyright © 2018 by Leonard Goldberg. All rights
reserved. Printed in the United States of America. For information,
address St. Martin's Press, 175 Fifth Avenue, New York, N.Y. 10010.

www.minotaurbooks.com

Designed by Omar Chapa

The Library of Congress Cataloging-in-Publication Data is available
upon request.

ISBN 978-1-250-10106-8 (hardcover)
ISBN 978-1-250-10107-5 (ebook)

Our books may be purchased in bulk for promotional, educational,
or business use. Please contact your local bookseller or the Macmillan
Corporate and Premium Sales Department at 1-800-221-7945, extension
5442, or by email at MacmillanSpecialMarkets@macmillan.com.

First Edition: June 2018

10   9   8   7   6   5   4   3   2   1

For Mia and Jackson, and the
I.M. in both of them

CONTENTS

AUTHOR'S NOTE

More than a few inquiries have been received regarding the relationship between the Edwardian-era Joanna Blalock, the daughter of Sherlock Holmes, and the modern-day Joanna Blalock featured in my earlier novels. Allow me to remove any confusion by stating that the Edwardian Joanna was the grandmother of the modern-day Joanna. The family history was recorded as follows. On reaching adulthood, the first Joanna's son, Johnnie, endeavored alongside his famous mother and became one of London's premier investigators. But over time his interest in the sciences grew more and more intense, and he was later to enroll at Cambridge University to pursue the study of aerodynamics. Prior to graduation, however, he enlisted in the Royal Air Force and eventually flew fighter planes defending Britain in World War II. After the war he returned to Cambridge and graduated with first-class honors before immigrating to San Francisco where he married and shortly thereafter was appointed to a professorship in theoretical physics at the University of California at Berkeley. Early in his tenure he founded an elite group of scientists who were pioneers in the development of supercomputers. His firstborn, the modern-day Joanna, inherited her father's brilliance and her grandmother's remarkable skill of deductive reasoning, both of which formed the foundation for her becoming a renowned forensic pathologist at Memorial Hospital in Los Angeles. The current Joanna was not told of her unique lineage, for her father believed its revelation was certain to bring unwanted publicity and unreasonable demands, which would work to his daughter's disadvantage. However, upon her father's death, Joanna found an antiquated copy of *The Daughter of Sherlock Holmes* in his safe-deposit box. In the novel, her father, Johnnie, was portrayed as the son of the first Joanna Blalock who was in fact the daughter of Sherlock Holmes. Like her father before her, the modern-day Joanna decided to keep her extraordinary bloodline a deep secret, for she too was aware of the undesired consequences that were sure to follow its disclosure. Nevertheless, with the illustrious history of the Blalocks now revealed, I think it fair to say that the genius of Sherlock Holmes has been passed down through the generations and is still with us to this very day.

There is nothing more deceptive than an obvious fact.

—Arthur Conan Doyle
The Boscombe Valley Mystery

A
STUDY IN TREASON
A DAUGHTER OF SHERLOCK HOLMES MYSTERY

INTRODUCTION

The case I am about to disclose was of such importance that
I, John Watson, Jr., M.D., along with my father and my wife
Joanna, were required to sign the Official Secrets Act, which
bound us to keep secret all matters revealed and committed
to us. Every twist and turn in this deep mystery centered on
a missing document so sensitive that the fate of Europe may
well have rested upon it, and thus the need of absolute secrecy
for all those involved. However, with the passage of time and
the onset of the Great War, these impediments have been removed and the story of *A Study in Treason* can now be safely
told.

1

The Document

Late spring, 1914

There was joy in our rooms at 221b Baker Street that frosty London morning, but it was to be short-lived and soon replaced by a most somber mood. My father, John Watson, M.D., the close friend and longtime associate of the now dead Sherlock Holmes, was gradually recovering from a stroke he had suffered months earlier, but he continued to have weakness in his right leg, which caused him to limp noticeably on exertion. Of greater importance, those closest to him could tell that his mind, although still quite adequate, had not yet returned to its former self. It was in this regard that an eminent neurologist at St. Bartholomew's suggested we use repeated brain stimulation to enhance my father's mental acuity. Dear Joanna pursued this goal with zeal and spent hours on end reading and discussing old Sherlock Holmes cases with my father. The two never seemed to tire of these exchanges, with my father adding anecdotes never before revealed to the public. But the most enjoyable cerebral exercise for them was standing at the window overlooking Baker Street and studying the individuals passing by below.

"I say, Watson," Joanna said, and directed his attention across the busy street. "What do you make of the fellow hurrying to the bus stop?"

"He is scurrying for a bus," my father remarked. "Which indicates he is a man of modest means."

"The cut of his clothes would tell us that as well," Joanna observed. "Did you notice the wrapped gift he is carrying?"

"How do you know it is a gift?"

"Because it has a ribbon tied in a bow around it."

"And nicely done so," my father said. "I would think it is for his wife."

"Then you would think wrong," Joanna rebuked mildly. "For the man is a widower, as evidenced by the black band on his hat."

My father groaned to himself. "I too saw the band, but failed to connect it to the gift."

"The finer connections will come, Watson," Joanna said. "You must be patient, for the process cannot be hurried."

My father's attention was suddenly drawn to another individual below. "Oh, my goodness! I now see an absolutely crazed man coming our way."

My curiosity got the better of me and I rushed to the window to gaze out over my father's shoulder. Running down the sidewalk, which was still covered with yesterday's freak snowstorm, was a short, portly man, hatless against the cold, who was wildly turning his head from side to side, while at the same time slapping at his legs and chest with both hands. He kept his balding head down to such an extent that those walking toward him had to quickly move aside in order to avoid a collision.

"He is obviously very disturbed," I commented.

"A sad exhibition of a madman," my father agreed.

"Should we notify the police?" I asked.

Joanna shook her head. "There is no need, for he is neither disturbed nor mad."

"But his actions say otherwise," my father argued.

"Look carefully once more," Joanna recommended. "Observe the repeated motions of his head and hands. They will explain everything."

I, along with my father, studied the man as he drew closer to our window. Neither of us saw anything other than an obviously distraught, middle-aged man who appeared to be making uncontrollable motions with his hands. He paused briefly to raise his arms and then dig his fingers deeply into his waistcoat.

"Obviously it is small and quite precious," Joanna commented.

"What?" I asked.

"The object he is searching for," Joanna replied.

My father glanced at Joanna oddly. "Is that based solely on the poor man reaching into the pockets of his waistcoat?"

"It is based on everything he has shown us thus far," Joanna told him. "He is a man desperately searching for something he recently lost."

"Pray tell how you reached these conclusions," my father requested.

"By connecting all of his motions, for they have a common denominator," Joanna explained. "He is running because of the urgency of the matter, and the fact that he is hatless, despite the cold, tells us he has just discovered the loss and dashed out frantically to search for it. He keeps his head down and moving from side to side in hopes of spotting the lost item in the snow. And finally, he is not slapping at his thighs and waist uncontrollably, but rather patting at the pockets of his pants and waistcoat to determine if the item slipped off and is still in his possession."

"But what is this object?" I asked.

"A small, precious item that will fit easily in the pocket of his waistcoat," Joanna answered.

"A timepiece!" my father exclaimed. "It not only would have fit in his waistcoat, but could have unintentionally found its way into his pants pocket. Also notice that as he takes his hand away, there is a gold chain dangling from the waistcoat and that it has nothing attached to its end. I dare say a gold timepiece was in all likelihood once clasped onto it."

"Nicely done, Watson," Joanna said, with a genuine smile. "I must declare that you are coming along wonderfully well."

"That is because I have a most excellent guide," my father praised. "And she reminds me in every way that she is truly the daughter of Sherlock Holmes."

"Do you really believe I could match him?"

My father hesitated a moment before answering, "I would pay a handsome price to view the contest."

Gazing at the two before me, I could not help but remember how my life had changed since I first met Joanna only months ago. At the time I was, and continue to be, assistant professor of pathology at St. Bartholomew's Hospital where I spent long hours, but always managed to look after my father who was still residing at 221b Baker Street and was unfortunately in declining health. Despite his retirement and the fact that his close colleague Sherlock Holmes was long dead, people still sought his advice on criminal matters, which he dealt with in a most gentle and adroit manner. It was in my presence that the highly placed Harrelston family begged my father to investigate the apparent suicide of their son. Although hesitant to do so at first, he leaped at the chance when informed that the man's fall to his death was witnessed by Joanna Blalock and her young son, Johnnie, who is currently attending a distinguished boarding school in the Midlands. As was known only to my father, Joanna was the product of a one-time assignation between Sherlock Holmes and Irene Adler, the only woman ever to outwit him. Joanna was given up for adoption at birth, after her natural mother's death, and raised as Joanna Middleton, the adopted daughter of a child-less physician and his wife. But Joanna obviously inherited her biological father's and mother's brilliance. She read voraciously on a wide variety of subjects and became a highly skilled nurse, one of the few professions that allowed her to use her finely turned brain. Her medical training led her to become an amateur forensic detective. In her early twenties, her name became Joanna Blalock when she married Dr. John Blalock, a respected surgeon from an aristocratic family. But John died in a cholera epidemic and Joanna was left to raise her son alone, albeit in a world of wealth and privilege.

During our investigation of the Charles Harrelston death, Joanna joined our team and demonstrated her remarkable deductive skills to us and to Scotland Yard. It was she who dis-covered that the young man's death was premeditated murder and not suicide. Indeed it was she who set the ingenious trap that caught the killer. Thus, as I was to later write, Sherlock Holmes was after all still with us.

In the bright morning sunlight I found myself staring at the loveliness of Joanna and was once again reminded of her unique attributes and from whence they came. While her incredible deductive mind was no doubt that of Sherlock Holmes, her most attractive face, with its soft, patrician features and flawless skin, belonged to the stunning opera star Irene Adler. Either of her biological parents could have been responsible for Joanna's inquisitive, deep brown eyes and tall, trim figure. She was in fact an ideal mixture of genes that only God himself could have put together.

"Where are your thoughts, John?" Joanna asked, interrupting my reverie.

"I was thinking how fortunate I was to marry you," I replied.

"You caught me at a weak moment," Joanna jested.

The three of us chuckled heartily at my wife's quick and endearing wit that made her all the more lovable.

Just then the hatless man, who appeared to have given up hope, spotted a police constable and rushed over to him. The man spoke in an animated fashion and seemed to be pleading in earnest. The constable nodded and reached in his coat pocket for a rather large, gold timepiece, which he gave to the man. We watched the hatless man jump with joy, then shake the constable's hand over and over before dancing away.

"A timepiece it was," I remarked. "From its glitter and size, I would guess it came from a bygone era."

"Most likely an heirloom, which would make it impossible to replace and thus even more precious," Joanna added.

The constable was about to continue on his rounds, but he abruptly stopped as an official government car pulled up to the curb outside 221b Baker Street. He quickly cleared the sidewalk of passing pedestrians, then stood at attention for the occupant of the Wolseley limousine.

The formally dressed driver hurried around to open the

rear door, and out stepped a highly decorated senior naval officer in full regalia. The constable tipped and lifted his hat in respect.

"Espionage," my father whispered.

"Based on what?" Joanna asked at once.

"My past experience with Sir Harold Whitlock, who happens to be First Sea Lord of His Majesty's navy," my father remarked. "Holmes and I were involved with Sir Harold many years ago when he was director of naval intelligence. The matter was so delicate that I can only say it centered upon a spy at the very highest level of government."

"Was he uncovered?" I asked.

"And hanged." My father ran a quick hand across his silver-gray hair and smoothed out the tattered maroon smoking jacket he was wearing. "Do I look presentable?"

"Almost," Joanna said, and moved in to center my father's tie, which had gone astray. "But your smoking jacket leaves much to be desired. You really should replace it before it becomes nothing more than threads."

"Then I shall happily wear my threads," my father said, with a twinkle in his eyes.

I remained silent, for I knew full well that my father would continue to cling to the very old smoking jacket until the day he died, because it was the last vestige of his happier, exciting days with Sherlock Holmes. He sometimes spoke of Holmes as if the famous detective would suddenly reappear as he did after his deadly struggle with Professor Moriarity at the Reichenbach Falls.

Hearing the approaching footsteps on the stairs, Joanna said quickly, "If Sir Harold wishes John and me to leave, we shall take a long stroll to give you complete privacy."

"Perhaps the case is not of such great gravity," I suggested.

"I can assume it is," Joanna said with certainty. "Here we have the First Sea Lord, the highest-ranking naval officer in all of Britain, arriving on our doorstep unannounced in the early morning, with no aide or attaché at his side. He is without papers or briefcase and walks at a hurried pace. Thus, we can safely say this man carries a secret of immense importance with him."

"Then it must be espionage," I concluded.

The footsteps stopped, followed by a gentle rap on the door.

"We shall know shortly," Joanna said.

Miss Hudson, our landlady, showed the visitor in, then backed away, obviously awed by the admiral's presence. He waited for the door to close before speaking.

"I hope I am not intruding, Dr. Watson," Sir Harold said.

"Not at all, sir," my father greeted. "It is always a pleasure to see you. Allow me to introduce my son and his wife."

Sir Harold nodded to our names, then came back to my father. "I must ask to speak with you alone."

"Espionage again?" my father asked.

"I am afraid this is a state matter that requires absolute secrecy and cannot be spoken of in the presence of others," the First Sea Lord admonished. "There can be no exceptions, even for those we consider to be most trustworthy."

"I take it you wish me to become involved," my father said.

"I do indeed."

"Then you must include my son and his wife, for they are invaluable associates on whom I greatly depend."

Sir Harold hesitated before saying, "I am aware of your recent illness, but was told you had made a nearly complete recovery."

"And so I have," my father responded. "But that does not lessen the value of Joanna and John."

Pondering his dilemma, the First Sea Lord glanced back and forth between my wife and me, as if he were trying to assess our qualifications. Seconds ticked by in silence.

Joanna stepped forward and interceded. "Sir Harold, you are wasting time that I believe you have precious little of."

"I beg your pardon, madam," said he, taken aback by Joanna's outspokenness.

"Please forgive my abruptness," Joanna went on. "But it is obvious that you bring with you a most urgent matter and wish either advice or help. You will receive neither unless you include the three of us."

Sir Harold gave Joanna a long, studied look. "I take it you are the long-lost daughter of Sherlock Holmes, whom Inspector Lestrade spoke of so highly."

"I am."

"He said you could solve anything."

"He said too much."

"According to Lestrade, you have a knack for seeing clues others don't."

"I see what everyone else sees," Joanna explained. "But I think what no one else has thought."

"And what happens when there are no clues left behind?"

"There is no such crime," Joanna said. "Every criminal act leaves a trail that awaits a discerning eye."

Sir Harold hesitated once more. He was a tall, broad-shouldered man, with a square jaw and a steely gaze. His expression showed no indication of worry, but there were dark circles of sleeplessness under his eyes. In an authoritative tone he said, "You will all have to sign the Official Secrets Act."

"Agreed," Joanna said. "Let us sit by the fire and hear every detail of your story."

As we took our chairs, I stoked the smoldering logs to life while my father filled his favorite cherrywood pipe with tobacco. Sir Harold and Joanna kept their gazes fixed on one another, each taking the other's measure.

"Everything revolves around a highly secret document that has gone missing," Sir Harold began. "Should it fall into the wrong hands, the consequences would truly be disastrous. It is possible that the disaster has already occurred, but we pray this is not the case. The document was last seen three days ago at the country estate of the Duke of Winchester where it was to be copied. Let me assure you that every precaution was taken to—"

"The document," Joanna interrupted. "We must know its contents."

"I cannot share that information with you," Sir Harold said firmly. "It is known to only those at the uppermost level of government and must remain so."

"Even though we signed the Official Secrets Act?"

"Even though."

"You are placing a blindfold on us, yet you expect us to see."

"I have no other choice."

"Nor do we," Joanna said, rising to her feet. "I know you must have other pressing matters to attend to, as do we, so I wish you good day and every success in locating the missing document."

"If you had an inkling of the document's importance," Sir Harold stressed, "you would not—"

Joanna waved away the First Sea Lord's urging. "You are

asking us to locate a berry in the forest, yet you refuse to describe the berry."

"It is more like a needle in a haystack," Sir Harold said frankly.

"Which is even worse," Joanna said. "Since the event occurred at a country estate, I would think the local police were called in and, with their lack of success, you were forced to summon Inspector Lestrade from Scotland Yard to join the investigation. In that I suspect neither were given the details of the document, they no doubt floundered about and have muddied the waters even further. I daresay that with each passing moment the chances of recovering the document grow dimmer and dimmer."

"You seem to imply that being aware of the document's contents will be of paramount importance in locating it," Sir Harold said. "I do not see how, and need to be convinced before I disclose its nature."

"It is a straightforward matter of deduction," Joanna informed him. "This was a crime of purpose, which always leaves behind a trail one can follow. In this particular instance, the document's contents will tell us who benefits the most by stealing it."

"I did not say it was stolen."

"Was it misplaced, then?"

"No. That possibility has been excluded."

"Could it have been intentionally destroyed?"

"Absolutely not."

"Or found its way to some hidden place, such as beneath a rug or behind a desk drawer?"

"All searched, top to bottom, along with every other square inch of the library."

"Which leaves us with the singular explanation that it was stolen," Joanna concluded. "Moreover, the theft had to have been committed by someone who was aware of the document's contents and value. We too must have this information, for without it there is no hope of discovering the thief and retrieving the document."

Sir Harold exhaled resignedly and slowly nodded. "I see your point."

"Excellent," Joanna said. "And rest assured not a word spoken here will leave this room."

"Let me again emphasize how sensitive this document is," said he, fixing his eyes on the blazing logs before him. "The winds of war are now blowing across Europe. Each side is arming itself in preparation for the terrible event, which appears to be inevitable. It is Germany and its desire to dominate the continent that has precipitated matters. At this very moment, Kaiser Wilhelm is building up a mighty military power, especially his navy, to pursue his goal of dominance. In an effort to thwart the kaiser's desires, Britain has entered into an alliance with France called the French Treaty."

"That is not surprising," my father said. "We have the same enemy, and certainly Germany would expect this."

"But what the kaiser does not expect is the plan we have to thwart him," Sir Harold continued on. "It might even prevent war and, if it does not, it will surely prepare us for the event. As I mentioned earlier, Germany is currently building up a powerful navy, so that it will have complete control of the Baltic Sea, which of course is all too close to Britain. As an integral part of the French Treaty, we will deploy several squadrons of His Majesty's fleet to the Orkney Islands off the northern tip of Scotland, where they will act as a counterbalance to Germany's primacy in the Baltic. Such a move would not only bottleneck the German fleet coming out of the Baltic, it could also hinder Germany's major ports from importing critically needed raw materials for its war efforts. Needless to say, this maritime strategy would be a major deterrent to the kaiser's grandiose idea of conquest."

"I take it that our fleet has not yet made its move," Joanna said.

"We are in the early phases, and the plan cannot be implemented further until new naval installations are established in Scotland," the First Sea Lord told her. "With these developments in mind, I am certain you can see how vital it is that Germany not learn of these ongoing plans."

"Indeed," my father said. "With our fleet sitting at the doorstep to the Baltic, Germany might have second thoughts about starting a war."

"That would be our hope," Sir Harold agreed. "But should war break out, our fleet will be more than prepared to confront the kaiser's navy.

"Now allow me to tell you how the document went missing," he continued. "After all was settled and agreed upon, our foreign minister, the Duke of Winchester, drew up a final draft of the treaty, of which multiple copies were to be made prior to signing. The task of producing the copies was left to the Duke's son, a highly placed undersecretary at the ministry. All this was to occur in absolute secrecy at the Halifax country estate in Hampshire. I myself, along with several members of naval intelligence, put in place all the security measures to be taken while the document was being copied."

"Were the naval intelligence officers aware of the contents of the document?" Joanna asked.

"They were not, nor were the security guards, one of whom was stationed outside the door to the library where the copies were produced, while others patrolled the outer perimeter of the grand house. They were in place around the clock. In any event, everything was going smoothly until mid-afternoon on the second day, when the undersecretary left the library to visit the lavatory. No one else was in the library at the time and the door was securely shut when the undersecretary departed. He returned five minutes or so later and discovered that the document was missing. A most careful search was undertaken at once and when the document could not be found, the police and eventually Scotland Yard were called in."

"Were there any other entrances to the library?" Joanna asked.

"None," Sir Harold replied. "And all the windows had remained shut and locked, and could only be unlocked from the inside."

"How many others were allowed to enter the library?" Joanna queried.

"Only three and always under the careful eye of the undersecretary and the security guard."

"Did the security guard ever enter the library?"

"Never. And the key to the door was held by the undersecretary. As I just stated, only three other individuals were permitted entrance. In addition to the undersecretary, there was his wife, the Duke of Winchester, and a trusted butler who has been in the family's service for over forty years. All visits were brief, lasting only minutes, and no one was allowed to carry any papers or books out of the library."

"Three unlikely suspects," my father commented.

"Please keep in mind, Watson, that unlikeliness does not equate with innocence," Joanna said, then arose from her chair and went over to a small desk where she plucked a

Turkish cigarette from its colorful box and, striking a match, lighted it.

Inhaling deeply, she began pacing the floor and left a trail of pale smoke behind her. Like her father, Sherlock Holmes, Joanna smoked heavily when involved in a difficult, problematic case, and could easily consume a pack of cigarettes a day until the solution came to her. My father suggested that the nicotine surge might stimulate the creative center of her brain, and I concurred with this since she rarely smoked when not occupied by a puzzling case.

Joanna paced for another minute, lost in her thoughts, then turned abruptly to Sir Harold. "On which floor of the grand house is the library located?"

"It is on the second floor, some thirty feet above the ground."

"Which excludes the windows as a point of entrance," Joanna said.

"That was clear from the onset since the windows were locked from the inside and had remained so."

Joanna gave the First Sea Lord a knowing smile. "Anything that can be locked can be unlocked by a clever enough thief. Nevertheless, it is most unlikely that the thief entered through the window because to do so would have required a rope or ladder. Such an adventure would have surely been noticed by your security men guarding the perimeter of the grand house."

"How then did he enter?"

"That is the key to your puzzle," Joanna responded. "For if we know the how, it may well point to the who, which will tell us the why."

Sir Harold's face brightened for the first time. "So you have confidence you can help us avert this disaster?"

"I make no promises," Joanna said. "We shall investigate and gather the clues and see where they lead us."

Sir Harold sighed to himself, with disappointment clearly on his face. "I was hoping for more, but of course will welcome any assistance you might give us. When will you depart?"

"On the train to Hampshire that leaves early tomorrow morning."

"Let us pray for the best," Sir Harold said, and rose from his seat. "Please keep me informed of any developments."

We watched the First Sea Lord walk gravely from the room. He was the picture of a man carrying the heaviest of burdens.

Once the door closed, Joanna turned quickly to my father. "Do you feel up to joining us on this venture?"

"I believe the country air would be quite invigorating," my father said eagerly.

"It will be more than invigorating, Watson, in that it will present an excellent opportunity to advance your physical therapy."

"Are you proposing we go beyond our daily strolls, which I must admit tire me a bit?"

"Precisely so, for it is now time to progress to a higher level in your recovery, which should improve both your strength and endurance."

"You sound as though you have worked with stroke victims in the past."

"Indeed I did while a nurse at St. Bart's," Joanna informed him. "Do you recall Reginald Alexander, the chief executive at the hospital, who suffered a cerebral embolus some years back?"

My father hesitated briefly before nodding. "He was badly paralyzed on one side I was told."

"But now he is walking because of an intensive physical program devised by a brilliant specialist at St. Bart's."

"Did you participate in his recovery?" my father asked, now keenly interested.

"I did so on a daily basis. The poor man came to the surgery ward because of a bedsore he developed while lying immobile for prolonged periods of time. Once the sore was cleaned out, we began him on a muscle-strengthening program while he recuperated. Slowly his muscles responded and, although he limped noticeably, he could walk. It was as if his brain was retraining itself. As his strength increased, so did his endurance and eventually he strolled about with only the slightest of limps."

I asked, "Do you recall every step used in the strengthening program?"

"I do," Joanna assured. "But to be certain, I consulted with the St. Bart's specialist and he told me I was spot on."

I turned to my father with an encouraging word. "Let us hope there are better days ahead."

"Let us hope I am not too old to learn such retraining," my father said. "I am afraid my brain may be quite set in its ways."

"We shall see, my dear Watson, we shall see," Joanna said with a smile that rapidly faded from her face. "Now tell me, do you have your service revolver at the ready?"

"I most certainly do," my father replied, and went to his room, only to return with his Webley Revolver No. 2 in hand. "Do you expect violence, Joanna?"

"I expect war," she said, and left it at that.

2

The Secured Library

Our train ride to Hampshire was a pleasant diversion from the noise and turmoil of London. For the most part we remained silent, with Joanna mulling over the few clues at our disposal, while my father and I scanned several newspapers to learn if the French Treaty had somehow found its way into print.

"No such mention in the *Standard*," my father announced.

"Nor in the others," I said.

"Perhaps the thief now realizes the gravity of his theft and is having second thoughts," my father suggested.

"And is seeking a way to return it without being discovered," I added.

Joanna came out of her reverie, saying, "That is wishful thinking. More likely, he is either haggling over the price to be paid for such a valuable document or at the least contemplating the best and most profitable manner to dispose of it."

"So you do not believe the Germans know the contents of the treaty," I surmised.

"Not as yet. But they shortly will," Joanna said grimly, then returned to her quiet deliberations.

I watched her steeple her fingers and rest her chin upon them, which she often did when consumed in deep thought. She rarely spoke while assembling limited clues in some sort of order, but when enough facts were at her disposal she would discuss the problem at length, believing that nothing clarified a puzzling case like stating it to another person. This was another trait she had apparently inherited from Sherlock Holmes. According to my father, the famous detective would not hesitate to awaken him in the middle of the night to exchange views at length on a mystery that had thus far evaded solution.

As our train sped along, I became enchanted with the bucolic beauty of the English countryside. There seemed to be miles and miles of open farmland and forests, among which were scattered small houses with red roofs that glowed in the bright morning sun.

"What do you stare at so?" my father asked.

"The quiet loveliness of the countryside, in such stark contrast to the tumult and pollution of London," I replied. "It is a most tranquil world out here where I am certain civility reigns."

"So you wish to imagine," Joanna said as her lidded eyes opened. "But permit me to assure you that crimes, every bit as vicious as those in London, take place in these peaceful surroundings. You see, isolation and separation give ideal cover for abuse, torture, and even murder. Who would hear the screams of the tortured or abused? Who would question the disappearance of a young son or daughter who has presumably left for London to seek fortune and a better life? Yet, in a crowded tenement, cries for help would be heard and screams of pain noticed, and the police summoned. And the sudden disappearance of an individual would cause worry to more than a few. Thus, in some instances, the confines of London offer more protection against evil than the apparent tranquility of Hampshire."

"You always see the worst of humans," I remarked.

"That is the side I have to deal with," Joanna said.

"But surely, at the countryside estate owned by one of England's most prominent families, such violence is most unlikely to occur," my father said.

Joanna gave us both a long, serious look. "Do you not remember the murderer Dr. Christopher Moran, a distinguished physician who used his medical skills to dispatch several of his colleagues in order to gain sole possession of a great fortune?"

"I do," my father and I said simultaneously.

"It is that case, more than others, which clearly demonstrates that position in society does not dissuade one from committing heinous crimes," Joanna told us. "We should keep that in mind here as well."

An hour later we alighted from our hansom and gazed up at the solemn Halifax mansion. It was not what we expected. The grand manor was constructed of dull, gray stone, with a large central section and two curving wings. On the second floor of the east wing was a broken window, through which a maroon drape could be seen, and a portion of the roof above was tattered and depressed. We were viewing a picture of partial ruin.

"I wonder why the exterior has been allowed to remain in such poor repair," I thought aloud.

"Perhaps the problems have arisen only recently," my father suggested.

"More likely it is evidence of the declining fortune of the Halifax family," Joanna said. "This estate was once among the richest in England, with borders that could only be measured in miles. But three successive heirs were of a dissolute and wasteful disposition, with the most recent downfall being brought about by the Duke's older, now dead brother, who was both an alcoholic and a compulsive gambler. All that is left here is a few hundred acres and a two-hundred-year-old house that is deteriorating. Of course the family still holds title to a dukedom that has been passed down through numerous generations of Halifaxes. The current holder is the seventh Duke of Winchester."

I looked at Joanna in astonishment. "How in the world did you learn so much about the Halifaxes on such short notice?"

"I asked my father-in-law," Joanna replied matter-of-factly.

My father and I nodded to ourselves, remembering that Joanna's father-in-law was Lord Blalock, an esteemed statesman who once held the offices of home secretary and Chancellor of the Exchequer. To this day he remained a valued advisor to His Majesty's government. In addition he was an established member of London's aristocracy and knew all their secrets and histories.

"My father-in-law also directed me to an historical foundation that maintains records on the great manors of England," Joanna went on, reaching in her purse for an index card. "I jotted down a few notes on the Halifax manor that you may find of interest. It was built in 1690 upon a huge land grant given to the Halifaxes during the reign of Charles the Second. The family was to fall in and out of favor with the hedonistic king who was known to chop off the heads of those who opposed him. Thus the Halifaxes were eager to keep their distance from the court in London and spent most of their time in Hampshire, continually looking over their shoulders for the sudden appearance of the king's henchmen."

"If they had such fears, they might well have built a secret escape passage from the manor," I surmised.

"My thoughts precisely," Joanna said. "And the purpose of my visit to the foundation. But alas, none were known or ever mentioned."

"Yet they obviously survived," my father said.

"And prospered," Joanna added. "They were eventually to increase the size of their land holdings to two hundred fifty thousand acres."

"Such unimaginable wealth, all concentrated in one family through the generations," said I. "Until their recent downfall."

"That is the point to be taken," Joanna noted. "Such a severe decline in wealth to those accustomed to it often leads to an overwhelming thirst for money."

"Surely you do not suspect the Halifaxes," my father said.

"I suspect everyone until they are proven innocent."

"But that contradicts Anglo-Saxon law, in which one is presumed innocent until proven guilty," I argued mildly.

"I am not interested in the law, only in justice, and, as now, safeguarding the country I love." Joanna pointed up to the broken window on the second floor of the mansion and asked, "What do you make of the open pane?"

"It is broken," I answered.

"And?"

I shrugged. "And what?"

"We should look for more broken windows, particularly on the first floor of the mansion. For if we find one, it would tell us how someone could unlock the window from the outside and enter undetected."

"But Sir Harold distinctly told us that the windows in the library were locked and undisturbed," I recalled.

"You miss the point, dear John," Joanna said. "Once inside the grand manor, a clever thief might find a hidden way into the library."

"But no such way was found."

"That does not preclude its existence," Joanna said, and walked to the stone steps where an elderly butler held an open door.

We were led up marble stairs and down a cavernous corridor before reaching a library that was most generous in size. Lining the walls were row upon row of leather-bound volumes, and interspersed among the shelves were hanging Persian tapestries and portraits of aristocratic personages from the Victorian era. Awaiting us by the fireplace was Inspector Lestrade, who was still wearing his topcoat and brown derby against the morning chill. Joanna briefly studied the fireplace, which was broad in width, but quite narrow in depth. It contained cold, unstirred ashes.

Tipping his hat, Lestrade greeted us warmly. "Good morning and thank you very much for coming on such short notice."

"I take it no progress has been made," Joanna said, skipping the usual amenities.

"None whatsoever," Lestrade replied, and removed his derby to rub at his bald head. He was a tall, middle-aged man with a pleasant enough face except for his eyes, which seemed fixed in a perpetual squint. "We remain in a quandary as to how the thief entered and departed with this most important document. We have diligently searched for a secret passage, but have found none."

"Yes, quite a quandary," Joanna agreed, and turned to the butler who stood by the entrance to the library. "You may leave now, and please close the door behind you."

Once the butler had departed, Lestrade said, "He is above suspicion. The butler has been in service here for over forty years, with an absolutely spotless record. We went to the trouble of carefully investigating him as well as all the other household staff, and I can assure you none were involved."

"Oh, I can assure you one is involved," Joanna said.

Lestrade looked at her oddly. "Based on what, may I ask?"

"That will become clear once we discover the secret entrance."

Joanna commenced with a thorough search of the half-dozen windows, examining each pane and testing all the locks. Next she went to the bookshelves and removed a volume every few feet, then tapped on the wall behind it and listened for a returning sound. None came, but I had to admire Joanna's ingenuity. She was percussing the wall the same way a physician percusses a patient's chest, except Joanna was not searching for a tumor or pneumonia, but for a hollow sound to indicate there was a vacant space on the other side of the shelves.

"You are simply repeating what has already been done," Lestrade informed. "There is no passageway hidden by the leather-bound volumes."

"I am afraid, Lestrade, that in this regard I trust only myself." Joanna moved back and forth across the hardwood floor with slow, deliberate steps, looking for any irregularity or opening. She even took up an expansive Persian rug in front of a mahogany desk and searched there as well, but to no avail. Stretching her neck, she closely studied the cathedral, beamed ceiling, which was a good fifteen feet above at its highest. "Was the roof examined?"

Lestrade followed her line of vision and remarked, "We inspected the ceiling and the roof above it on two separate occasions. There was no opening or aperture to be seen. And even if there were, the distance from the ceiling to the floor is such that the thief would have required a long, unwieldy ladder to reach the document, which you must admit would be out of the question here."

"And that?" Joanna asked, and motioned to a closed door that was well off to the side of the desk.

"A closet," Lestrade responded. "Which was thoroughly searched top to bottom."

Joanna opened the door and peered in. The closet was rectangular in shape and quite spacious, with the sides measuring five-by-five feet in width and depth. In the dimness we could see that the walls and ceiling were covered with a fine layer of dust and mold, the latter of which gave off a most disagreeable odor. Joanna waved away the pungent smell and carefully percussed each of the walls within. Finding nothing of interest, she closed the closet.

"I see that you too are having difficulty uncovering a secret entrance into the library," Lestrade noted.

"It is here," Joanna insisted.

"We held the very same opinion but, as time has passed and no such passageway discovered, I now wonder if we are overlooking an unconcealed way through which the thief may have gained entrance."

"Are you suggesting this passageway is before our very eyes?"

"That is a possibility we must consider."

"But all the evidence tells us otherwise."

"How so?"

"Permit me to demonstrate an exercise in logical deduction. You will agree the thief could not have entered the library through the door, which was locked and under twenty-four-hour guard."

"That is obvious."

"And that entrance through the locked windows or roof is impossible."

"Quite so."

"And that the brick fireplace is far too narrow to allow a person to pass through?"

"Clearly."

"Then how did the thief find his way in?"

Lestrade shrugged.

"There has to be a hidden entrance," Joanna concluded. "You must remember, one of my father's cardinal rules posits that once you have eliminated the impossible, whatever remains, however improbable, must be the truth."

"I fear that even our dear Sherlock Holmes, were he here, would have difficulty unraveling this puzzle," Lestrade opined.

Joanna ignored the comment and thought aloud. "We are missing the obvious here."

The door to the library opened and the Duke of Winchester, whom I recognized from his photographs in the newspapers, entered. Behind him was his son, who bore a striking resemblance to his father. The age difference of twenty or more years was plain to see, yet both were tall and lean, with chiseled, aristocratic features and jutting chins. Their expressions were fixed and resolute.

While Lestrade was making the introductions, the Duke approached Joanna and said warmly, "I recall you from some years ago during a happier time."

"And I, you, Your Grace," Joanna replied. "I believe it was at the wedding of your son, Harry."

"Indeed."

Joanna nodded to Harry Halifax who gave her a half bow in return. "It is good to see you again, Harry, but of course not under these trying circumstances."

"I too wish it were a more pleasant situation," Harry said formally, without a hint of geniality in his voice. He took a deep breath, as if preparing himself for an unwanted action, then gave Joanna a most critical gaze. "You have been sworn to secrecy and know that nothing revealed here can ever be spoken of or written about. With that in mind, let me say that both my father and I are very much aware of your excellent detective skills, as chronicled by your husband, and only pray that you can help us find a way out of this terrible dilemma."

"I shall do my best," Joanna said, and turned to the foreign minister. "Allow me to begin with you, Your Grace. Please do not hold back any information, for to do so may well hinder our investigation and place our efforts in vain."

"Agreed."

"I have been told that only those at the highest level of government knew of the French Treaty."

"Knowledge of the treaty was limited to the prime minister and his most senior cabinet members, none of whom I can assure you breathed a word."

"Were they informed that copies were to be made?"

"Of course. But no one knew where and when the copying would be done, nor who would perform the task. That information was available only to myself, my son, and the prime minister."

Joanna thought for a moment before asking, "Was the copying of the treaty ever spoken of outside your office at Whitehall?"

"Never," the Duke said. "All discussions with my son were brief and always held in my office, with no one else present."

"And did the same hold true here at your Hampshire estate?"

"It did. Any talk of the treaty was done here in the library, in complete privacy."

"Were questions not asked regarding the sudden appearance of security guards both within and outside the mansion?"

"Not by the staff."

"Did not other family members inquire?"

"Not to me."

"Nor I," Harry added. "Only my wife was in attendance, and she made no such inquiry. My sons are off to boarding school, you see."

"Very good," Joanna said. "This information is most helpful."

"If I am not needed further, there are other urgent matters I must attend to this morning," the Duke said.

"Of course. And thank you for speaking so openly."

The stone-faced Duke turned to leave, then abruptly came back to Joanna's side. For a brief moment, the resolve left his face and he whispered a plea meant only for her ears. "For God's sake, Joanna, do all you can for us and for all England."

With his heavy burden, the foreign minister strode glumly to the door.

"I too have urgent matters awaiting me," Harry said in an authoritative voice. "Thus, I trust you will excuse—"

"You must stay," Joanna said firmly. "For none of your affairs are nearly as urgent as the one we are facing."

The aristocratic undersecretary was taken aback, clearly unaccustomed to receiving orders from a woman, but the stern expression on Joanna's face told him it would be in his best interest to do so. "Tell me the information you wish."

"I want every detail of your routine from the very second you arrived at the country estate until the document went missing. Leave nothing out, no matter how insignificant it might seem."

Harry paused a moment, as if to gather his thoughts, then said, "We stepped through the door at 10 A.M. Monday morning and I immediately went to the library to begin my task of making twelve copies of the French Treaty. I am certain of the time because the grandfather clock in the hall struck ten."

"Was the security guard already stationed at the door to the library?" Joanna asked.

"He was, with strict orders not to admit anyone other than the butler, Charles, and my wife."

"What were their duties that required admission?"

"Charles was to serve afternoon tea promptly at 3 P.M. and return an hour later to clear the tray. His visits were to be brief and only for that purpose."

"Please show us where the tea was to be served."

Harry walked over to a large coffee table positioned some ten feet to the side of the mahogany desk. "This is the path he took. After putting down the tray and pouring tea, he stood back and waited to make certain all was satisfactory, then departed."

"Good," Joanna approved. "Now would you please summon the butler and ask him to serve tea in the usual manner."

"But it is still morning," Harry objected.

"So it is."

Harry sighed heavily and grumbled his annoyance. "Is this truly necessary?"

"If it were not, I would not have made the request," Joanna replied. "And may I suggest we stop wasting time since we have so little of it at our disposal?"

"The waste of time is having a trusted butler go through the charade of bringing afternoon tea in mid-morning," Harry groused. "It serves no purpose."

"We shall see," Joanna said without inflection.

The butler was called, and while we waited Joanna retraced her steps, again examining the windows and walls and floor for hidden passageways. If her failure to uncover a secret entrance caused her any bother, she gave no evidence of it. But for some reason the ceiling drew her attention once more and she continued to stare at it.

Lestrade said, "I can assure you that both the ceiling and roof were carefully studied and no openings were discovered."

"Have you yourself examined the roof?" Joanna asked.

"Thoroughly, madam," Lestrade assured. "It contains no possible entrance into the library."

"I would very much like to see the roof, if only to satisfy my curiosity."

"Of course. This way, madam."

As we turned to leave, my father reached out for the arm of a leather-upholstered chair and slowly eased himself down into it. He took several deep breaths to gather himself.

"Are you all right, Father?" I asked concernedly.

"Just a bit fatigued from our early start this morning," he replied in a tired voice.

"Perhaps you should rest while we climb the stairs to inspect the roof."

"A capital idea, John," my father agreed. "I shall wait here to learn of your and Joanna's findings."

Departing the library, I glanced back at my father and was again reminded of the toll that age and illness had extracted from him. He seemed old and worn, with deeply grayed hair and moustache. His jawline was still firm, although it was now partially covered with hanging jowls. Fortunately, his spirits remained strong despite his lagging endurance.

"Go, go," he encouraged. "I shall be fine."

Lestrade led us down the corridor to a spacious supply room in the midsection of the manor. Mops, brooms, dusters, and cleaning materials were neatly stacked against the walls. Large containers of bleach and solvents stood on wide shelves that surrounded a single flight of stairs that opened onto the roof.

As we climbed up the staircase, Joanna noted, "There is very little space between the ceiling and the roof."

"A mere two feet, with thick beams above and below," Lestrade said. "There is scarcely enough room for a young child to crawl about."

We exited through a sturdy trapdoor and stepped out onto a expansive slate roof whose only openings were for chimney stacks. The roof itself was gently sloped, but enough so as to make walking about hazardous. To prevent missteps, Scotland Yard had constructed pathways consisting of long lengths of rope suspended on stationary poles that one could hold onto should the need arise. There were no external ladders leading to the stories below.

"As you can see, there is absolutely no way a thief could enter the library via the roof," Lestrade stressed. "He could not have come this way."

"So it would seem," Joanna said, and with her head down, began to slowly pace back and forth over the entire expanse of the slate roof. I followed close behind and inspected every slate tile, but could discover no breaks or openings. All of the fittings were well joined and the stone slabs appeared to be of the same age. Near one of the chimney stacks, Joanna stopped abruptly and called over to Lestrade. "Inspector, why has the slate beside this chimney been disturbed?"

Lestrade hurried over and examined the area in which newer slate tiles had been placed between several badly chipped ones. "That was done months ago," he informed. "There was a crack in the chimney below the roofline that had to be sealed. We contacted the repairmen and they confirmed the work they performed. They also confirmed that the space between the roof and the ceiling was quite small, no more than a few feet."

"Did you inquire into the background of the repairmen?" Joanna asked.

"Indeed we did," Lestrade said. "It was a father and son, well known and well trusted, who have been in business for over twenty-five years. The son, by the way, fought in the Second Boer War and was decorated for gallantry."

Joanna nodded to herself and slowly gazed around the entire slanted slate roof. "Thus it would seem the thief's point of entry was neither the roof nor the walls nor the floor."

"We reached that very same conclusion, madam," Lestrade said. "Which would indicate he had no way to make his entrance, yet he did. Somehow he performed the impossible."

"The thief did not do the impossible," Joanna countered. "He simply found a way in that we have overlooked."

We returned to the library where my father remained seated, but now his posture was upright and he appeared to be a bit brighter. Nevertheless, I could still sense his fatigue.

"Did you find anything of interest?" my father asked us.

"I am afraid not, Watson," Joanna said. "There was no secret way in."

"I could have told you that," Harry said with a dismissive shrug. "The only thing up there is a wide spread of slate slabs, some of which are unfortunately beginning to leak."

Joanna's eyes narrowed. "Where have these leaks occurred?"

"Not in the library, if that is what—"

Our conversation was interrupted by Charles, the butler, who after a gentle rap on the door entered the library carrying a silver tray laden with the essentials for a splendid tea.

"Thank you, Charles," Joanna said. "Would you be kind enough to pour tea?"

"For all, madam?" Charles asked in a soft, but clearly heard voice.

"Only for the undersecretary."

"Very good, madam."

With white gloves on, Charles prepared the tea perfectly as he had no doubt done thousands of times before, then stepped back from the coffee table and positioned himself to the side of the massive mahogany desk. As if by magic, he produced two newspapers and placed them atop the desk.

"Excellently done," Joanna praised.

"Thank you, madam," Charles said, with a bow at the correct level.

Joanna glanced over to the desktop. "Is that a copy of the morning *Standard*?"

"Yes, madam."

"May I see it briefly?"

Charles reached over to the desk and without squinting selected the *Standard* and handed it to Joanna.

"Thank you, Charles," Joanna said. "Your presence is no longer required."

"Very good, madam."

Once the door closed, Harry again showed his annoyance with the butler's reenactment. "And exactly what was the purpose of that charade?"

"It clearly demonstrated that your butler in all likelihood saw the French Treaty," Joanna explained. "After pouring tea, he stepped back and placed two newspapers on your desk. Doing so enabled him to see and perhaps even read a portion of the French Treaty. His vision is quite excellent in that he was able to pick out the *Standard* from the other newspaper without hesitation."

"Are you implying that our forever loyal Charles is guilty of stealing the treaty?" Harry asked exasperatedly.

"I am implying that he could have unwittingly been involved," Joanna said. "Having read part of the treaty while you were distracted with tea, he might have spoken about it to others on staff here, as members of the household tend to do. They love gossip and delight in spreading important news. And this news could have reached the wrong person's ears."

"I had not thought of that," Harry admitted.

"It simply shows there is no such thing as absolute security despite one's best efforts," Joanna said. "The smallest leak is all that is required."

"But Charles could not possibly be involved," Harry muttered, shaking his head at the very notion.

"At this point no one in the household can be excluded," Joanna went on. "Now tell us what duties your wife had that required her visits to the library."

"She stepped in to say hello and inquire if I had any needs she might attend to," Harry said, then pointed to a vase of colorful flowers that, though wilted, had remained quite lovely. "Or she would bring in flowers to brighten the room."

"Exceptionally well arranged," Joanna commented.

"My wife has a gift for it."

"Might we have a word with her?"

"Elizabeth is in town shopping, but should return by early afternoon."

"We shall see her then," Joanna said, and gazed around the expansive library once more. "So, only your father, your wife, and the butler were allowed in. Correct?"

"Without exception."

"Not even the security guard?"

"He remained outside the door at all times."

Joanna nodded, but something in her expression told me she was not completely satisfied with Harry's answers. "Let us return to your copying routine. I take it the first day went well?"

"Quite so," Harry replied. "There were no interruptions and that allowed me to make four copies of the rather lengthy document."

"And on the second day?"

"Things again went very smoothly until the very moment I left for the lavatory."

"Did you lock the door behind you?"

"I always do."

"And you have the only key?"

"That is correct."

"And when you returned the document was gone?"

"I could not believe my eyes," Harry said, wincing at the memory. "Only the original had disappeared with the four copies remaining in place. We searched high and low in every possible crook and crevice, but to no avail. It was the beginning of our nightmare."

"Did you notice anything unusual upon your return to the library?" Joanna asked.

"Such as?"

"Were the other papers on the desk ruffled about?"

"No."

"The desk drawers opened?"

"They remained closed as I had left them."

"The windows shut?"

"And locked."

"Were there any unusual noises?"

"Not that I recollect," Harry said, then abruptly held up a hand. "But there was one thing I found somewhat bothersome, although I do not believe it is of any consequence."

"Describe it," Joanna said at once.

"For a moment I thought I detected tobacco smoke," Harry said. "It was quite faint and then faded away. I suspected the aroma had drifted in through the ventilation duct that connects the library to the room next to it."

Joanna asked, "What is the use of the adjoining room?"

"It serves as a temporary lounge for the security guards, and I know one of them smokes, for I have detected that odor on his attire."

"Was the aroma you noticed present throughout the library?"

"It was not," Harry answered without hesitation, then corrected himself. "Let me be more precise and say that the smell was more noticeable between the desk and the fireplace."

"Could you have mistaken it for smoke from the fireplace?"

Harry shook his head. "The chimney has a most excellent draft and virtually no smoke from the burning logs enters the room. Unless I am mistaken, the faint aroma was that of tobacco smoke, for I have asthma and am very sensitive to it. For this reason, I avoid tobacco smoke in every way possible."

"This is most important," Joanna stressed. "You are absolutely convinced the smell was that of burning tobacco and not burning wood?"

"I would swear to it," Harry said. "Besides, the day the treaty went missing was quite mild and we saw no need to light a fire."

"Show me your exact position when you detected the aroma of tobacco smoke," Joanna urged.

Harry moved over to the left side of the desk and took a step toward the closet. "Here," he announced.

"Did you look into the closet?"

"Most certainly," Harry said. "All I detected was the odor of mold, so I rapidly closed the closet, for mold too can set off an asthmatic attack."

Joanna gazed up at the highest point of the cathedral ceiling and followed it down as it sloped toward the closet. She performed this maneuver once again before a Mona Lisa–type smile crossed her face. "It was in full view of our eyes all the while, and we simply chose to overlook it."

"What?" Lestrade asked.

"The attic that no doubt holds the secret passageway into the library," Joanna said.

"But, madam, there is virtually no attic here," Lestrade argued. "We could only find a space of two feet between the roof of the manor and the ceiling below, which is not nearly enough for a man to travel through. Even a very small man could not do it."

"You miss the important clue, Lestrade, as I did at first," Joanna said, and gestured to the top of the ceiling. "At its highest, the cathedral ceiling is twenty feet from the floor and above it a space of two feet before one comes to the roof. But notice how the ceiling slopes down acutely as it approaches the area of the closet." She moved over to the door of the closet and raised her arm up to its fullest. "At this point the ceiling is only eight feet or so in height, yet the gently sloped roof of the mansion is no less than fifteen feet from the library flooring. Thus, there is a space of seven feet above the ceiling in the closet that is unaccounted for, and that is where in all likelihood the attic and secret passageway is located."

"But how did the thief gain entrance into the library?" Lestrade asked.

"Through the closet," Joanna replied, and stepped into the enclosure. "I will need a torch."

Lestrade handed her a metal torch that gave off a surprisingly strong beam of light. She shone the light above the entire enclosure before focusing the beam on a long, barely visible crack in the mold-covered ceiling. "There it is!" Joanna exclaimed. "Your walking stick, please, Watson."

My father gave her his walking stick and watched as she poked with force at the ceiling. On the first effort, the wood in the ceiling stayed put and budged not an inch. On the second try, a trapdoor large enough to admit a man cracked open.

"Blimey!" Lestrade said.

"Bravo!" my father cried out.

"So obvious now," I muttered, more to myself than to the others.

"It is the obvious that is so often overlooked," Joanna told us. "We neglected the closet because we did not take into account the rather steep sloping of the beamed ceiling. And Harry missed the aroma of tobacco smoke in the closet because it was overwhelmed by the stench of mold."

"You are every bit as skilled as we were informed," Harry praised her. "But I must admit that at first I underestimated you."

As have others to their downfall, I thought to myself. In our busy months together, Joanna had solved four cases Scotland Yard could not. Two were brutal murders, two involved greed at the highest level. All perpetrators were currently in jail, except for one of the murderers who had been hanged some weeks ago.

"Now we must carefully search the hidden passageway," Joanna said.

"Surely the thief and document are long gone," Harry opined.

"But there will be a trail he left behind."

"Do you believe it will lead to the document?"

"That remains to be seen, but I have a strong suspicion this is only the first step down a long, difficult path."

The Duke returned to the library and, when he saw us gathered around the opened closet, rushed over. "What has transpired?"

After being told of the secret passageway Joanna had uncovered, the foreign minister could not contain his excitement. "Outstanding! I must say, Joanna, you have outdone yourself."

As was her custom, Joanna showed little response to praise and adulation, for simply arriving at a solution gave her all the satisfaction she required. However, in this instance, she did permit herself the briefest of smiles.

"May I ask how you were able to make this important discovery?" the Duke asked.

"The faint aroma of tobacco smoke," Joanna replied, and described the deductive steps that led to the hidden trapdoor. "It was your son Harry's acute sensitivity to this type of smoke that proved to be the decisive clue."

"But it would seem so trivial."

"To some it would appear to be entirely trivial," Joanna agreed. "But I dare not call it that since most of Sherlock Holmes's classic cases had the least promising commencement, and the same held true for one of ours. Recall the dreadful Laverne murder in which the most revealing clue came to my attention because of drops of water remaining in an umbrella despite the bright, sunny day outside?"

"Do you believe your discovery will lead to a successful conclusion of our current dilemma?" the Duke asked hopefully.

"I am afraid we are only at the beginning, Your Grace, but nonetheless the concealed location of the trapdoor provides us with a most important clue."

A puzzled look crossed his face. "What can we hope to learn from its hidden location?"

"A great deal," Joanna replied. "You must keep in mind that very few individuals are aware of the secret trapdoor and what lay behind it. This observation narrows down the list of suspects considerably. Simply put—one amongst the few who knew is responsible for the theft."

"Pray tell, how do we go about uncovering this scoundrel?" the Duke implored.

"In every crime there are key questions whose answers lead to resolution. As a rule, the more complicated the case, the more numerous the questions. Here we are faced with five." Joanna held up her hand and, with her fingers, counted off the queries. "One—who was aware of the trapdoor and attic space? Two—who knew the precise moment the library would be vacated? Three—who had knowledge of the document's importance? Four—who benefits from its possession? And five—who might have the desire to guide the document into the wrong hands? Answer these questions and the case is solved. Until then, I fear we are swimming about in murky waters."

"The answer to your first question—who would know of the trapdoor and attic space—would no doubt point to a member of the household," my father reasoned. "Only they would be aware of the inner structure of the mansion. Yet no one mentioned the attic space when the staff was interviewed. Perhaps they were hiding their collusion."

"But that person may not have known of their involvement," Joanna countered. "Remember, one loose tongue is all that is required for this information to be heard by the wrong ears. It is important to keep in mind that all of the questions must be answered before we can draw the correct conclusion."

"This will be no simple matter," my father said.

"Answering five separate but interconnected questions never is," I concurred.

"We must not attempt to answer all five at once, for it would surely be an exercise in futility," Joanna instructed.

"Think of it as a puzzle that has to be assembled piece by piece. Come up with one definite answer and determine if it will be a link that leads to another."

"I have some recently obtained information that may relate to your fifth question," the Duke said. "I do not wish to bear false witness, but according to naval intelligence, my groundskeeper, Henry Miller, is a naturalized British citizen who was born in Munich and immigrated to England in his late teens. His prior name was Heinrich Mueller, which he Anglicized because of the strong anti-German sentiment across all of Britain."

Joanna's brow went up. "Has he returned to Germany recently?"

"That is being investigated."

"Is he a known German sympathizer?"

"Not that I am aware of, but that too is under investigation."

"But certainly a groundskeeper would not have knowledge of a trapdoor and crawl space in the grand house," I interjected.

"But other household members would and could have informed him," Joanna said, then addressed the foreign minister. "I am sure that naval intelligence is being most thorough, but do make certain they look into whether Henry Miller is a member of any German society or club hereabouts or in London. These may have been kept in the shadows for obvious reasons."

"I shall," the Duke said and sighed heavily. "Henry always appeared so solid and trustworthy."

"The best of criminals usually do," Joanna said and gazed up at the trapdoor once more. "And now I believe a careful search of the crawl space above the ceiling is in order."

"Do you have any hope the document will be there?"

Joanna shook her head. "The treaty is gone. The question is how far."

"It would seem that you are of the opinion that the treaty has now left the estate," the Duke said gloomily.

"Not necessarily."

"So there is hope yet of recovering it?"

"Just a glimmer," Joanna warned. "And that too will disappear if we do not make haste."

3

The Secret Passage

Climbing a sturdy ladder, Joanna entered the crawl space above the ceiling, with me, the principal torch bearer, a step behind. Inspector Lestrade brought up the rear and he too held a powerful torch, which afforded us excellent lighting. As we expected, the space was large and had a height of nearly seven feet, which could easily accommodate a standing man. What was unexpected was the strong, pungent odor of bleach.

"It seems the thief attempted to bleach out the mold," I surmised.

"So he was a rather neat fellow, I would say," Lestrade opined.

"I would think it was more than neatness that drove him to the task," Joanna said. "More likely, he did not wish for any of the mold or its odor to come off onto his clothes, which would have been noticed and raised questions. Bleach is also a powerful solvent that can wash away clues left behind."

"Then we are dealing with a clever thief indeed," Lestrade said.

"Let us see how clever," Joanna said, and began surveying the dust-covered floor. She stopped abruptly in front of footprints, some coming, some going, and many superimposed on one another. "From the length of his stride, I would estimate him to be near six feet tall, and his shoe size would indicate a rather large man. Unfortunately, the level of dust is thin, making it impossible to accurately measure the depth of the shoeprint and thus judge his weight. He shows no limp or peculiarity in gait."

"Next you will be telling us the color of his eyes," Lestrade jested.

Joanna stooped down and examined a footprint more closely. "I cannot describe his eye color, but I would confidently predict he is a working man as evidenced by the square toe on his boots and the roughness of their soles."

"Can you determine the type of work he performed?" I asked.

"Not with what is before me, but I can tell you that he, in all likelihood, did manual labor on the outside, for there are particles of yellow, dried mud in the dust print."

"Why are you so convinced the dirt is from the outside?"

"Because of its claylike consistency, which is not to be found in a dusty attic space," Joanna replied. "Were your father here, he would be most helpful on this point, for he and Sherlock Holmes once unraveled a rather nasty case by correctly identifying soil from the murderer's shoe."

"I too wish he were present," I remarked. "He would have surely enjoyed relating the particulars on the case you just mentioned."

"It is best he took your advice and rested," Joanna said as

she moved closer to the outer wall where something had attracted her attention.

"A brief repose should do wonders for him," I agreed, and once again was reminded of the infirmities that came with my father's advancing years. It was most fortunate that I had earlier arranged for him to have a room at a nearby inn where he might rest and regain his strength.

"Hello!" Joanna called out. "What do we have here?"

Lestrade and I hurried over and found Joanna kneeling down, with her face close to the floor. For several moments she sniffed at a powdery product and rubbed a pinch of it between her fingers to test its texture.

"Havana," she declared. "Most definitely a Havana."

"The Cuban cigar?" I queried.

"A very fine Cuban cigar and he smoked it here while he waited. And this answers two of our five questions. Namely, how did the thief know of the document's importance and how did he know when the library would be vacated? The cigar ash tells us he was perched here, listening to every conversation between Harry and his father, and waiting for the moment Harry would leave for the lavatory."

Lestrade stepped in for a nearer inspection of the small, fluffy, gray-white pile of ashes. "Is the ash that remarkable?"

"Quite so," Joanna said. "In my father's monograph on this subject, he stated he could identify one hundred forty different brands of tobacco by their ash alone. There is an entire paragraph devoted to the Havana's distinctive aroma and the residue it leaves behind. You should read it, Lestrade, for it may serve you well in the future."

"And you yourself have the same talent?" Lestrade asked skeptically.

"I am almost as well versed on the subject as he was, and

I daresay I could easily hold my own against any of today's supposed experts."

"But you smoke only cigarettes," I interjected. "While, according to my father, Sherlock Holmes indulged in pipes, cigars, and cigarettes, each in large measure, which gave him experience with all forms of tobacco."

"True enough," Joanna said. "But there was no law preventing me from purchasing over a hundred types of tobacco used in pipes, cigars, and cigarettes, and putting a match to them to determine what type of ash and aroma they would leave behind. A tightly rolled Havana is among the most distinctive. There can be no doubt that our thief has a taste for the finer things in life."

"In addition, he seems to be a rather brash fellow," Lestrade commented. "He lights up an expensive cigar and puffs away while waiting at his leisure to strike."

"I believe you to be correct in that there was no nervousness on his part, for all of his steps are measured and unhurried," Joanna said. "He was simply biding his time."

"A moment, please," I interrupted. "I see a very odd discord among your findings, Joanna. First, you tell us the thief is a working man, which dictates a limited income, then you have him smoking a most costly cigar. The two simply do not fit together."

"Very good, John," Joanna agreed, obviously pleased with my reasoning. "A man making a pound a month is unlikely to spend it on a fine cigar."

"Then how do you put the two together?"

"I don't. But I shall remember and docket the information, for it may be of consequence later in this investigation." Joanna released the cigar ash and turned her attention to the wall. "Now where did he strike it?"

"Strike what?"

"The match to light and perhaps relight the cigar." Joanna carefully searched the outer wall and, finding nothing of significance, gazed up to a high, wide beam that went across the entire attic space. Pointing to a long scratch mark in its midsection, she stood on her tiptoes and inhaled deeply. "If I am not mistaken, it still retains the faint odor of sulfur dioxide, which of course is a combustion product of a strike-anywhere match."

"Well, he had to light his cigar somewhere," Lestrade said with a shrug.

"The scratch mark adds two features to the description of our thief," Joanna went on. "First, we can assume he reached up well above his brow to strike the match head, and thus avoid any sparks coming to his eyes. The height of the mark indicates I was correct in estimating that our thief is nearly six feet tall. Furthermore, the slant of the scratch to the right tells us the striker was left-handed. You will also note that there are no matches on the floor."

"But a man who smokes an expensive cigar would never be expected to pocket a burned match," I argued. "It would appear we have another set of contrasting clues here."

"Which can be most informative, for it tells us we are dealing with a man who is not what he appears to be."

"A riddle within a riddle," I commented.

A Mona Lisa smile came across Joanna's face. "Oh, I can think of at least three explanations for these disparate clues, but each will have to be tested to assess its value."

"But how will you test them?"

"With additional clues, of course."

As we moved slowly down the dimly lighted attic space, the pungent smell of bleach was replaced by that of mold and dust. Joanna kept her eyes riveted to the floor, searching for more trapdoors that could have been used for entrance or exit, but none were to be seen. Off to the sides were thick clusters of broken, dangling cobwebs, which indicated we were following the path of the thief. Something up ahead caught Joanna's attention, for she stopped abruptly and motioned for me to direct my torch to a thick support beam that went from ceiling to floor. At the lower end of the vertical beam, both cobwebs and dust had been wiped away.

Joanna knelt for a closer inspection and, using her magnifying glass, examined the lower portion of the column at length. "Bring the torch down a bit, please, John."

I focused in on the inferior-most surface of the supporting column, but could see only partially rotten wood. But Joanna saw an object of obvious interest and carefully plucked it off the wood before holding it up to the light. It appeared to be a long thread of some sort. "Pray tell, what is it?"

"A coarse strand of rope that was caught in the splintered section of the support beam," she replied.

"Is it of importance?" Lestrade asked.

"Quite, for it tells us how the thief lowered himself down into the library," Joanna elucidated. "He tied a sturdy rope around the beam to support his weight and down he went. He of course removed the rope when he returned to the attic space and fled. But, in his haste, he left a thick strand of hemp behind."

"If he was six feet tall, as you say, why did he not simply hang by his arms and drop to the floor of the closet?" Lestrade asked. "It would have only been a distance of a few feet."

"An excellent question," Joanna said. "But remember, silence can at times be a thief's worst enemy, such as in this case when the library was dead quiet and a security guard just outside the door. A dull thump or the noise of a misfall on the hardwood floor might be heard and all would be lost."

"I had not thought of that."

"And then, most importantly, if he were to lower himself down by his arms, how was he to return to the attic space? He could not begin to reach the trapdoor with a jump, so he would find himself trapped in the closet. Our thief is no fool, and we would all be wise to remember that."

"There is one more question here that gnaws at me," Lestrade said. "Why didn't the thief do his sordid work in the middle of the night when there was no risk he would be caught?"

"Another good question that crossed my mind as well," Joanna replied. "As a precaution, I assumed the document would be locked away at day's end, and the Duke confirmed this to be the case."

"In a safe?" I inquired.

"In a sturdy Chubb, which would present a problem to the best of England's safecrackers."

We continued along the dust-laden space that now held thicker clusters of cobwebs. In the dim stillness, we scanned every foot of the ceiling, wall, and floor, searching for the thief's exit. Approaching the very end of the passageway, we were about to give up hope when a faint glimmer of light appeared in the floor. As we drew closer, the light dimmed further, then reappeared.

"What do you make of it?" Lestrade asked in a whisper and reached for his service revolver.

"It is a trapdoor that is not well placed and allows the light from below to enter," Joanna explained.

"But why does the light seem to come and go?" Lestrade asked.

Joanna stepped forward and pressed her foot on a wooden plank next to the trapdoor. The light abruptly dimmed. When she removed her foot, the light strengthened. "The glimmer lessened because the weight of our coming steps caused the wooden floor to give just a bit and allow the door a better fit."

Joanna opened the trapdoor widely, and the three of us peered down into a small room that appeared to have once been a secluded office. There was a dust-covered desk and chair, and off to the side were bookshelves filled with leather-bound volumes and binders. Sunlight streamed in through a closed window that overlooked a motor garage. The additional light allowed us to see a length of rope that descended from the attic space to the top of the desk.

"His way down," Joanna noted.

"Hardly a hiding place," I ventured.

Joanna pointed to a narrow staircase beyond the window. "It was his escape route."

We hurried out of the attic space and along the main corridor of the second floor before reaching the secluded office. Its door was unlocked and showed no evidence it had been tampered with. On entering we were met with the musty odor that was characteristic of a poorly ventilated space. We quickly searched the desk and bookshelves and, finding nothing of interest, descended the tight staircase one abreast. At its bottom we came to yet another door that was easily opened. The three of us stepped into a large, well-stocked pantry, from which arose the mixed aromas of spices and exotic foods. No one was present, but a wide side window was partially opened. The noise and chatter from the nearby kitchen could clearly be heard.

"The trapdoors were the way he entered and exited, with

not a soul close enough to see or hear him," Joanna said. "And the open window provided him an avenue in and out without being noticed by those in the kitchen."

"Do you believe the pantry window remains open all the time?" I inquired.

"It most likely does throughout the day which allows for excellent ventilation and minimizes the odors that could drift into the remainder of the manor."

Lestrade nodded in agreement. "I must say our thief truly knows how to dot his *i*s and cross his *t*s."

"He knew every inch of the manor," I commented.

"And how to enter and exit it without being seen," Joanna added.

As we hurried back up the stairs, I could not help but be impressed with the number of overlooked clues that Joanna had uncovered during our one brief visit to the Halifax mansion. That she had outdone Lestrade and Scotland Yard was no surprise, for her detective talents were tenfold better than theirs. But she had also outperformed naval intelligence, which had no doubt been called in by the Foreign Office. Yet, despite all these new findings, I did not feel we were any closer to uncovering the traitorous perpetrator.

"You are very quiet, John," Joanna said.

"I am lost in my thoughts."

"No doubt concerned that the identity of the thief continues to elude us."

My jaw dropped in astonishment. "How in the world would you know this?"

"By your involuntary actions," Joanna elucidated. "You continue to look around, floor to ceiling, wall to wall, as if hoping to discover some new, revealing clue about the thief. And your fists are tightly clenched, indicating you are anxious and concerned over the thief, and perhaps angry that he continues to evade us."

"As you can see, Inspector Lestrade, my wife is a most excellent mind reader," I said.

"Oh, but I am more encouraged than you by our findings thus far," Lestrade said. "We now have a partial description of our thief to work with. He is six feet or so tall, of a goodly size, left-handed, and is an outdoor laborer who enjoys expensive cigars."

"Very good, Lestrade," Joanna praised. "You are to be commended for assembling our clues in such fine order."

Lestrade basked noticeably.

"However," Joanna went on, "you have neglected a most telling clue."

"Which is?"

"The rope."

A puzzled look crossed Lestrade's face. "And exactly what does this sizable length of rope tell us about the thief?"

"That he is quite strong and in all likelihood muscular," Joanna replied. "Think about it, Lestrade. This large man had to lower himself, hand under hand, down a rope from the trapdoor to the floor below. This is not a simple task, to be performed by one with ordinary strength. And even more difficult, he had to climb up from the secluded office, hand over hand, to enter the attic. So you see, our thief must have powerful arms and this may well be one of his most distinguishing features."

"And powerful arms might relate to the man's duties as an outdoor laborer," I added.

Joanna smiled pleasantly at my deduction and said, "It is most helpful when the meaning of one clue reinforces the significance of another."

On reentering the library we found Harry Halifax and a woman I presumed to be his wife awaiting us. She was quite lovely, although a bit short and broad across the middle. With her flawless skin, sparkling blue eyes, and blond hair, she seemed the picture of good health, which contrasted greatly with her husband's haggard appearance.

"Any trace of the treaty?" Harry asked in a rush.

"I am afraid not," Joanna replied. "But that was to be expected. No worthwhile thief would dare to leave such a valuable document behind."

"That was wishful thinking on my part," Harry said wistfully, then introduced only me to his wife, Elizabeth, for she and Joanna were already acquainted with each other.

"It is always good to see you, Joanna, but of course not under these dreadful circumstances," Elizabeth said.

"I too wish it were otherwise," Joanna said.

"If I can be of any help whatsoever, I would be delighted to do so."

"I have only a few questions that might lend us some assistance," Joanna began in a soft, unintrusive voice. "On the first day, did you arrive at the estate with your husband?"

"I did."

"And went directly to putting everything in order?"

"All was already in order, for the staff had been notified of our imminent arrival."

"Did you accompany your husband to the library?"

"No. I went about other duties while he went directly to work behind the closed door of the library."

"Did you enter the library on the first day?"

Elizabeth shook her head. "There was no need."

"And on the second day?"

"Twice," Elizabeth replied without hesitation. "Once in

the morning to see if Harry wished any refreshments. Then on a second occasion in the early afternoon, to freshen up the air with a floral arrangement. Both visits were quite brief."

"Were the flowers picked from your garden?"

"Oh, yes. Flowers are planted here in such a fashion as to ensure that some are in bloom year round." Elizabeth pointed to a vase near the window and said, "I brought those in and arranged them where the light was best."

Joanna strolled over to the vase holding a variety of colorful flowers, and studied them at length. "The white roses and pink valerians are perfectly matched with the violet Canterbury bells, are they not?"

I was greatly surprised by Joanna's sudden attention to the flowers, for she had never shown such interest in the past. If anything, she tended to ignore natural elements, no matter the beauty, unless they somehow were related to criminal activities. In particular, she had never demonstrated the least affection for botany or practical gardening.

"Were you trained in floral arrangement?" Joanna continued on.

"Indeed I was," Elizabeth said. "I had the good fortune to learn it from a Japanese master while on an extended visit to Tokyo as a young girl. You see, my grandfather was once Queen Victoria's ambassador to the imperial house of Japan."

"I have been told that the Japanese consider floral arrangement the very highest form of art," Joanna said. "In their vocabulary they have the word *ikebana,* which to the Westerner means skillfully arranging flowers. But to the Japanese, the word denotes bringing life to flowers. In a deeper sense, it refers to placing the elements about us into a more perfect order. Looking at your exquisite arrangement, I would hazard a guess that you had studied ikebana."

"Why, indeed I did," Elizabeth said, obviously pleased with Joanna's compliment. But in an instant her face turned serious. "Do the flowers offer any hope of solving the terrible problem before us?"

"Ah, yes, the mystery," Joanna murmured, coming back to the most perplexing puzzle we were facing. "We shall see if it somehow fits in." She gave the flowers another long look before asking, "By the way, were you ever told of the document or had knowledge of its immense importance?"

"Never," Elizabeth answered at once. "We only knew that it required my husband's close attention and that any disturbance was to be held to a minimum."

"I have one final question," Joanna said. "Have there been any visitors to the manor since your arrival?"

"Not that I am aware of," Elizabeth replied.

"No other family members?"

"None."

"Thank you, Elizabeth," Joanna said. "You have been very helpful."

As Harry and Elizabeth departed, Lestrade turned to leave as well, saying, "I too must be on my way, for the commissioner at Scotland Yard insists on a daily briefing by phone. Is there anything in particular I should draw his attention to?"

"He will be most interested in the secret passageway," Joanna replied. "But please ask him to hold its details in highest confidence."

"Shall I inform him of the thief's description?"

"I would hold that in abeyance until we have a more complete picture."

"No need to make a mistake here. Correct?"

"My point exactly," Joanna said. "For the very last thing

we wish to do is misinform Scotland Yard. The consequences could be most serious."

Lestrade nodded gravely.

I nodded as well, for Joanna had firmly sealed Lestrade's lips and limited the knowledge of our most important findings to a precious few. Like her father before her, Joanna knew that a secret told to Scotland Yard remained a secret no more.

Once the door to the library closed, Joanna returned to the vase holding the flowers, then moved over to the mahogany desk, and from that point stared straight ahead to the window. "Our dear Elizabeth is being less than honest with us."

"Are you saying she is a liar?" I asked.

"I am saying she is not telling the whole truth on two counts," Joanna replied. "First, she clearly stated she was unaware of the document's great importance, which of course is nonsense. When a man locks himself in the library to do official government work and an armed guard is stationed in the corridor outside the door, even a dullard would realize something of vast importance is taking place in that room. And I can assure you that Elizabeth is no dullard. She is quite bright, with a deep intellect as witnessed by her knowledge of ikebana, a term very few people would have knowledge of."

I shrugged. "She learned it while in Japan."

Joanna shook her head. "She did not simply learn it, but mastered it and that, dear John, is the measure of her intellect. The art of ikebana is not just a matter of plucking flowers and seeing how the colors match. It requires touch and vision and endless *patience* so the various flowers can be arranged and rearranged until perfection is attained. Notice that I emphasized the word *patience* because it is not unusual for such an arrangement to occupy hours of time."

"So all of her visits could not have been brief," I concluded. "The floral arrangement demanded a stay of some length."

"And the lighting in the room is a critical component of ikebana," Joanna continued on. "That is why I viewed the arrangement from the mahogany desk, which showed me how sunlight coming through the window would reflect off the colorful petals."

"Thus, she had to be very near the desk," I said, following Joanna's line of reasoning.

"And for a goodly amount of time," Joanna added. "It would have presented no problem for Elizabeth to glance down and read sections of the document."

"And the obvious security measures would have heightened her curiosity to the point where a glance at the document would have been irresistible."

"So it would seem."

"But why lie?"

"To cover something that, at this time, is beyond our reach."

"These waters appear to become murkier by the moment."

"But there are several clarifying clues before us as well."

"Such as?"

Joanna gestured to the large window overlooking the front of the estate and strode over. "Tell me what you see out there. Be so good as to include every detail."

My gaze went to the expansive green lawn that stretched on and on until it came to a thick forest of tall trees. Off to the side was a stone bridge that crossed a narrow stream. And everywhere there were police searching the grounds, some with dogs straining at their leashes. A few men using ropes and hooks were dredging the stream for submerged objects.

Muted shouts and whistles could be heard in the distance. Before I could describe my sightings, Joanna prompted me.

"It is the terrain, not the people, that is of interest," she said.

"What portion of the terrain?"

"The distance between the manor and the forest."

"It is a good hundred meters."

"And?"

I shrugged and looked even more diligently for the important feature, but it escaped me. The landscape was flat and well cared for, with no statues or fountains visible. Much of the space was taken up by police searching the area, but there was nothing remarkable about them. "I see nothing worthy of comment."

"It is the openness," Joanna said.

The Duke of Winchester entered the library, looking even more grim. The lines in his face seemed to be deepening by the hour.

"My son tells me that your search of the attic space proved in vain," he said unhappily.

"The document was not recovered," Joanna told him. "But I do believe we are nearer to a solution."

The Duke suddenly brightened. "You have a suspect?"

"Not as yet."

"But you appear to have some confidence that the matter can be solved."

"The outlines are beginning to come into view," Joanna said carefully. "But there are crucial pieces of the puzzle yet to be discovered."

"Can I be of assistance?" the Duke asked eagerly.

"Perhaps," Joanna replied. "Please describe for me again

the events that transpired just before and just after the theft was noticed. The exact timing in minutes is most important here."

His Grace paused a moment, as if to clearly organize the events in his mind. "My son left the library for the lavatory and returned approximately five minutes later. He searched the library for another minute or two and, when the document could not be found, sounded the alarm."

"Was the estate closed down at that time?"

"That was done immediately. No one was permitted in or out, and a thorough investigation of the house and grounds undertaken."

"Can you approximate the number of minutes that passed between your son leaving the library for the lavatory and the sounding of the alarm to close down the estate?"

The Duke silently moved his lips and counted to himself. "Seven minutes at the most."

"Thank you," Joanna said. "This information may be quite important."

His Grace waited for Joanna to say more and when she didn't, he asked impatiently, "Does this lead us to a more definite suspect?"

"At this moment, I cannot be that hopeful."

"I see," the Duke said, as the last trace of optimism left his face.

Joanna turned to the window and, moving in closer, seemed to focus her attention on the wooded area beyond the stream. "Is there forest at the rear of the manor as well?"

"There is indeed," the elder statesman replied. "Off to the rear of the manor are the cottages for the butler and grounds-keeper, and behind them the motor garage and stables. It is at this point that the woods begin, which I am sad to say have become quite thick and overgrown from lack of use. This was not the case some years ago, for the forest was full of game, such as deer and hares, which we hunted on a regular basis. But now the family shows little interest in the sport and only poachers roam the woods, which present somewhat of a problem."

"How so?" Joanna asked at once.

"On occasion they trespass onto the grounds with ill intent, but are frightened off by the shotgun of the grounds-keeper, who keeps a sharp eye on the premises when it is vacant."

"Has there been any evidence of forced entry?"

"Not at the Halifax manor, but it has occurred at adjacent estates with loss of valuable items, I am told."

"Were the local constables called in?"

The Duke nodded. "But with little result. None of the trespassers have ever been apprehended. So even if one of them was responsible for the theft of the document, we do not have the faintest description of him."

"We do have some clues about the thief," I volunteered. "We know that he—"

"Is a most cunning fellow, who was sure of foot, as he came and went through the passageway," Joanna interrupted abruptly. "Perhaps more information will be forthcoming when we reexamine the space with a brighter light."

"Let us hope that will be the case," the Duke said. "So very much depends on this, Joanna, so very much. I do not exaggerate when I tell you the outcome of the war, which is sure to come, and the fate of England may well hang in the balance. The stakes could not be higher." The elder statesman's face sagged for a moment before regaining its composure. "God help us if the treaty falls into the wrong hands."

As he turned for the door, Joanna held a finger to her lips, indicating to me that nothing more should be said regarding the clues we had uncovered.

Joanna spoke again, but only when she heard the nobleman's footsteps in the corridor. "I would not tell too much," she said in a quiet voice. "Politicians are never to be trusted, not the best of them."

"But surely those who hold such high office can—"

"Those least of all," Joanna said, and returned to the window. Something on the estate grounds remained of interest to her. "And we should not trust his close family members either."

"Are you referring to Harry?"

"And Elizabeth."

I looked at Joanna quizzically. "Based on a floral arrangement?"

"Based on her family history," Joanna replied. She walked away from the window to light a cigarette, then turned to me. "Elizabeth's maiden name is Stanhope. What do you make of that?"

I was taken aback by the stunning revelation. "Is she related to Horace Stanhope whose brokerage firm was ruined by scandal?"

"His daughter."

My mind raced back five years in time to the scandal that caused the downfall of one of London's oldest and most prestigious brokerage firms. It all revolved around the New England Holding Company, which owned large stretches of real estate outside of New York and Boston that were said to be ripe for development. The Stanhope brokerage, led by the eldest son, Ian, made huge commissions from the sales of the New England stock, and they themselves purchased sizable blocks of the shares, which they sold at peak value prior to the holding company being exposed as a fraud. Its vast stretches of so-called valuable real estate turned out to be mainly swamps and bogs. The Stanhopes were believed to be aware of the deception and were facing indictment when an arrangement was reached. Their brokerage firm and the Stanhopes in particular were forced to return all profits and given a huge fine, which was said to be in the six figures. The family was disgraced and bordering on bankruptcy from which they barely escaped. News of the scandal and all its details was the talk of London for weeks on end.

"Greed," I thought aloud.

"But there is even more to this tragedy. According to my father-in-law who was Chancellor of the Exchequer at the time, Ian Stanhope had convinced the Duke of Winchester to invest in the scam, which cost the Halifaxes dearly and forced them to sell off yet more of their estate. It has been a bitter pill for them to swallow."

"So there must be real dislike between the families," I concluded.

"I think it is fair to say there is no love lost between them."

"Do you believe it has affected Elizabeth's marriage?"

"How could it not?"

"Thus it would appear this fiasco has left both families mired in deep financial straits."

"By all accounts they are drowning in debt."

Joanna returned to the window once more and stared out. There was something in the distance that continued to draw her attention.

4

A Prime Suspect

The Hampshire Inn, where we had rooms, possessed a most inviting dining area. Particularly impressive were its dark paneled walls and large brick fireplace with its blazing logs that gave off the aroma of burning hickory. There were six tables in the room, spread well apart, with space for six more if needed. It was here that we enjoyed a dinner of nicely seasoned lamb and a hearty claret. My father had recovered completely from his bout of fatigue and was again his chipper self, regaling us with Sherlock Holmes stories, some of which had never been chronicled. By far the most fascinating adventure involved Queen Victoria and Leonardo da Vinci.

Joanna and I drew our chairs in closer so as not to miss a word.

"As you may know, the Crown owns one of the most valuable collections of art in the world," my father began. "It is particularly strong in paintings by the Old Masters, notably works by Raphael and Michelangelo. But believed to be the most valuable by far are the six hundred sketches by Leonardo da Vinci. When one of those sketches went missing and turned up on the London black market, Queen Victoria had to pay a handsome price of ten thousand pounds for its return. Now, who could possibly be the thief? Was it an art curator at Buckingham Palace? A member of the royal court? Or perhaps a common thief who somehow found his way into the palace? In their quandary, the royal family wisely called in Sherlock Holmes to solve the crime before another sketch mysteriously disappeared. Of course to Holmes it was a simple matter that could be brought to conclusion in a matter of days. He borrowed the most prized of the da Vinci sketches from the Crown and, using his underworld contacts, spread the word that yet another of the great artist's works was available for purchase. Holmes knew that a dishonest art dealer had to be involved in the initial sale to ascertain the validity of the sketch and to serve as a middleman. Several notorious dealers vied for the prize, but one called August Upshaw drew particular attention, for Holmes knew he was connected to the mastermind criminal Moriarity. Holmes in disguise met with Upshaw in the shadows of East London, and when the authenticity of the sketch was validated, another ten thousand pounds changed hands. At that point Holmes revealed himself and demanded to know the identities of the seller and buyer of the initial da Vinci. Of course Upshaw resisted, but relented when Holmes threatened to turn the matter over to Scotland Yard. The art dealer and buyer were promised immunity on return of the ten thousand pounds."

"But who was the thief?" Joanna asked.

"Would you care to hazard a guess?" my father asked back.

Joanna pondered the problem for a moment. "It had to be someone who knew the value of the sketch, and that individual had to have free access to the collection and could come and go without arousing suspicion."

"Which points to the art curator at the palace," I proposed.

"I think not," said Joanna. "An art curator would be far too clever to place the sketch on the London black market where it could be easily traced. He would take it to either a foreign market or have a private buyer lined up in advance. We can exclude the curator."

"Who then?"

"Someone higher up in the palace."

My father nodded at Joanna's assessment. "It was a private secretary in the queen's court who had come over from Germany with Prince Albert at the time of the prince's marriage to Victoria. He was not only a cousin to the prince, but one of Albert's closest confidants."

"Don't tell me he was given immunity as well," I bemoaned.

"He was, as soon as the ten thousand pounds was returned," my father said. "He was banished back to Germany and told he would be imprisoned if he ever returned. The only reason he avoided punishment and public humiliation was that it would have sullied the now dead Prince Albert's name, which the queen would have never allowed, for she remained deeply devoted to Albert for the remainder of her life."

"It should be mentioned that the British people were always suspicious of Albert's German heritage," I noted.

"Indeed, there were more than a few who considered him a foreign intruder," my father added. "Publication of this adventure might have fueled the public's animosity to the prince and thus was thought too sensitive to be published."

"Was the ten thousand pounds returned to the Treasury?" I asked.

"It was not, for that might have raised questions as to its source," my father replied. "Rather, Holmes suggested it be donated anonymously to the newly formed science section at the Victoria and Albert Museum. The queen was delighted to do so."

"Perfect," Joanna said, obviously pleased.

The conversation remained light until we sat back, with cigars for my father and me, while Joanna enjoyed one of her Turkish cigarettes. It was only then that we delved into the mystery of the missing French Treaty.

"I truly regret my condition prevented me from joining you in the attic space," my father said.

"As you well know, Father, some degree of weakness may persist after even a mild stroke," I consoled. "With more and more activity your strength will return."

"Let us hope your prognostication is correct," my father said, then lowered his voice although we were the only diners in the room. "Now tell me of your progress."

"It is certain beyond any doubt that a member of the household is intimately involved," Joanna began.

"Of course, someone with a loose tongue could have unintentionally uttered words that fell into the wrong hands," I proposed.

"I have excluded that possibility, for the nature and timing of events was too precise to be carried out by an opportunist."

"You are losing me here," my father said.

"Let us begin with the timing," Joanna said, and looked over her shoulder to make sure the waiter was not present. "According to all, Harry Halifax left the library for the lavatory and remained away for five minutes. After returning and finding the document missing, he searched about for another minute or two, then sounded the alarm, at which time the estate was immediately closed down. Thus, from the moment he last saw the document to the moment of the alarm, a total of six or seven minutes at the most had passed." Joanna paused to allow my father to assimilate the new information, then went on. "Now, let us examine the event from the standpoint of the thief. He waited patiently in the attic space for Harry Halifax to leave, before climbing down a rope and into the closet. I would think he stayed in that position for a minute or so to be certain Harry would not suddenly return. Only then did he rush over to the desk to gather up the pages of the document, which must be quickly read to ensure they are complete and authentic. Next, he must neatly fold them and perhaps bind them before securing them under his coat. Thus, two more minutes are gone. Now he must climb up the rope—no easy task, mind you—to reach the attic, close the trapdoor, and untie the rope. Another minute has passed, for a total of four. Then he must quietly and carefully traverse a hundred and fifty feet of darkened attic space to return to the area above the secluded office, and another minute or so has elapsed. Thus far he has used up at least five minutes and still has to secure the length of rope from the attic to the secluded office, descend onto the desk below, and quietly make his way down a flight of stairs to the pantry, from which he escaped. All of these various tasks together would have required a to-tal of seven minutes at a minimum to accomplish, which is the exact time the alarm sounded. With all this in mind, Watson, what do you make of the thief?"

"To act in such a rapid, organized fashion, he must have had remarkable knowledge of the mansion and, in particular, every inch of the attic space," my father said. "I would think he had been in the attic a number of times before, and may have even had several practice runs prior to the actual theft. All of this tells us the thief's familiarity with the surroundings indicate he was or had been a longstanding member of the household."

"Spot on, Watson!" said Joanna. "Lestrade would say you have crossed all the *t*s and dotted all the *i*s. But unfortunately, you have failed to reach by far the most important conclusion."

"Which is?" my father asked.

"We now know that the document has not left the estate," Joanna informed us, and seemed to enjoy the puzzlement on our faces. "Come now! It is the timing that is everything here. Our thief rushed to the open window in the pantry some seven or eight minutes after the theft. He has the document in hand, but the alarm has sounded and the estate is shut down. What is he to do?"

"He cannot run across the expanse of lawn, which is wide open, and now under the scrutiny of the security officers," I said, as I recalled the front of the estate I viewed from the library at Joanna's urging. "He would have surely been seen and apprehended."

"And he cannot return to the secluded office or attic space, for he would have been trapped within the manor," my father added.

"Which leaves the open window as his only escape route, and he took it," Joanna concluded. "As we departed the manor this afternoon, I glanced over to the area of the pantry window and noted there is thick, tall shubbery beneath it. Most likely our thief went through the window and into the thick bushes below, then slinked along the side of the house to a safer position. I can assure you he wasted no time hiding the document."

"Has the Duke been so notified?" my father asked.

"He has not and should not be, nor should anyone else, including Inspector Lestrade," Joanna said. "It is best not to let this information slip out, for a fox not aware of the hounds is much easier to catch."

"But surely the Halifax family can be excluded as suspects," my father argued mildly.

"Not altogether," Joanna said. "For although they are unlikely suspects, keep in mind their financial difficulties are deep and grow deeper by the day."

"But they are one of England's most prominent families who are—"

"Rapidly declining into bankruptcy," Joanna reminded us. "Just think of the value of this document to the Germans who would pay virtually any price to learn of its contents. Then imagine how a windfall of a hundred thousand pounds could turn around the fortunes of the Halifax family."

"And their desperation would be magnified by the substantial loss they suffered in the Stanhope brokerage scandal," I noted.

"Which forced them to sell off even more of their estate, of which precious little remains," said Joanna. "I should also draw your attention once more to the financial ruin of the Stanhope family. A hundred thousand pounds would be like a godsend to them as well. Even if they had to split that amount with a needy coconspirator, it would still be most welcome and ensure their salvation."

My father's brow went up. "Are you suggesting that Harry and Elizabeth may be acting in concert?"

"I have not excluded that possibility. Nor should we exclude Elizabeth's brother, Ian, who is a known scoundrel and might also be involved."

"Greed is a strange transformer of the human character," I said, recalling one of Sherlock Holmes's famous lines.

"Indeed," Joanna agreed. "And the half-truths told to me by Elizabeth Halifax prevent me from declaring their innocence."

My father abruptly sat up. "Half-truths, you say?"

"It has to do with the two visits she made to the library on the day of the theft," Joanna explained. "She claimed both were quite brief. The first visit was to determine if her husband wished any refreshments, which he did not. Thus, her entrance and exit took no time at all. The second visit was to complete a delicate floral arrangement, and therein is the lie."

"It seems our dear Elizabeth is an expert on arranging flowers," I elucidated. "And the floral arrangement was of such beauty, it no doubt required at least an hour rather than minutes to accomplish."

"Do people truly spend an hour on the placement of flowers?" my father asked.

"Even more if they feel they have not yet reached perfection," Joanna replied. "In Japan, where Elizabeth studied, the floral arrangement ikebana is a treasured form of art. She is a master at it, as evidenced by the moving loveliness of the flowers she arranged for her husband. Beyond any question, Elizabeth Halifax spent considerable time in the library the day of the theft."

"Would it be too much for me to inquire how you came by all this knowledge?" my father asked. "And please do not simply say you read about it."

"But that is so," Joanna insisted. "Although I must admit I was greatly prompted by a very skilled Japanese gardener. When I was a nurse at St. Bartholomew's, one of the patients I cared for was a sweet Japanese woman who was slowly wasting away from some unknown disorder. Her husband, the gardener, was most appreciative of the manner in which I looked after his wife, and rewarded me by bringing beautiful flowers on his every visit. He would tell me about the origins and arrangements of flowers, with particular emphasis on the Japanese art of ikebana, which means *bringing flowers to life*. So I began to read about these topics, more out of curiosity than anything else. But then I came across a section on Japanese plant poisons and this stirred my interest for obvious reasons. One of the deadliest toxins was produced by the Japanese yew, and lo and behold, the symptoms induced by ingestion of that toxin matched those of the gardener's wife."

My father and I leaned forward so as not to miss a word of this fascinating story.

"And I can clearly see your next question," Joanna went on. "The answer is yes. She was correctly diagnosed with Japanese yew poisoning, which was administered in the tea he served his wife daily. Unfortunately she died, but not before the gardener confessed to the dastardly deed. He was later convicted and sentenced to death. But while imprisoned, he committed suicide, or seppuku, by self-disembowelment, and thus saved us the expense of a well-deserved hanging."

My father smiled and nodded happily. "You are so much like your father. He too had an interest in botany, but primarily in plant poisons, such as belladonna and opium. He cared nothing for practical gardening and even less for those who toiled endlessly in the soil. But were he involved in the case you just mentioned, I can assure you he would have filed away every possible reference on Japanese plant poisons."

"There are volumes written on this very subject," Joanna informed us.

I asked, "Was there a reason for the gardener to poison his wife?"

"Money," Joanna replied. "He had purchased a sizable life insurance policy on her a year earlier. Clever fellow that he was, he had taken out the policy with a small Japanese company to cover his tracks. So, at the bottom of it all was pure and simple greed. And it is greed that brings us back to the missing document and perhaps to the misstatement of Elizabeth Halifax. She was less than truthful with us and we must find out why."

"But surely not greed," I thought aloud.

"Do not exclude that possibility so readily," Joanna cautioned.

"But I cannot connect greed, theft, and floral arrangements in some traitorous act," I said.

"Nor can I," Joanna said. "But her lying is a loose end that needs to be tied. When one leaves a dangling question unanswered, it often comes back to haunt you."

"I believe your father made a similar comment in his volume *The Whole Art of Deduction*," my father said.

"I find it strange that Sherlock Holmes would refer to his deductive talents as an art," I mused. "One usually thinks of art as being a creative endeavor which has a visual appeal."

"I thought that as well and once asked Holmes why he used that very term," my father said. "He told me he purposely selected the word *art* in the title, for he considered his skill of deduction to be an art form that he inherited."

"Were there other Sherlocks before the famous Sherlock?" I asked.

"Not in the true sense," my father answered. "I only knew the barest of his family connections, which included the fact that his ancestors were country squires who lived the life that was natural to their class. Yet he was certain his inquisitive, deductive mind may well have been acquired through the genes passed down from his grandmother, who was the sister of the famous French artist Vernet. Sherlock Holmes believed that art in the blood could take the strangest forms, and that this accounted for his deductive skills."

"I have read that my biological father had a brother named Mycroft, whose deductive skills surpassed even those of Sherlock's," Joanna recalled.

"That is true, but the brother had little ambition and even less energy when it came to solving crimes."

"A layabout, then?"

"Quite the contrary. Mycroft had a brilliant mind for figures and audited the books of several of the government's highly placed departments. But that was the only faculty to which he applied his extraordinary mind."

"Is he still alive?"

"Long dead, from massive heart failure."

Joanna puffed thoughtfully on her cigarette before saying, "So my son and I are the last of the family line."

"To the best of my knowledge," my father said, then a gentle smile came to his face. "But do tell me, have you heard from young Johnnie lately?"

"A letter arrived the day before we left for Hampshire that I should have shared with you," Joanna replied. "He has now completed the initial term at his most demanding middle school, where he has excelled in virtually all subjects."

"A remarkable brain for a lad not yet eleven," my father said. "Please let him know how much I miss his visits."

The warmth of my father's voice was clearly evident. There was a strong bond between him and young Johnnie

Blalock, which I believe in large measure reflected the tight bond my father had had with Sherlock Holmes. During the recovery from his stroke, my father spent a great deal of time with young Johnnie, while the lad was on leave from his boarding school, and the attachment between the two grew even greater. I wondered if this bond was also acquired from genes present in the blood of both.

At that very moment my thoughts were interrupted by Inspector Lestrade, who burst through the door and hurried over to our table.

"I do believe we shall all be going back to London shortly," he announced.

"Do you have a suspect?" I asked.

"A prime suspect who now appears to be on the run." Lestrade removed his derby and waved away the approaching waiter. "I must say, all the pieces are now fitting together very nicely indeed."

"Pray tell us the details," Joanna requested.

"Allow me to begin by demonstrating the vital role Scotland Yard played in bringing this case to a successful conclusion," Lestrade said. "For it was our records-investigational unit that provided me with the most important clue. They discovered, you see, that the butler Charles's son had a criminal past for major theft, and had spent time in prison several years ago because of it."

"Describe the theft," Joanna implored.

"Artworks and other valuables were taken from a nearby estate by the young scoundrel, then hidden in the forest on the Halifax land," Lestrade recounted. "The thief was seen coming and going into the woods on several occasions, which raised suspicions and led to the discovery of the stolen goods."

"Were all the items recovered?"

"All except for the two most valuable paintings, which were never found," Lestrade replied. "It was believed the thief disposed of the artworks on the black market, for a considerable amount of money was in his possession when he was apprehended."

"Do you recall how much cash?"

"Over fifty pounds, which would be a fortune to a butler's son who worked as a stable boy."

"And the lad admitted his guilt?"

"At first the teenager steadfastly proclaimed his innocence and wanted the constables to believe he was paid for simply hiding the goods, which he had no idea had been stolen. All of which was pure rubbish, of course." Lestrade paused to light a small cigar before continuing. "He changed his tune very quickly when given the choice of spending twelve months in a local jail or standing trial in front of a hard-nosed magistrate who was almost guaranteed to place him in Pentonville for five years or more."

"But surely there is more to this story than a theft that took place five years ago."

"Oh, there most certainly is, madam," Lestrade continued on. "Over the past month there has been a rash of break-ins and burglaries in the surrounding villages that resemble the one for which the stable boy was convicted. And of course this made us wonder if the lad had returned to his bad habit of taking other people's belongings. In addition—and this point is most important—on the very morning the document disappeared, Roger Bennett told his father he had to go to London on most urgent business that he would not discuss further, despite being pressed to do so. Then, and please pay attention to this event, a deliveryman whom we just questioned recalled seeing a young fellow running on the lawn near the forest only minutes before the alarm was sounded. And he was clutching papers or a note folder of some sort. And for a bit of icing on the cake, the thief was known to be very friendly with Henry Miller, or Heinrich Mueller I should say, the German-born groundskeeper on the estate. Of course Scotland Yard is now delving into the background of Mr. Miller to determine if he has continued loyalty to the fatherland."

"A very good summary," Joanna praised. "All events and facts seem to be in order."

"Thank you, madam," Lestrade said. "I take it you rather like the pudding I have put together."

"It is not bad at all, Lestrade, but I would hold it in even higher regard if a few of the key ingredients were not missing."

"And exactly what are those ingredients?"

"The ones I will sleep on," Joanna said, and rising from her chair added, "And with that, I will wish you a pleasant good evening."

5

The Servants

If one were to search all of England I do not think you could find a more distraught face than that belonging to Charles Bennett, the trusted butler. His son's guilt was weighing so heavily upon him, he found it difficult to speak.

"I cannot believe my dear boy is involved in this despicable act," he said in a voice so low it was almost inaudible. "Being such a good lad, it would be so unlike him."

"Even with his criminal past?" Joanna asked directly.

"That is a black mark against his name, to be sure, but it is a false one."

"Yet he was imprisoned because of it, which makes the stain quite permanent," Joanna pressed.

"Only because he was forced to choose between the lesser of two punishments," Bennett explained. "He was a victim of an evil deceit that was brought upon him by a friend who was a stable boy at a nearby estate. The friend told my son that he had inherited a variety of household goods from an aunt and had no place to secure them. Both he and my son knew of a small shed in the forest on the Halifax estate and it was decided to hide the goods there until they could be disposed of at a local market. My son would periodically go into the forest to make certain the items had not been disturbed and was seen doing so. This somewhat unusual behavior aroused suspicions and led to finding the goods in the shed. My son was arrested and charged, for you see the items had not been inherited, but stolen from the grand house at the nearby estate."

"What of your son's friend?" Joanna asked. "Was he not taken into custody and questioned?"

"He disappeared and was never heard of again," Bennett replied. "Thus, the entire burden of guilt was placed upon my son."

Joanna squinted a suspicious eye. "Yet your son, a convicted criminal, was allowed to return to work on the Halifax estate. I would think that the family would want no part of him."

"His Grace, the kind man that he is, also believed my son had been deceived and was not guilty of any theft. I pleaded with him to allow my son to return to gainful employment, and he was good enough to grant his permission," Bennett said, then shook his head sorrowfully. "And now look at what his kindness may have brought upon him and his household."

"I am afraid it is more than a matter of *may have* at this point," Joanna said frankly. "For his coconspirator was never apprehended, and he might have backed up your son's story."

"That is a sad fact," the butler had to agree.

Joanna asked, "Was the individual who bought the artworks found and questioned?"

"Unfortunately not, for he too had disappeared into the shadows."

"How convenient," Joanna said, and glanced around the small sitting room in the butler's cottage that was located at the rear of the estate. It was simply furnished, with a couch and stuffed chairs surrounding a well-used fireplace. On the wall were framed photographs from a generation ago. "I take it your son lives here with you."

"Yes. It is just he and I."

"Your wife is no longer with you?"

"She died some years ago from typhus and I had no choice but to raise my son on my own."

"Is there other family?"

"Only a brother, a dockworker in Liverpool, who passed away five years ago. His wife died soon after."

"Did they have children?"

"A daughter who perished young from scarlet fever and a son who left home as a teenager and turned out to be a bit of a wanderer. He was last heard to be working with a traveling circus in Scotland." The old butler sighed sadly. "I am afraid my family is all gone, save for my son who will soon leave me."

Joanna thought for a moment before asking, "Did you son spend every night in his room without fail?"

"He did. I can vouch for that, for his bedroom is next to mine. Would you care to see it?"

"We would indeed."

The butler led the way into a small, cramped bedroom, with barely enough space for an unmade bed and a narrow chest of drawers, above which was a miniature British flag. Tacked onto every inch of wall were posters of English athletes wearing their track uniforms. One showed a discus thrower, the others pictured slender, well-conditioned runners.

Joanna tilted her head back and sniffed the air. "I see your son enjoyed the sport of track."

"It is the love of his life," Bennett said. "He belongs to a local track club and is considered their very finest miler. He trains regularly, with hopes of someday joining His Majesty's Olympic team."

"I would assume he keeps himself in the best of physical shape," Joanna said.

"He is obsessed with it," Bennett replied. "He carefully watches his diet and weight, and when he is not running, he exercises with weights to build up his muscles."

"So tobacco use would be out of the question."

"He would avoid it like the plague."

We thanked the butler for his time and left him with his heartbreaking misery. Outside the air was crisp and the sky a deep gray that heralded approaching rain. As we strolled to a nearby cottage where the groundskeeper Henry Miller awaited us, I watched Joanna's expression change. Now there was a Mona Lisa–type smile on her face, which as usual was impossible to decipher.

"Was there some observation in the butler's cottage that I did not notice?"

"The air in the son's bedroom," Joanna replied.

"It was fresh," I said, with a shrug.

"Quite, with no aroma of smoked tobacco."

"But Joanna, the son is a track athlete in training," my father interjected. "One would never expect him to be a smoker."

"That is the key observation, Watson," Joanna said. "Jot it down in your memory, for it may become most valuable to our investigation."

The door to the groundskeeper's cottage was open, so

after a brief knock we entered and found Henry Miller seated by the fire, reading a German newspaper.

He quickly arose and greeted us with a Teutonic half bow before proclaiming his innocence. "I had nothing to do mit the theft," he said, involuntarily substituting the German *mit* for its English counterpart *with*. "I only know what I have been told about it."

Joanna said, "What makes you believe that we think you guilty?"

"Because of my German ancestry," Miller replied promptly. "Although I am a British citizen now, I was born in Munich and immigrated here many years ago. Still, the English people are very suspicious of anyone with a German background. And with the kaiser's desire to dominate Europe, these suspicions are growing."

"Our visit here is not to determine your guilt or innocence, but to learn if you might be helpful in recovering the missing document."

"But I know nothing of it," Miller pleaded.

"But you do know Roger Bennett, with whom we understand you were quite friendly."

"That is true," Miller confirmed. "He and I both shared a great interest in the sport of track. As a young man in Germany, I excelled in throwing the javelin, but had to withdraw because of an ailing knee. Roger is a miler who I believe has excellent prospects. That is what we talked about most of the time."

"Never about politics?"

"Never." Miller reached for a well-used pipe and slowly lighted it. He was a broad-shouldered man, with blondish-red hair and skin that was tanned and lined by exposure to the sun. "All we spoke of was his upcoming preparations to join the British Olympic team."

"Did he ever discuss the shed in the forest?"

Miller shrugged. "We both knew of its location and that it served to store infrequently used equipment, such as devices to dredge the stream. I doubt he would hide the stolen document there, for, although secluded, it could be easily broken into."

"Do you think he is guilty of theft?" Joanna asked.

"Everything seems to point that way," Miller said, showing no emotion. "I believe your Inspector Lestrade thinks that Roger is on the run and may try to leave the country and go to somewhere on the Continent. The inspector kept questioning me about Germany because of my background."

Joanna's brow went up. "Did Roger Bennett ever express a desire to travel to Germany?"

"Not that I remember," Miller replied. "His main interest was German athletes and how they trained, particularly in cold weather."

"Did he make any attempt to learn the German language?"

"Never."

While Miller reached for a match to relight his pipe, Joanna asked, "Do you ever indulge in cigars?"

"On occasion I enjoy one from America, but rarely so because they are out of my price range."

"Have you ever smoked a Havana?"

Miller forced a laugh. "Only in my dreams, for they are far too costly for me."

"As they are for most," Joanna said, and quickly took inventory of the furnishings around her. Like the butler's cottage, the groundskeeper's sitting room was small and sparsely furnished, with a couch and several well-worn chairs around a fireplace containing smoldering ashes. There were no books or radio or gramophone to be seen, nor any pictures or artwork on the walls. Joanna turned back to Henry Miller and asked, "Did you see Roger Bennett on the day of the theft?"

"Only briefly," Miller responded. "He was running laps around the outer perimeter of the estate, and waved to me from a distance. We did not speak."

"Had the alarm already sounded?"

Miller shook his head. "It did so several minutes later."

"Was Roger carrying anything in his hands?"

Miller thought for a moment before answering. "Only his notebook, which he used to record the length and time of his daily runs. As I told the inspector, I could not be certain it was his notebook, but assumed so since it was part of his routine."

"Was he near the forest at that moment?" Joanna asked.

"He was at the edge of it, close to the stream," Miller replied, then added, "and of course he had coils of heavy rope wrapped around his waist."

"Why the rope?" Joanna asked at once.

"For additional weight," Miller elucidated. "That makes the running even more difficult and builds up the muscles in his legs, so when the weight was removed he could run like the wind. True runners, you see, go to extraordinary lengths to improve their performance."

"From where did he fetch the rope?"

"From the stable where old, used rope is in abundance."

"And would not be missed if taken."

"Exactly, madam."

"You have been most helpful," Joanna said, and led the

way out. We strolled some distance from the cottage before speaking, so we could not be overheard. A few raindrops were beginning to fall and the rapidly darkening sky told of more to come.

"Do you believe the rope Roger Bennett used for training is a length from the same rope he employed to slip up and down from the attic space?" my father asked.

"It seems to fit, doesn't it?" Joanna replied. "Except for one point. Why parade around in an instrument you have used in a robbery?"

"Perhaps he mistakenly thought no one would ever make the connection," I suggested.

Joanna waved away the notion. "I believe our thief is too clever for that."

"And stable boys are not noted for their cleverness," I agreed. "Particularly one who is so easily duped into participating in an obvious robbery on an adjacent estate. One has to wonder if the lad is a bit slow-witted."

"Indeed, hiding valuable art in an unprotected forest shed is not the smartest of moves," my father added.

"So," Joanna summarized, "we are presented with a not-too-bright stable boy with little education who we must assume knows the exceptional value of the treaty and how to dispose of it."

"Not a good fit," I thought aloud.

"Not a good fit by any measure," Joanna said.

Before we could delve further, the rain intensified and we dashed for the main house. Inspector Lestrade hurried out with a large umbrella to afford us protection against the sudden downpour. Once inside the Halifax manor, the inspector could not wait to tell us of the new evidence incriminating the butler's son.

"We are in the process of putting yet more nails into the prime suspect's coffin," he announced proudly. "First and foremost, we now have the testimony of the local tobacconist who swears a Havana cigar was sold to Roger Bennett days before the theft. Imagine that, if you would. A stable boy lucky to earn a pound a month, yet he purchases the most expensive cigar available, which he plans to smoke in the attic space while waiting to steal the document."

"And unwittingly leaves its ashes behind," my father noted.

"Exactly right, Dr. Watson," Lestrade continued on. "And the next nail is even more damaging. One of the older German societies in London has been under surveillance, and its manager questioned yesterday. After being shown a picture of Roger Bennett, he instantly recognized the young man as a recent visitor to the society who requested information on the city of Berlin. And when did this visit take place, you ask? Why, on the very day the document was stolen." Lestrade paused and nodded to himself, as if to bask in the new evidence. "I must say that the noose around the lad's neck grows tighter and tighter."

"So it would seem," Joanna said. "But pray tell how did a stable boy from the countryside find his way to a German society in London?"

"A most excellent question, for it appears we may well have a conspiracy in the making," Lestrade went on. "You see, it was the groundskeeper, Henry Miller, who is a member of the Deutsche Society and who directed Roger Bennett to it."

"So the groundskeeper lied to us," I thought aloud. "He and Roger Bennett had talked of matters other than German athletics. Perhaps Miller's allegiance to England is not nearly as great as he professed."

Lestrade nodded at my conclusion. "A German down to the marrow, it would seem."

"Are you suggesting he used Roger Bennett to gain possession of the vital document?" my father asked.

"I am, for the two were no doubt thick as thieves," Lestrade said. "The question now is whether the German espionage ring is larger than we could have ever imagined. We must be very careful here, for if they learn of our newfound knowledge all would be lost. If they are as clever as we believe, they could vanish into thin air. With this in mind, I shall leave the London portion of this investigation to my counterpart at Scotland Yard, while I concentrate on securing even more evidence against Roger Bennett to make certain our case is airtight in every way. There can be no mistakes here, for if he shown to be a traitor it will earn him a place on the gallows."

"Alongside Henry Miller, if your assumptions are correct," said I.

"We shall keep a watchful eye on him as well," Lestrade said. "For it is he who may lead us to the whereabouts of Roger Bennett." He turned to Joanna with a request. "I think we would do well to work closely together on this aspect of the investigation. Delving into Henry Miller could provide us with important information."

"I would approach this case in yet another way," Joanna said.

"How, may I ask?"

"Oh, for now I should not influence your line of inquiry. I think it best for you to go on your line and I on mine. We can compare notes later and each could well supplement the other."

"Excellent!" Lestrade proclaimed. "Of course, I shall have to take the lead."

"I would have it no other way."

As Lestrade departed, Joanna waited until he was out of earshot before saying in a low voice, "Let us hope he does not muck it up."

I looked at Joanna in surprise. "Do you not feel he is on the correct path?"

"It is not the path that is of paramount importance, but the evidence," Joanna said. "Much of what Lestrade has presented to us is circumstantial rather than something that would stand up before a hard-nosed British jury."

"And it does seem a bit far-fetched to believe that a simple stable boy and a trusted groundskeeper would conspire to steal and profit from such an important document," I opined.

"Far-fetched indeed," my father agreed. "Yet Lestrade appears intent on building a case of collusion between Roger Bennett and Henry Miller, all based on a string of evidence that is neither convincing nor compelling."

"He takes that track because it is the path of least resistance and offers the quickest resolution, both of which Lestrade finds very appealing," Joanna told us. "He plucks pieces of information here and there that fit with the puzzle he has fixed in his mind, while ignoring those that contradict." She sighed softly before adding, "In his haste I fear he will muddy the waters even more and further obscure that which awaits us in the shadows."

"Which is?" I asked.

"The firsthand and indisputable evidence required to send a man to the gallows."

6

The Tobacconist

When I awoke the following morning, Joanna was still pacing our room at the inn, having smoked an endless number of Turkish cigarettes, which had filled the air with dense smoke. Like her father before her, she required little or no sleep for days on end when she had an unsolved case on her mind. With total concentration, she would turn the facts over and over, rearranging and studying them until she either solved the puzzle or was convinced the data was insufficient to do so. I feared the latter as I watched her light another cigarette from the one she was smoking, then drop down into an over-stuffed chair and stare out into the smoky haze.

I quietly walked over to a large, stone fireplace and stoked the smoldering logs to life, then added another, for there was a definite chill in the room. Outside, a cold rain was falling and splattering heavy drops onto the window, which obscured my view of the nearby forest. Glancing back at our four-poster bed, I could tell Joanna had not slept upon her side of the goose-down mattress.

"I take it you have made no progress," I said, wrapping myself in a thick robe against the morning chill.

"To the contrary, I now have a firm grasp on the important clues—particularly the butler's and groundskeeper's observations—and believe the conclusions Lestrade has drawn from them are incorrect."

"Are you referring to the rope he had around himself while running laps?"

"Among other things," Joanna replied. "But let us begin with the rope. The suspect, Roger Bennett, was seen running near the forest, with thick lengths of rope tied around his body to increase his weight and strengthen his leg muscles. And mind you, this occurred only minutes before the theft was discovered and the alarm sounded. It is rather absurd to believe a thief racing away with his most valuable stolen goods would choose to burden himself with added weight and slow down his escape."

"He would be racing for his life," I agreed.

"And he was out in the open where he would be seen, no less," Joanna went on. "Of course Lestrade immediately assumed that young Bennett was dashing into the forest to hide the document in the shed, the very same shed he used in the past to secure the goods he had supposedly stolen from the nearby estate."

"You used the word *supposedly* while describing his prior theft," I interrupted. "Do you doubt his earlier guilt?"

"I have questions that we can visit another time, but for now let us continue to examine Lestrade's poorly constructed conclusions. I can assure you he believes that the notebook Roger Bennett was carrying was in fact the missing document or at least held the document within its covers. Again, what thief of any merit would expose himself and his stolen item in such a foolhardy fashion? A thief worth his salt would keep in the shadows and hide the document quickly in a pre-determined place."

"But you have no solid proof that your conclusions are correct and Lestrade's are not."

"The proof will come later, but for the present I have to base Roger Bennett's actions on logic, as it pertains to how a clever criminal would behave. And trust me when I tell you our thief is a most accomplished one and not a stable boy who from his past appears to be quite gullible." Joanna crushed out her cigarette and studied it at length before speaking again. "No, my dear John, there are too many loose ends that Lestrade wishes to ignore. Rather, he is fixed on forcing all the pieces of evidence into an acceptable solution that will not stand up to close scrutiny. But despite my spot-on deductions, I am faced with one striking clue I cannot get around."

"The tobacconist's testimony that Roger Bennett had recently purchased a Havana cigar, the ashes of which we found in the attic space," I surmised.

"And which he could ill afford," Joanna added. "Here is a determined young athlete, training in earnest, who would avoid any tobacco use for obvious reasons. Yet an eyewitness says he purchased a costly Havana that he apparently smoked in the attic space while waiting for his opportune moment. That points the finger of guilt directly at Roger Bennett."

"So perhaps Inspector Lestrade's conclusion was not incorrect, after all."

"Perhaps. But when a single piece of evidence contradicts all others, one would do well to reexamine the contradictory piece," Joanna said, rising to her feet. "And that is exactly what we must do."

While Joanna changed clothes, I shaved and went about trimming my moustache in a small mirror. As I studied my face, I could not help but see the resemblance I had to my father. Our noses were straight and aquiline, our lips full, and our jawlines strong with prominent chins. The hair was different of course, with mine being thick and brown whilst his was totally gray and thinning.

"Why do you stare so in the mirror?" Joanna asked.

"Because I was seeing my father's face in the reflection," I replied.

"You are most fortunate in that regard," Joanna said, and kissed my cheek. "Good genes are a true blessing."

That remark caused me to smile, for the genes Joanna carried had to make her the most blessed person on the face of the earth.

"Now you must finish your trimming," Joanna urged. "There are important matters awaiting our attention."

At breakfast we were joined by my father, upon whom Joanna tested her conclusions regarding the odd behavior of Roger Bennett. My father listened with keen interest and delight, for it must have reminded him of how his old colleague and friend Sherlock Holmes would use him as a sounding board when attempting to reason through confusing data. With each confirmatory clue, my father nodded his agreement until Joanna came to the testimony of the tobacconist.

"The single piece of evidence that throws everything into disarray," he commented.

"And perhaps the most incontrovertible clue we have at our disposal," Joanna said. "Everything else is supposition."

"Perhaps the tobacconist was mistaken in identifying the young man."

"Unlikely," Joanna said at once. "In such a small village, everyone knows each other. It was not as if a stranger happened into the tobacco shop."

"But still, it is possible that—"

"One must never make exceptions, for they disprove the rule. Until shown otherwise, the word of the tobacconist stands."

"And makes Roger Bennett guilty."

Our conversation was interrupted by the chatter of French tourists who were being led to their tables by the innkeeper, a talkative, jolly Scotsman, with a thick, gray moustache and heavy muttonchops to match. After seating the recently arrived group, Trevor MacGregor came over to our table to assure we were enjoying the comforts of his inn.

"I trust you are finding everything to your liking," he greeted in a strong Scottish accent.

"It suits our needs very well," Joanna said. "And the food is beyond expectations."

"We pride ourselves on that," MacGregor said with a smile before gesturing to the new guests. "But the French always present a dining challenge, and I no doubt will soon hear complaints from them, in that they are unhappy already. They specifically requested a ground-floor room, for the old man has a bad knee and will have difficulty climbing the stairs. But I could not provide this because the two first-floor rooms are taken."

"Perhaps the guests on the first floor would consider moving to the upper rooms," my father suggested.

"Oh, if life were only so simple," MacGregor said, sighing

to himself. "One of the rooms is occupied by a frail, elderly woman who requires a wheelchair, and the other by a guest whom I never see."

Joanna's brow suddenly went up. "How can a guest here remain unseen?"

"By his request," MacGregor replied. "The room was let by a London agent who told me in no uncertain words that the guest insisted on a first-floor room, with the window facing the nearby forest. He requires only one meal each day and that is dinner, which has to be served promptly at 7 P.M. The dishes are left at the door and removed an hour later. The explanation given was that the guest needed absolute quiet and solitude as he wrote continuously on his book about Elizabethan England. So, he got exactly what he wanted, after paying for a two-week stay in advance."

"Very odd," Joanna remarked.

"Very odd, indeed."

"Surely the room had to be cleaned."

"Of course, but again there were restrictions," MacGregor said. "The room is to be cleaned and aired twice a week on Monday and Thursday between six and six thirty in the afternoon."

"And neither the waiter nor chambermaid ever saw him?"

"They never laid eyes on him. Nor did I, for that matter, because the agent himself checked the man in and took the key with him. In all my twenty years at this inn, I never had a stranger guest. But then, with business so slow during the cold months, all visitors are most welcome." MacGregor glanced over to the door of the dining room where several more guests appeared. "Now, if you will excuse me, I must attend to the last of the French group."

"One final question, if you will," Joanna requested hurriedly. "Has this structure always been an inn? Was it ever part of the Halifax estate?"

MacGregor thought for a moment, then slowly nodded. "Way back when, in 1750 or so, it was initially built to house visiting dignitaries to the Halifax manor when they had overflow at their large gatherings. It later became an inn that was frequented by some rather famous people, the most notable of whom was none other than the writer Charles Dickens."

"Do you know the purpose of Mr. Dickens's stays?" my father asked, keenly interested.

"It is rumored that while here he visited the factories at nearby Basingstoke where he was made aware of the ongoing child-labor abuses," MacGregor recounted. "Some say it formed the basis for his novel *Oliver Twist*."

"So writers have been guests here before," Joanna said.

"We have had our share, but none nearly as strange as the current one," MacGregor replied.

"What an interesting history your inn carries," said Joanna. "Would it be possible for us to be given a tour of its surrounding grounds?"

"I could show you around this afternoon, if you wish."

"That would be most kind of you."

"Then let us gather at four o'clock in the front entrance."

"We shall look forward to it."

MacGregor glanced over his shoulder at the French guests who were now gesturing impatiently to him. "The French," he groaned under his breath as he stepped away.

With the innkeeper out of earshot, I quickly asked, "What do you make of the strange guest?"

"A man who clearly wishes not to be seen by anyone," Joanna said.

"Or perhaps not interrupted," my father suggested. "As a

writer, I can tell you that any interruption can break your train of thought and bring your writing to a standstill. That would explain his desire not to be disturbed by the cleaning and dining schedules at the inn."

"But it would not explain his insistence for a room on the ground floor, with a window that faced the forest," Joanna countered. "I would propose he uses that window as an entrance and exit, thus avoiding being seen by anyone. In the darkness of the evening, when the room is being cleaned and dinner served, he would climb out and disappear into the nearby forest."

My father and I quickly leaned forward, but it was he who asked the question on both our minds. "Are you implicating him in the theft of the document?"

"I am saying we must find a reason for his strange behavior, for it seems most unlikely that he demanded these restrictions only to isolate himself while he toiled over some historical novel." Joanna slowly shook her head as she furrowed her brow. "There is something sinister here and we must uncover what it is."

"And how do we go about that?"

"With guile."

After fortifying ourselves with more dark, rich tea, we strolled to the nearby village on a gray, chilly day. The main street was narrow and lined on both sides by quaint, well-kept shops. Half a block down we passed by women queueing up in front of a thrift store that had a sign in its window advertising a sale on newly acquired secondhand goods. Joanna peered in briefly, for something had caught her interest, but she did not enter and we moved on. Only a few people were up and about and those who were, were bundled in heavy coats against the weather. They paid scant attention to us as we hurried past them and hoped we would not run into Inspector Lestrade. Earlier we had decided not to inform the inspector of our intentions to visit the tobacconist, for he might have alerted them and put them on guard, thus assuring their story would not change.

Up ahead we saw a hanging sign, with its illustration showing a lighted meerschaum pipe. The shop was definitely upscale and not one that would be visited by a stable boy. As I reached for the door it suddenly opened, and much to our surprise an obviously harried Charles Bennett rushed by us. He appeared to barely notice our presence and uttered a mute greeting through tight lips before continuing on his way.

"Rather odd behavior for a butler," I commented.

"Something in the shop has clearly upset him," my father noted.

"Yes, something has," Joanna said, her eyes still on the butler who now seemed to be breaking into a trot. "And we must determine what has so aroused him."

"Do you believe it has great significance?" I asked.

"It does to Charles Bennett," Joanna said. "And thus it does to us."

The air inside the shop held a delightful aroma of fresh tobacco. One section was devoted solely to pipes of all varieties, another to cigars and their accessories, including holders and cutters, and a third section displayed cigarettes and loose tobacco. Joanna immediately purchased a goodly supply of Turkish cigarettes and enchanted the shop owner with her considerable knowledge of the dark tobaccos from Turkey and Syria that produced such a strong, distinctive aroma.

After putting the shop owner, Mr. Brandon Hughes, at ease, Joanna introduced us and our affiliation with Scotland Yard, then inquired about the health of Charles Bennett.

"I just saw Charles Bennett leaving and he seemed quite ill. Is he all right?"

Hughes, a short, stout man with a round face, shook his head sadly. "I am afraid Charles is greatly upset over his son's involvement in the Halifax theft. It is almost too much for the poor man to bear."

"I take it he was here to confirm his son's purchase of a Havana."

"Yes, yes," Hughes said unhappily. "But there can be no doubt of it. We sell very few of those cigars because of their steep price, and when we do we carefully note the buyer."

"So it was you who served him?"

"No, madam. It was my son, Lawrence, who has become quite an expert on cigars. Would you care to speak with him?"

"If it is not inconvenient."

Joanna waited for the shopkeeper to disappear behind a hanging curtain at the rear before speaking in a rapid, quiet voice. "Do not mention the butler's son further. Allow them to bring up the subject and talk freely about it."

"And what if they do not?" I pondered.

"Oh, they will," Joanna assured. "Roger Bennett is now the main topic of conversation in the village, and Mr. Hughes and his son will wish to know every morsel of information so they can add to the local gossip."

As the curtain parted, Joanna brought an index finger to her lips, then strolled over to the cigar section of the shop and peered intently into a glass-covered showcase. I turned my attention back to the approaching shopkeeper and his son who, unlike his father, was quite thin, with a most serious expression that was accentuated by the gold-rimmed spectacles he wore.

The son introduced himself, all the while keeping his eye on Joanna and her apparent interest in the cigar display. "Is there anything in particular that so draws your attention, madam?"

"Indeed," Joanna said pleasantly. "It is the remarkable variety of exotic cigars, which I did not expect to find in a village of this size."

"We are surrounded by a number of well-to-do estates, the members of which favor the finest cigars," Lawrence Hughes explained.

"Which accounts for the Havanas and other Cuban cigars," Joanna remarked. "But I also note a splendid array of cigars from the Dutch East Indies that are somewhat less expensive, yet provide a well-balanced and full smoke."

"The Dutch are less popular because of their rough, unorganized ends," he said, clearly warming to the subject.

"But I am told they still maintain their mellow flavor."

"My, my! You do seem well informed on foreign tobacco. How did you come by such knowledge?"

"From my father," Joanna replied.

"Which cigar did he favor?"

"He was primarily a pipe smoker and preferred rough-cut shag tobacco, although on occasion he would indulge in the best of the Havanas."

"As any gentleman of standing would."

"Precisely," Joanna said, with a firm nod. "Which made it so surprising when we learned that Roger Bennett had purchased the same from you."

"I too was stunned when he laid down a five-pound note for two of the finest Havanas we have in stock."

"Two, you say?"

"Two."

Joanna rubbed at her chin pensively. "Are you quite certain it was Roger Bennett?"

"Most certainly. I had seen him about the village on a number of occasions and had even spoken to him briefly."

"Were you friends?"

"Oh, no, madam. We were more like passing acquaintances."

"Had he ever been in your shop before?"

"Never. Most of our products are on the costly side, so we see little trade with common laborers."

"Did Roger Bennett wish to see a variety of cigars?"

"He had no interest in anything other than the Havanas."

"Did he speak of the qualities of the cigar, like a true connoisseur would?"

"No, madam. There was no conversation at all. He abruptly ordered the cigars, then paid and left, which is most unlike the usual buyer of the finest Cuban."

"So, you noticed nothing unusual about him?"

The son hesitated for a moment, as if thinking back. "He did have a somewhat peculiar hue about his complexion. It was pale and pasty, like someone who had been confined to the indoors. I wondered if he had been ill."

"Did you so inquire?" Joanna asked without inflection.

"Not to him, but to his father just a moment ago. It seemed that the mention of his son's drawn, pallid appearance caused the old man to become most upset." The son shrugged to himself. "I meant no offense, but was concerned because of the possibility of illness."

"I am certain that in retrospect the butler will see that you were simply worried about the state of his son's health."

"Let us hope so."

"I have one more question," Joanna said. "Did Roger Bennett make any other purchases during his visit?"

"He bought nothing else."

"No holders or cutters?"

"None whatsoever. Although I did find it odd that he had no idea what a cutter was when I offered to show him one. I mean, after all, most smokers of fine cigars use a cutter to nip off the head before lighting. Strange, eh?"

"Quite," Joanna agreed.

"And what was stranger yet was his outburst when I attempted to explain the purpose of a cutter," the son went on. "He became most upset, with his face turning red and filled with anger. He leaned in toward me in such a threatening fashion that I feared for my safety."

"Did he actually strike you?"

"No, ma'am, but I do believe he was on the verge of doing so. However, another customer entered our shop at that very moment and this fortunate occurrence may have dissuaded the stable boy from committing any violence."

"Do you have any idea what set off this uncalled-for behavior?"

"None in the least. I wondered if he had misinterpreted my explanation on the use of the cutter, believing that I was being condescending and speaking down to him. But he ignored my apology and, without a final word, snatched up the cigars and left in a huff." The son shook his head at the unpleasant memory. "I of course discussed the incident with my father and he was of the opinion that the violent outburst may have been brought on by the boy's illness. Sick people at times can be quite short-tempered, my father reasoned."

"Indeed they can," Joanna said, and thanked the son for being so helpful to the investigation.

Outside, a warming sun was beginning to peek through the clouds and the brisk breeze we had felt earlier had died down. We waited until we were well clear of the main street and out in the countryside before discussing the comments of the shopkeeper and his son.

"There are so many contradictions here that it is impossible to put together a cogent scenario," Joanna mused. "Every fact and clue we gain seems to be disputed by yet another fact or clue. Let us begin with why a well-conditioned athlete in training would purchase two of the finest cigars, which he most certainly could not afford."

"Particularly a mile runner who depends entirely on the power of his muscles and strength of his lungs," my father said. "The effect of cigar smoke on his bronchi would be disastrous and cut his wind and endurance substantially. Yet here he is, buying not one but two cigars that give off a quite strong smoke."

"And where did he acquire the money to purchase the cigars?" Joanna asked. "As a stable boy, his monthly salary would not begin to cover the cost of one Havana, much less two."

"Perhaps he was prepaid for his part in the theft of the document," my father proposed. "He was delighted with his newfound fortune and decided to celebrate by buying two very expensive cigars."

Joanna shook her head vigorously. "It still does not fit. A highly trained athlete, who lives for his sport, does not celebrate with strong cigars. His fondest dream is to be invited to join His Majesty's Olympic team. Why would he ruin his chances to do so? Recall that the walls of his bedroom were covered with posters of Olympic athletes, so it was the first thing he saw in the morning and the last at night. And there was a British flag tacked to the wall demonstrating his love of country, which is hardly the hallmark of a man about to commit a traitorous act."

"But there remains abundant circumstantial evidence supporting his guilt," my father argued. "I am of the opinion the case against him is strengthened by his father's anguished reaction to the eyewitness account of his son's purchase of Havana cigars. The man looked as if he had witnessed the lad's execution."

"In a way, perhaps he had," I said.

"I see both of your points, but please reconsider with these facts in mind," Joanna said. "First, there is the color of his complexion. Distance runners have rosy, glowing cheeks that radiate good health, not the dull, pallid skin that Roger Bennett demonstrated, and that was duly noted by the shopkeeper's son. Also recall that the father's reaction was not to the mention of his son's name, but to his peculiar hue suggesting illness. That is what so agitated the butler. Why would it do so?"

Her question was met with silence from both of us.

"This is a most important clue, for it relates to something disturbing that suddenly appeared in the stable boy," Joanna continued. "As a surgical nurse at St. Bart's, I myself saw such abrupt changes in skin color when a patient suffered rupture of a great artery or met with some horrendous traumatic event. But neither of these occurrences are present here, so we must seek another cause." Turning to my father, she said, "At this point, Watson, I must impose on your medical expertise from many years of practice and ask the following—what could bring such an abrupt change to one's complexion?"

"Several disastrous disorders come to mind," my father replied. "Both a massive heart attack and a stroke can induce a deathly hue to one's facial appearance. A so-called gray face mask can also result from the prior ingestion of certain poisons or mind-altering stimulants."

"A mind-altering stimulant!" Joanna cried out. "Are you saying that a powerful drug could so transform an individual?"

"It is a well-known phenomenon, particularly when such drugs induce profound hallucinations."

"Such as described in the story of Dr. Jekyll and Mr. Hyde?"

"Precisely."

Joanna nodded to herself and said, "And that could explain the butler's reaction to his son's complexion. Charles Bennett had seen the transformation before and knew he was again looking at the two sides of Roger Bennett—a Dr. Jekyll and Mr. Hyde, the latter being drug-induced and capable of committing criminal acts."

"It could also explain the stable boy's near violent behavior in the tobacco shop," said my father, nodding back. "We may well have two separate personalities existing in the same individual."

"One being the diametric opposite of the other."

"But how do we prove it?"

"By demanding the truth from Charles Bennett."

7

The Stable

We joined Trevor MacGregor at the front entrance of the inn
at four sharp. In the late afternoon sunlight, all details of the
fine structure were now clearly visible. The Hampshire Inn
was a broad, two-story building that was whitewashed and
surrounded on three sides by dense woods. The open side
faced a road that led to a thoroughfare half a mile away. On
the lawn before us stood a wooden sign that gave directions
to the stable.

Joanna asked, "Is the stable still in use?"

"Less and less these days, as you can see from the condition of the bridle path." MacGregor pointed to a path on the
side of the inn that was partially hidden by weeds and overgrowth. "I once had three horses and two dogcarts available
for my guests. Now I have one of each and I sometimes wonder why I bother to keep those."

We walked another dozen paces before reaching the stable
with its straw-covered floor and three stalls, two of which

were vacant. The third held a gray mare who paid scant attention to us. By contrast, a nearby border collie quickly got to her feet and, crouching low, fixed her eyes and nose on the intruders. On recognizing MacGregor she relaxed and came over for a gentle scratch on her head.

"Border collies make excellent watchdogs," MacGregor remarked. "They are smart and keen and friendly to their human family, but not to others. If strangers enter the stable, they will regret it."

"Have there been unwanted visitors lately?" Joanna asked.

MacGregor nodded. "A few weeks back a vagabond slipped into the stable at night, seeking shelter from the cold and rain. Sally raised quite a ruckus and chased the poor bugger into a corner."

"So you apprehended him?"

"And fed him and sent him on his way," MacGregor said, with a shrug. "I also instructed him not to tell others of my kindness, for if he did, I would not call Sally off the next intruder."

While Joanna gazed about the well-kept stable, it was a bicycle in the far corner that drew my father's interest. The bike rested on wooden blocks and appeared to be partially restored, with rusted handlebars and its front fender and wheel missing. A polished leather seat was torn, but still serviceable. My father strolled over to examine the metal name tag on its frame.

"Ah, it is a Military Humber, I see," he remarked.

"Indeed it is," said MacGregor.

"But I read that these sturdy bikes were made specifically for His Majesty's army."

"They were, which leads to an interesting story behind this particular bicycle," MacGregor continued on. "A truckload of Military Humbers were being transported when a major accident occurred on the nearby thoroughfare. The bikes were tossed about and run over by passing trucks and motorcars, leaving many torn apart and damaged beyond repair. Most were carted away by the military, but a few of the badly mangled bikes were overlooked, and Roger Bennett found one in the tall grass by the roadside and brought it here in an attempt to restore it. The lad is known to be very good with his hands."

The innkeeper walked over to the bike and climbed aboard, fitting his feet into the leather straps on its pedals. He then began pedaling vigorously, causing the rear wheel to spin smoothly and noiselessly. After a half minute or so, he applied the brakes and the wheel stopped instantly. "In another few weeks it would have been good to go and ready for use. Roger and I formed a partnership, you see, with me paying for the tires and paint while he did the repairs. Once it was fully restored, we planned to rent it out to guests and split the proceeds fifty-fifty. But alas, that is not going to happen now, is it?"

"So it would seem," Joanna replied, watching the innkeeper dismount and step over a wool blanket that covered odd-shaped objects. Pointing to it, she asked, "Spare parts?"

MacGregor nodded. "Which unfortunately will never be used."

As we passed by the stalls, the mare nearby inhaled quickly, then puffed the breath out through her nostrils, producing a soft, purring sound.

"She does that when she wishes attention," MacGregor informed us. "I am afraid she is becoming a bit lonely for human companionship. And now with Roger Bennett's troubles, this will only increase."

Joanna's brow went up. "How was Roger Bennett connected to the mare?"

"I paid him half a crown a month to look after the stable," MacGregor replied. "It was not much work and only required that he feed and water the horse and clean the stalls. As I mentioned, he is also quite handy with tools and could repair the dogcart when needed."

"So he was a good worker."

"Quite."

As we turned away from the mare, the animal snorted and whinnied gently, then moved her head up and down.

MacGregor came back to the mare and rubbed her snout. "She has not been comfortable since going lame."

"When did this occur?" Joanna asked.

"Sometime yesterday, I would think," MacGregor replied. "Walter, our waiter who also helps out in the stable, reported it to me this morning, but swears the mare was fine the morning before. We are waiting for the visiting veterinarian to have a look."

"Thus it would appear the injury must have happened after Roger Bennett's troubles began," said Joanna.

"So it would seem," MacGregor said. "But the reason is beyond me. It is most unusual for a horse to go lame while in their stall."

"Most unusual indeed," Joanna agreed as a faint smile came and went from her face. "I would be curious to learn the veterinarian's opinion on the cause of the lameness."

"Once I know I shall inform you."

Joanna strolled over to the dusty dogcart and studied it at length. It was a two-wheeled, horse-drawn cart with cross seats back to back. For some reason, it was one of the wheels that drew her attention. "This cart has seen better days."

"But it remains sturdy enough for service," MacGregor said. "Of course it is much more appealing when washed."

Joanna rubbed a finger over the wheel and examined the mud that came off it. Then she reached for her magnifying glass and, leaning forward, closely inspected the entire circumference of the wheel. "Do the gouges I see cause a rough ride?"

"Not that one would notice, for the paths here and about are somewhat rocky and uneven."

"Who would drive the dogcarts for your visitors?"

"That would depend on who was available. At times it would be Roger Bennett, on other occasions Walter."

"The two of them got along well, did they?"

"Oh, yes. But now and then they would have a good-natured wrestling match to see who was the strongest and would thus be favored by our most attractive chambermaid." MacGregor chuckled briefly to himself. "Which of course was in their fantasies. The chambermaid had her man and would not show the slightest interest in a poor stable boy or under-sized waiter."

"You mentioned that the chambermaid had her man," Joanna inquired. "Is she married?"

MacGregor shook his head. "She fancies a man from a nearby estate whom she meets on a side path near the inn."

"Did you recognize him?"

"I never saw him myself, but only learned of the secret meetings from Walter."

"It is difficult to keep secrets in a close-knit inn, is it not?"

"It is impossible, madam."

MacGregor led the way out and paid no attention to the adjacent bridle path, but Joanna did. Some aspect of the weed-covered path was of interest to her. I saw nothing remarkable other than its lack of use and puddles of standing water. We strolled to the rear of the building and passed a large storeroom and expansive kitchen before coming to the wooded area that faced the northern exposure of the inn.

"The forest extends to the Halifax estate itself," MacGregor told us. "As a matter of fact, a fair amount of it is owned by the estate."

"Are there paths in and out?" Joanna asked.

"Only a few narrow ones that I am told are under close watch when the Halifaxes are in residence."

"So, for the most part, people do not venture in."

"I request my guests not to do so for, as I have mentioned, most of it is private property."

"Do the Halifaxes make a big issue of this?"

"Their security guards do, for the Duke holds a much-esteemed position in His Majesty's government."

"And with the winds of war swirling about us, one cannot be too cautious," said my father.

"Exactly right, sir," MacGregor concurred. "My French guests tell me that war is imminent and the Germans will soon be on the march."

"Again," my father noted sourly.

"It is in their blood."

Joanna stepped in closer to the wooded area and motioned to a small clearing no more than ten yards across. It was protected by a stretch of canvas that was held aloft by thin poles. "May I ask the purpose of this tentlike structure?"

"We cut away the brush and small trees, hoping it would be used as a picnic area," MacGregor replied. "But our guests have shown little interest."

"Yet I see footprints in the wet soil," Joanna pointed out, and leaned down for a closer look.

"Perhaps someone just wandered in," MacGregor said, then, with a worried expression, added, "Let us hope they do not become lost."

"That did not occur," Joanna assured. "For I see footprints exiting as well."

"Aye," MacGregor said, glancing over Joanna's shoulder at the prints. "They are probably made by someone on an inquisitive stroll."

"That would explain it," Joanna agreed, but her eyes remained focused on the footprints.

MacGregor reached for his timepiece and said, "I hope you will be good enough to excuse me, for I must now make preparations for our early diners."

"Of course," Joanna said. "And thank you for the most informative tour."

Once the innkeeper was out of earshot, Joanna quickly turned to me and spoke in a low voice. "Look carefully at the footprints and tell me what you see."

I knelt down and closely inspected the footprints in the mud. "They were made by a man wearing workman shoes. The depth of the footprints say he was a large man and the length of his stride would indicate a height of near six feet."

"Spot on, John. But there is more."

I examined the footprints once again, looking for details I might have missed, but could find none. "Pray tell, what has escaped my inspection?"

"The fact that the prints you just studied are remarkably similar to the prints we discovered in the attic space."

I quickly reached for pen and paper, which I kept in my coat pocket. "I shall make an exact copy of this print so we can compare it to that found in the attic."

"Please note that the left heel is a bit more worn than that on the right."

"Would the wear be enough to cause a change in gait?"

"A very good question, John, but I think not. Nevertheless, it may still serve a purpose. We should reexamine the footprint in the attic and see if it too shows a worn left heel."

"Which would strongly suggest they were made by the same individual."

"But why would the thief take a walk in the mud outside—" my father was turning to ask Joanna when the answer came to him. "I say! Do you believe those mud prints were made by the secret lodger on one of his concealed journeys?"

"That, Watson, is a most intriguing possibility."

"So this little venture with MacGregor may turn out to be quite productive," my father noted.

"But we are not done yet."

"Oh?"

Joanna smiled at my father. "How are your muscles holding up, Watson?"

"They are a bit tired, but willing to carry on."

"Excellent! Then let us return to the bridle path where more clues await us." As Joanna stepped away from the clearing, she abruptly stopped and turned back to us. "Do not look at the inn while we walk away. Appear to be gazing at the sky or woods, for behind a first-floor window I saw a figure staring out at us."

"Could you make out his face?" I asked quietly.

"That was not possible, but it was the figure of a man," Joanna replied. "A large man."

"Might it be the secret lodger?"

"That is to be determined," said Joanna, and walked away from the clearing with her eyes averted from the inn.

We strolled back to the stable at a slow pace, so as not to stress my father's endurance further. But it still required effort for him to keep up with us, which was evidenced by him leaning more heavily on his walking stick. On our approach to the stable, the border collie came to the door and eyed us carefully before letting out a low, menacing growl.

"Quite territorial, is she not?" I commented.

"Make a note of that for future reference," Joanna said, and guided us to the muddied bridle path. The first ten yards were covered with weeds and brush, but beyond the overgrowth the earth could be seen more clearly. It was this portion of the path that drew Joanna's interest. She walked back and forth along its outer edges, head down, her gaze fixed on the muddy trail. She made the journey three times, appearing to scour every inch of the ground.

"More footprints?" I called out.

Joanna shook her head. "Dogcart tracks."

"What do you make of them?"

"Everything," Joanna responded. "For I now know where and when the horse went lame, and who the driver was."

My father and I moved in for a closer inspection of the marks that had been left behind by the dogcart and horse. There was a confusing array of tracks in the mud, for some were crisscrossed while others ran in opposite directions. No human footprints could be seen.

"I observe no telltale signs," said I.

"Nor I," my father agreed.

"What of the crisscrossed tracks made by the horse and dogcart?" Joanna asked.

My father and I gave the matter thought, but could not come up with an answer.

"There is only one possible explanation," Joanna continued on. "The horse and cart left the path, turned around and came back onto it. This is evidenced by the pressed-down vegetation on the opposite side of the path." She pointed to the indentations in the grass and weeds that were made by wheels and hoofprints. "Thus we can conclude the dogcart and horse were driven off the path here and then returned to the path, resulting in the crisscrossed pattern you observed."

"But why?" I asked. "Did something frighten them?"

"No, dear John," Joanna replied. "They returned to the stable because the horse went lame."

"That scenario fits," my father concurred. "But that is only an assumption, is it not?"

"The proof is before your eyes," Joanna said, coming to our side and motioning to the hoofprints in the mud. "Allow me to draw your attention to the hoofprints leading away from the stable. You will note that the four prints are all even and virtually identical to one another. On the return journey, however, only three are the same. The fourth is not as deep and obviously drawn out. This is the certain sign of a horse gone lame, for it will not place weight on the injured hoof and will simply drag it along."

My father gave Joanna an admiring look. "May I ask how you came across this information?"

"My father-in-law and I took to the riding path in Hyde Park with some frequency, and on occasion a horse around us would go lame. It was then that I noticed the indisputable evidence of an injured hoof."

"However, we cannot be certain that the tracks we see

were produced by MacGregor's dogcart," I argued mildly. "There must be others in the vicinity."

"That are drawn by a lame horse?" Joanna countered.

"Unlikely, but not out of the question."

"But there is further proof," Joanna went on. "First, there is wet mud on the wheel of the dogcart in the stable that Mac-Gregor tells us has not been in use for weeks. Thus, someone must have taken the cart out of the stable without his permission. Since it rained last night, but not the day or night before, we can reasonably conclude that MacGregor's dogcart was very recently on the bridle path, from which it collected mud."

"It is still not conclusive evidence," I persisted. "Logic by itself will not stand up in a court of law."

"But the distinctive track made by the dogcart will," Joanna said, and gestured to a deep indentation in the mud caused by a wheel. "You will note that at approximately six and twelve o'clock there are obvious gouges. These very same gouges were present on one of the dogcart's wheels in MacGregor's stable."

"Thus the dogcart had to have come from MacGregor's stable," I agreed. "And since the border collie did not raise a ruckus on its preparation and departure, it must have recognized the driver. It could not have been MacGregor or Walter, the waiter, which leaves us with the stable boy, Roger Bennett."

"That is undeniably the case," said my father.

"Furthermore," I reasoned on, "there is only one explanation that would link all these facts and occurrences together. Please follow my line of logic here. It goes as follows. Roger Bennett, desperate to escape, crept into the stable late last night in the rain and prepared the dogcart and mare for travel.

Sally, the border collie, did not bark, for she knew the stable boy well. In the quiet of night, down the bridle path they go until the mare comes up lame, forcing Roger Bennett to turn the dogcart around and return to the stable."

"Well done, John," my father praised. "But unfortunately that does not bring us any closer to the missing document. In that we already have doubts about the stable boy's guilt, it now seems the unknown secret lodger is our most likely suspect."

"Then we are faced with a most confusing conundrum," I thought aloud. "Assuming the secret lodger is the thief in the attic and the same person who strolled onto the clearing in the forest, it cannot be he who took the dogcart for its midnight ride."

My father nodded at my conclusion. "For the secret lodger would have surely aroused the border collie."

"That depends, my dear Watson," Joanna said.

"On what, pray tell?"

"On whether you have excluded the possibility that the secret lodger previously encountered the border collie under more pleasant circumstances," Joanna replied.

"But how could he bring this about?" my father asked.

"Via Walter, the waiter, who leaves dinner for the lodger outside his door every night," Joanna answered. "It would be a simple matter for the lodger to exit through the window in his room, slink along the walls of the inn to the stable and feed the dog lamb bones that would render the secret lodger a most welcomed friend. You must remember that in dogs nothing supersedes their stomachs."

"Do you truly believe this happened?" I inquired.

"I am only raising the possibility," said Joanna.

"But you must admit this sequence of events is quite unlikely," my father contended.

"Dear Watson, please recall Sherlock Holmes's advice in this particular regard," Joanna said. "His exact words were, 'Once you eliminate the impossible, whatever remains, no matter how improbable, must be the truth.' Now, have you eliminated the possibility that the secret lodger previously befriended the dog?"

"I have not."

"Nor have I. We should keep in mind that we are dealing with a very clever thief. And the cleverest of thieves always has an unanticipated escape route."

As we strolled back to the front entrance, my father began to falter and limp noticeably. Out of concern, I offered my arm and he accepted it. Joanna and I exchanged worrisome glances, both of us now fearing he would never have a complete recovery. I took some comfort, however, in the knowledge I had had my father far longer than most sons and should be grateful for that.

Stepping into the inn, Joanna saw Trevor MacGregor at the reception desk and hurried over to him. My father and I rested on a comfortable couch in the lobby and waited for Joanna to conduct her apparently important business. Moments later she returned and motioned us away from the other guests in the lobby.

"What was your conversation regarding?" I asked, quietly.

"The man staring out at us from the first-floor window."

"And?"

"He is the secret lodger."

8

An Unexpected Death

It was in the midst of breakfast the following morning that we received the most unexpected news.

A local constable hurried to our table and said in a clearly urgent voice, "Inspector Lestrade requests your immediate presence at the Halifax estate. I have a hansom at your disposal."

"Did the inspector give a reason?" Joanna asked.

"Oh yes, madam. The butler, Charles Bennett, has been found dead."

On the ride out we wondered if and how the sudden demise of Charles Bennett might be connected to the missing document. Joanna reminded us that all deaths fell into four categories—natural, accidental, suicidal, and homicidal. If the butler's death was caused by suicide or homicide, it would surely be part and parcel of the investigation, with the *how* it was related to be determined. We were all eager to learn the circumstances surrounding the butler's end, but Joanna thought it best to hold our questions until a thorough examination could be performed. One of her cardinal rules was to neither accept nor seek secondhand information, for it tended to be inaccurate and only served to lead the investigator astray.

For most of the journey, Joanna kept her head buried in the morning newspapers, only to conclude with an indecipherable hum.

"Is there something of interest?" I asked.

"There is one somewhat curious notice," she replied.

"Which is?"

"The Deutsche Society of Edgware Road has been closed for renovations."

"What is so curious about the renovations?"

"The timing."

On arrival at the estate, we were not driven to the main house or to the butler's cottage, but rather to a large motor garage where Inspector Lestrade awaited us. Standing next to him was a tall, well-built man, with a ramrod posture and a very short haircut. His expression could best be described as stern and resolute.

"What we have here is quite obviously suicide," Lestrade said, and pointed to the closed rear window of a quiet limousine. "In the backseat you will see the body of Charles Bennett, who apparently could not bear the disgrace his son has brought upon the family. He was discovered this morning exactly where he sits, with the motor running. The cherry-red color of his skin, which I have encountered on numerous occasions in the past, indicates he died of self-induced carbon monoxide poison. The gentleman to my right is Lieutenant Dunn from the Office of Naval Intelligence who has been sent to join our investigation. The lieutenant has also seen his share of carbon monoxide poisonings and confirms my suspicions."

"There can be no doubt of it, as you can see for yourself," Dunn said, and gestured to the corpse. The motion exposed a multicolored tattoo on his wrist.

Before I could study the tattoo further, Lestrade opened the rear door of the limousine, giving us a clear view of the body in the bright morning light. Charles Bennett was sitting upright, his eyes wide open and staring out into vacant space. The skin about his face, particularly his lips, was colored cherry red. His gloved hands were unclenched. "No one can deny what has occurred here," the inspector concluded.

Joanna moved to the rear of the limousine and leaned over to examine the exhaust pipe. Something must have caught her eye, for she reached over to a nearby yardstick and inserted its length into the pipe without meeting resistance. "I note the exhaust pipe has not been blocked."

"The motor's fumes could still accumulate overnight within the car's cabin," Dunn said. "And this of course would allow the level of carbon monoxide to rise to a lethal concentration."

"But is it not true that in the majority of carbon monoxide–induced suicides, the exhaust pipe is occluded to ensure a toxic level of the poisonous gas?" Joanna pondered.

"There are exceptions," Dunn countered.

"One must be careful with exceptions, Lieutenant, for they are at times used to explain away an important clue." Joanna strolled over to the rear windows and closely examined the ones on each side of the limousine. She next inspected the sliding glass panel that separated the open driver's compartment from the rear cabin. "The fittings on one window and on the panel are not well sealed. There are narrow gaps between the window and panel and the roof above. These openings could provide cross-ventilation."

"But you still must explain the cherry-red complexion of the corpse," Lestrade challenged.

"I must admit that it is a characteristic of carbon monoxide poisoning, but the other clues I mentioned do not fit with this diagnosis. Thus we must search for another cause." Joanna turned to me, saying, "You are an experienced pathologist at St. Bartholomew's, John, and this should fall within your area of expertise. Are there other diagnoses that are associated with the acute onset of a cherry-red complexion?"

"None that come immediately to mind, but allow me to have a quick look at the corpse; it might prove revealing."

I climbed into the rear cabin, careful not to disturb the position of the body. The gloved corpse of the butler was upright, his expression peaceful, his mouth partially open, with his chin resting on his chest. There was no outward evidence of trauma except perhaps for a drop of dried blood on his lower lip. But it was his eyes that caught my attention. They were open, and should not have been. Individuals exposed to lethal levels of carbon monoxide drift into a coma, with their eyes closing as they were falling asleep. There was nothing else remarkable, but my line of vision went back to the spot of crusted blood on the corpse's lip. How did it get there? People slowly lapsing into coma do not bite their lower lip nor have seizures. I next considered the possibility that a superficial lesion on the mucosa had oozed blood, which would account for its presence. Using a piece of tissue paper, I pulled the lower lip down and peered in. A front tooth looked chipped, but that could have been old. I moved in closer for a better view of the palate and pharynx. It was at that moment I detected the distinctive aroma of bitter almonds. Bitter almonds!

I came back to the group and announced, "It was not

carbon monoxide, but cyanide that killed Charles Bennett. This is not suicide, but unmitigated murder."

"What are the signs?" Joanna asked at once.

"There are two," I replied. "The major finding was the distinctive odor of bitter almonds emanating from the corpse's mouth. No other poison causes this unique scent."

Lestrade quickly entered the rear compartment of the limousine and sniffed at the butler's open mouth. "Blimey! It does smell of bitter almonds. Are you quite certain, Dr. Watson, that only cyanide can be held responsible for this aroma?"

"Quite."

"But what of the cherry-red color to his skin?"

"That too on occasion can be a consequence of cyanide poisoning, and much resembles that which is induced by carbon monoxide," I explained. "However, the mechanism that causes the discoloration is different for the two toxic agents. Carbon monoxide combines tightly with the hemoglobin in an individual's blood to form carboxyhemoglobin, which has a cherry-red color and so taints the skin. Cyanide, on the other hand, poisons the body's cells so they cannot take up oxygen, so the oxygen content in the blood remains very high and thus results in a bright red color."

"How do we know the cyanide was not self-administered?" Lestrade asked. "Perhaps he wished to make double certain of his death."

"That would be most unlikely, Inspector," Joanna said. "Cyanide causes instant and certain death, while carbon monoxide must accumulate unpredictably over hours to reach a lethal level. Surely the butler would have swallowed the cyanide first, and thus had neither the need nor opportunity to construct a second mechanism for his suicide."

"But if the poor man was murdered, how was the cyanide forced into him?" Lestrade inquired.

I attempted to suppress my smile as all the pieces of the puzzle came together. *Forced* was the key word here. "The corpse had a chipped front tooth and a spot of blood on his lip, both of which would have occurred while the victim was resisting having his mouth pried open."

"Excellent, John!" Joanna proclaimed, then began to pace back and forth as she gave the matter more thought. There was some aspect of the murder scene that seemed to be bothering her. She lighted a Turkish cigarette and was about to start off again, then quickly turned to me. "Were there any signs of a struggle?"

"None about his face, other than the spot of blood. And his hands were gloved, so his nails could not have been broken nor would there be blood beneath them from fighting off his assailant."

"He had to be held down," Joanna surmised. "His head had to be stationary, at least for a moment or two, so the cyanide could be forced into his oral cavity."

"I could see no bruises about his face."

"What of his neck?"

"There were no marks on the lower portion, but I did not examine the jawline area, for fear of altering the position of the head at this early stage of the investigation."

"Please examine that area now, John," Joanna said. "I am certain Inspector Lestrade would have no objection."

Lestrade gestured his approval.

I reentered the rear compartment of the limousine and gently lifted up the corpse's head. Just below the angle of the mandible on both sides were deep bruises that were circular in nature and most likely produced by fingers on a tight grip. "There are bruises here under the jawline."

"To hold the head steady," Joanna concluded. "And since the butler would have continued to resist, I think it fair to say our killer had most powerful hands."

"And arms," Lestrade added. "Which he employed in climbing up and down a length of rope to enter and exit the attic space."

"Thus it would seem," Joanna agreed. "So now we not only have a thief, but a vicious murderer as well."

"But why kill a harmless butler?" Lestrade asked.

"Because he knew too much and may well have uncovered something incriminating," Joanna responded.

My father and I exchanged quick glances, both of us wondering if the episode at the tobacconist had somehow brought about the murder of the butler. Joanna said nothing further on the matter, so we too remained silent.

"Nicely done," Dunn said, but the tone of his voice carried scant praise. "Yet I am afraid your quick deductions bring us no closer to the missing document."

"It would appear you do not approve of my methods," Joanna said, taking no offense.

"I believe rapid deductions have their place in uncomplicated crimes, but are of little value in more complex cases, such as the one we are facing."

"Rapid deductions can be of great relevance if they are based on fact, and this holds true for all criminal acts, regardless of their complexity," Joanna countered. "For example, if there was a Chinese suspect in this case who spoke only the Mandarin dialect, I would know to call on you to be the interrogator."

Dunn was taken aback. "How are you aware that I speak Mandarin?"

"By the tattoo on your wrist, which makes all so obvious."

"Do you speak Mandarin?"

"Not a word," Joanna said, and turned her attention back to the corpse of Charles Bennett. "John, do you think it worthwhile to remove the butler's gloves to make sure there is no evidence of self-defense?"

I carefully took off the white gloves and noticed that the corpse's skin was now turning a dark brown color. This finding confirmed the diagnosis of cyanide poisoning. Unlike that of carbon monoxide toxicity, the cherry-red color from cyanide fades quickly because the oxygen content in the blood dissipates at a rapid rate and thus induces the skin to darken. "His arms are clean and there are no scratch marks on his hands," I called out.

"Most unfortunate," Joanna called back. "For the butler's attention to proper dress, even in death, may have robbed us of an important clue."

"Such as?" Dunn asked.

"Such as deep scratch marks on the hands and arms of a prime suspect," Joanna answered. "So you see, Lieutenant, one clue, no matter how trivial it may seem, could lead to another clue and yet another, which when all pieced together offer a solution to the crime. That is my method and the method of my father before me."

"Inspector Lestrade warned me of your unique talent," Dunn said, his voice more appreciative now. "But pray tell, how could you possibly know I speak Mandarin?"

"By a combination of clues," Joanna recounted. "First, your posture and bearing, along with your short haircut and sharply creased trousers, all tell of a long military background. Secondly, your tattoo consists of a blue anchor that signifies you were either a sailor or marine, with your strict orderliness pointing strongly to the naval sector."

"I served and continue to serve in the Royal Navy," Dunn said. "But how can you relate this to my knowledge of Mandarin?"

"There is more," Joanna went on. "Now, below the anchor is Chinese script, which is characterized by red lettering that is quite square and dense, with no flowery component that is common in written Japanese. This difference was delineated most excellently by my father in his monograph on tattoos. So, with these clues, we have a well-polished naval officer who spent considerable time in China. And this begs the question— what were his duties while stationed there? Well, the best career officers would in all likelihood be assigned as naval attachés to the British Embassy in Peking where Mandarin is the commonly spoken dialect. Since the script below the anchor is written in Chinese, rather than English, I think it reasonable to assume you are familiar with Mandarin."

"The personification of Holmes," my father whispered under his breath.

"So you see, Lieutenant, it was all in the clues that were laid out before me," Joanna concluded. "Trivial clues, you might call them, but they become quite important when placed in proper order."

"I am still not convinced that a few rapid deductions will solve this most complex case," Dunn persisted.

"You will be when all is said and done," Joana responded. "Now tell us, is your visit here connected to the temporary closing of the Deutsche Society on Edgware Road?"

"How did you learn of the closing?" Dunn asked in a rush.

"It was duly noted in the morning edition of the *Daily Telegraph*."

"I am not at liberty to share that information with you," Dunn said, his face closing.

"No matter," Joanna said nonchalantly. "I will call the First Sea Lord who will provide me with all the necessary details. You see, I am here at his request."

Dunn sighed so heavily it sounded like a groan. "I was not informed of this. Please forgive me for being so secretive, but the fewer people here who know of my mission, the better."

"I understand, but your information might be most helpful as I continue in my line of investigation," Joanna said. "Rest assured that not a word spoken will leave this garage, for I, along with my husband and Dr. Watson, have signed the Official Secrets Act."

"Very well, then," Dunn said, lowering his voice while glancing over his shoulder at the door to make certain no one was within earshot. "It all revolves around the grounds-keeper, Henry Miller, or Heinrich Mueller if you prefer, and his membership in the Deutsche Society, a German club he helped establish and one in which we have a reliable informant. This club has a membership of over twenty-five men, half of whom still hold citizenship in their native Germany. To a man they love the fatherland and praise Kaiser Wilhelm's desire to dominate the entire continent. They disparage England and its ways, but never talk openly of sedition, although there is no doubt whose side they would be on should war with Germany ever break out."

"That Teutonic fervor never leaves them," my father growled.

"I am afraid you are correct in that, sir," Dunn said. "But now the trail becomes even more enticing. Our prime suspect, Roger Bennett, visited the club at Henry Miller's urging where by all accounts he was warmly welcomed. Miller, you see, is beloved by the other members and his allegiance to Germany remains quite strong, for he is the one who sings *Deutschland Uber Alles* the loudest. In any event, whilst visiting the society, Roger Bennett spoke fondly of Germany and its athletic accomplishments and requested information on living there. He even asked if they could provide a visa form for him to apply. They could not, but directed him to the German embassy where he was spotted and we assume sought the visa application. With all this in mind, we believe Roger Bennett may well be collaborating with members of the society, and thus we have closed it down while we interrogate its members. We also believe that they, along with Henry Miller, may lead us to the whereabouts of our prime suspect. I am here to question Henry Miller who might know the most about Roger Bennett."

"Such an open investigation could cause the collaborators to bolt," Joanna proposed.

"Which is our intent, for we have eyes on all twenty-five-odd members and will look for the ones who run."

"Quite clever," Joanna said. "But the fox who becomes aware of the hounds often seeks deeper cover."

"That is the risk we must take, for time is of the essence."

"Chancy," Joanna murmured to herself.

"Do you disapprove?"

"I neither approve nor disapprove, but will for now concentrate my thoughts on the evil deed just committed by our villain. There is a reason behind this murder that I believe will lead to the thief and the missing document."

"Aye," the naval officer concurred. "The murderer and the thief must be one and the same."

"And a nasty piece of work he is," Lestrade said, glancing back at the corpse of Charles Bennett. "What sort of animal kills his own father?"

A drug-crazed one, I was tempted to say, but held my tongue.

9

The Shed

We spent most of the day searching through the butler's papers and belongings, in hopes of uncovering clues that could lead to his son's whereabouts. In the top drawer of an oak cabinet we found old letters from the butler's brother who was a dockworker in Liverpool. They spoke mainly of the brother's family and how much they enjoyed their summer visits to Hampshire. But the last of the letters had been mailed five years earlier. It contained only a short obituary that stated the brother had died in an accidental fall. We went through all the shelves and other drawers and even turned the cushions of an old couch, but discovered nothing of consequence. As we walked toward the son's bedroom, we again noticed two framed photographs on the wall, both of which appeared quite dated. One showed a long line of uniformed rugby players, with their coach, the other a large group of family members, with a younger Charles Bennett in the center. There were far more children than adults in the picture from a generation ago.

The son's bedroom had already been rummaged through by Lestrade and Dunn. If there were any findings of note, they did not disclose them to us. For reasons unknown, the inspector and the naval officer kept us at a distance while they pursued their avenue of investigation. This did not seem to bother Joanna in the least, for she was not impressed by either of them.

"Lestrade is rather unimaginative, and one has to place a subtle clue under his nose before he sees its significance," Joanna said without rancor. "Dunn is brighter, but very straightforward and by the book, as one would expect with his military background. They refuse to leave the beaten path, which is unfortunate because that is where most of the answers lie. So, for now, it is best they go their way and we go ours."

"But they may stumble onto something of importance," my father suggested.

"Which they will share with us when they run into a dead end."

"And what makes you so certain that will happen?"

"Our past experience with Lestrade is he must be led to the correct deduction," Joanna replied. "When the tight knot has to be untied, he knows where to turn."

"Indeed," my father said, with a nod. "Like his father's dependence on Sherlock Holmes."

"It runs in the blood," Joanna said, and began viewing the disarray in the bedroom left behind by Lestrade and Dunn. Drawers were open and their contents strewn about the floor. The mattress had been lifted and remained askew, a pillowcase removed and thrown aside. Even the posters of track athletes on the wall had been taken down and in some instances torn into pieces.

"Thorough, but messy," Joanna commented, then looked

over to my father who was grimacing and rubbing at his shoulder. "Is your war wound acting up again, Watson?"

"I am afraid so," my father said, then sat down heavily on the mattress and stretched his arm for relief. "It decides to misbehave at the strangest moments."

The war wound Joanna referred to was caused by a Jezail bullet that found its mark during my father's participation in the Second Afghan War. The bullet had shattered bone and grazed the subclavian artery which resulted in great tissue damage that to this day incited intermittent painful episodes. "Perhaps a pain pill would be helpful, Father," I advised.

"No need," he refused. "It is passing."

But I could see the sharp discomfort was taking its toll on my father's endurance. It seemed to have sapped his strength even further and at the moment he seemed quite old and weary. Joanna noticed the change as well.

She placed a gentle hand on my father's shoulder and said, "If you wish, Watson, you can lie down for a few minutes and wait for the pain to leave altogether."

"It is gone now," he said, and after taking several deep breaths, his vitality gradually returned.

As my father positioned his arm on the mattress to raise himself, he partially crushed an open map of Germany, with the city of Berlin circled in black ink. "His interest in Germany is quite obvious," my father remarked, and turned the map over. On the back was scribbled a name and partially legible address.

Eric Stoltmann

Alexanderpl

Berl

I leaned in for a closer look. "The *Berl* no doubt stands for Berlin. Should we assume that *Alexanderpl* represents Alexanderplace?"

"If you wish to Anglicize it," Joanna said. "The Germans do not name their streets with a *place,* but rather with a *platz.* More likely, the address is Alexanderplatz."

"This could be Roger Bennett's contact man," I thought aloud.

"It could be," Joanna replied in a dubious tone. "But why leave it out in the open? If it was the name and address of a German operative, even a dullard would know to keep it secret and hidden."

"Perhaps he had no such hiding place," I said.

"Everyone has a hiding place," Joanna said, and returned to the search. She began with the small closet where she carefully inspected a single hanging suit and shirt, and found only a soiled handkerchief. With patience, she went over every foot of the wall and floor, looking for a crack or crevice, but discovering none. Finally she removed every drawer and peered into the rear of the cabinet, but saw only dust. As she replaced the drawers, one refused to slide in completely. Joanna quickly pulled out the drawer and examined its rear section. There was a small envelope glued in place that contained an old, neatly folded five-pound note. Holding it up, she asked, "What do you make of this, Watson?"

"A life's savings for a stable boy," my father answered.

"And one he would hardly leave behind if he were on the run," Joanna said, then furrowed her brow in the deepest thought before adding, "The contradictions continue to mount, yet I am convinced there is a single link that eludes us and will explain all."

We heard heavy footsteps hurrying into the cottage and

turned to find Henry Miller at the bedroom door. He paused to catch his breath, then said in a gasp, "Someone has broken into the forest shed."

"Is Inspector Lestrade aware?" Joanna asked.

"Yes, madam. He sent me to fetch you."

We dashed across the expanse of green lawn and over a narrow stone bridge beneath which ran a slow-moving stream. At the edge of the forest was a well-traveled path that wound its way through thick woods until it came to an open belt of grass, beyond which lay a red-colored shed. It was smaller than I anticipated, with dimensions of approximately twenty-five-by-twenty-five feet. Within, everything seemed in order and showed no evidence of tampering. But to Joanna, as I could tell by her peering eyes, there were many clues waiting to be read. She moved quickly around the shed, like a hound picking up a scent, ignoring the dredging equipment and heavy tools that hung from the walls. It was the ground within the shed that held her closest attention, although I must admit I saw nothing of interest. Her gaze went to the door as she asked Henry Miller, "Was the entry lock broken?"

"No, madam. It was intact when I entered for a pickax to clear a small stump. It was then evident to me someone had been in here."

Joanna stepped over to the door and carefully examined its heavily rusted lock, using her magnifying glass. "No scratches," she observed, before asking the groundskeeper, "Do you carry the key to the lock with you?"

"No, madam. The key is kept in the corner of the ledge above the door."

"Do others know of its hidden location?"

"Most of the people who work the grounds do."

"Thank you, Miller. You may return to your duties now."

Joanna waited until the groundskeeper was out of earshot, then turned to Lestrade and Dunn and asked unhappily, "Was it truly necessary for you to trample back and forth over every foot of earth in the shed?"

"It was required in order to perform a thorough search of the premises," Lestrade replied.

"Which in the process removed important clues," Joanna rebuked mildly. "You two have stomped over any recently made footprints, and thus we cannot match them to those made by the thief in the attic."

"Do you doubt that the thief and the intruder are one and the same?" Dunn challenged.

"I doubt everything I cannot prove," Joanna said as her gaze went to a woolen blanket in the dirt next to the dredging equipment. "I also note that the blanket has been ruffled and cast aside. Was that your work as well?"

"A neatly folded blanket was found where it now lies," Lestrade replied. "The groundskeeper assured us it was not an item usually kept in the shed, so we shook it loose looking for clues and found nothing."

"But disturbed everything," Joanna said, and moved over to inspect the blanket, which was obviously of good quality. Using her magnifying glass, she carefully pored over the blanket, then sniffed at the wool before dropping it to the ground. "There are no strands of hair that could have defined the hair color of the intruder and perhaps his approximate age. In addition, I detected the aroma of tobacco smoke, but it was so faint I could not identify its origin. Did you find ashes within the shed?"

"No, madam," Lestrade said.

"Did you examine the blanket for traces of ashes before you vigorously shook it?"

"We did not," Lestrade replied. "At that moment we were anxious to learn if the blanket contained the missing document or clues to its whereabouts. Ashes, I am afraid, were the last thing on our minds."

"Clues, clues," Joanna muttered softly. "Even the most trivial ones may count later on."

"We do not have time for *later on,* madam," Dunn groused. "The vital document remains missing, and it is quite clear that the stable boy, Roger Bennett, came back in the middle of the night to fetch it."

"Was that before or after he murdered his father?" Joanna asked.

"He could have done both," Dunn responded sharply. "But I suspect he had help as well, for by all accounts he was not bright enough to pull off such a clever theft by himself. He had an associate who I believe was none other than the groundskeeper, Henry Miller."

"But it was he who alerted us to the intruder in the shed," I argued.

"Perhaps to cover his own tracks and throw suspicion elsewhere," Dunn said. "You see, we now have indications that Henry Miller or Heinrich Mueller was involved and deftly persuaded the stable boy to become an accomplice."

"Might you share your indications with us?" my father implored.

Dunn hesitated for a moment before nodding. "Please remember that you are sworn under the Official Secrets Act."

"We are aware."

"Good, then," Dunn said, but kept his voice low. "It appears that Henry Miller may well be caught up in a web of conspiracy. When I questioned him earlier, he was less than forthright in describing his activities in the Deutsche Society, for some of his statements contradicted those of our reliable informant. For example, Miller denied urging Roger Bennett to visit the society, saying that he mentioned that only in passing. Yet the club management was expecting the stable boy's visit and treated him most warmly, even inviting him to return. Then there is the name Stoltmann that Miller could only vaguely remember, despite the fact that Eric Stoltmann is a well-known German track coach who once guided Miller during his javelin-throwing days in Munich. Now the Stoltmanns are of great interest to the allies' intelligence services, for it was Hans Stoltmann, Eric's older brother, who was an attaché at the German embassy in Paris and who was recently expelled from France because of presumed espionage activities."

"We saw the name Eric Stoltmann written on a map of Berlin in the stable boy's bedroom," I recalled.

"As did we," Dunn went on. "And so the pieces of the puzzle come together to form a more complete picture. It now seems clear that the stable boy and the groundskeeper are implicated up to their teeth, and I shall report so when I return to London. I shall also have the sad duty to report that in all likelihood the missing document has been taken from the shed by the thief and may well be on its way to the wrong hands."

"With all due respect, Lieutenant, your premise of guilt will not hold up in a court of law," Joanna said. "You will require far more solid evidence than you have at hand to squarely place the blame on Henry Miller and Roger Bennett."

"I plan to obtain it," Dunn said firmly. "And when I do, I shall have the pleasure of watching the two hang."

Dunn hurried out of the shed, with a most determined look on his face. Lestrade tipped his derby to us and had to break into a half-trot to catch up with the naval lieutenant. Only after the pair had disappeared into the woods did Joanna begin to shake her head.

"They rush to judgment so quickly while choosing only those shreds of evidence that suit their purposes," she said. "You must admit that a stable boy and a groundskeeper are the most unlikely of coconspirators."

"Surely you do not exclude them as suspects," my father argued.

"To the contrary. I continue to include them, but I do not give them the highest level of suspicion, which Dunn and Lestrade have bestowed upon them." Joanna's gaze went to the blanket on the ground and she studied it once more at length. "How could they see so much and observe so little?" she asked. "The clues were set in front of their eyes, yet they ignored them. That is the curse of having a preconceived notion."

"Are you referring to the blanket?" I inquired, following her line of vision.

"The blanket that was *folded,*" Joanna said. "Pray tell, who bothers to carefully fold a blanket of good quality and leave it behind, rather than taking it with him?"

My father and I stared back at Joanna in puzzlement, for neither of us had an answer to her question.

"Come now, Watson," she implored my father. "Why did the thief depart without the blanket? Why would anyone leave it behind?"

My father's eyes sparkled. "Because he planned to use it again!"

"Excellent, Watson! And what does that tell us?"

My father smiled broadly as the answer came to him.

"That he did not obtain what he came for and would have to return to fetch it."

"Ah! You have outdone yourself, Watson, and confirmed a vital piece of information that I must admit crossed my mind the moment I spotted the blanket lying on the ground," Joanna continued. "But the blanket tells us a great deal more. In particular, it clearly demonstrates that the missing document was never hidden in the shed, for if it were the thief would not have brought along a blanket to ward off the night's chill while he waited. Were the document here, he would have simply retrieved the stolen goods and been on his way. Since the thief planned to return, we can now rest assured the missing French Treaty remains on the Halifax estate. And as long as it is here, it cannot fall into the wrong hands."

"Which should give some comfort to the foreign minister and his fellow cabinet members at Whitehall," said I.

"As well as hope that the document will soon be recovered," my father added. "I believe the prime minister himself will no doubt be encouraged."

A hint of the Mona Lisa smile came to her face, but it quickly faded. "You should hold your optimism until we have the missing document in our hands and the thief in handcuffs. Please keep in mind that we are at a disadvantage, for time is against us, in that the thief knows where the document is and we do not. Thus, we must make haste if we are to avoid a disastrous end."

"But at least we know that the esteemed Lieutenant Dunn was wrong in his belief that the document had disappeared from the Halifax estate," I concluded.

"Obviously," Joanna said.

"But he was not wrong about the guilt of the stable boy

and the groundskeeper," my father noted. "The mounting evidence certainly points to their involvement."

"What evidence is that, Watson?" Joanna asked.

"A number of findings that are supported by the recent break-in into the shed," my father replied. "They both knew where the key to the shed's lock was located and could thus enter without doing damage to the door."

"Tut! Tut! I can quickly reason that away, Watson," Joanna said. "Every laborer on the grounds knows the location of that key, not to mention all the young people who no doubt used the shed for their secret, romantic encounters. That piece of evidence will not stand."

"But what of the groundskeeper's attempt to hide his knowledge of Eric Stoltmann, the German track coach, who guided him in the art of throwing a javelin?" I asked. "Surely he should have remembered that."

"So it would seem," my father agreed. "Athletes often have fond memories of their earlier coaches."

"Perhaps," Joanna said dubiously and turned to me. "You were a boxer in your younger days, John, and quite good at it from what I have been told. Can you give me the name of your boxing coach when you were in middle school?"

"Mar-martin or Marshall," I stammered. "That was his first name, as I recall."

"And his last?"

"It escapes me."

"And it probably escaped Henry Miller's memory while he was under the intense pressure of being cross-examined," Joanna said, and flicked her wrist dismissively. "Such evidence against the groundskeeper is weak at best."

"But who else could be responsible?" I asked.

"Someone who has an extensive knowledge of the Halifax estate and the family who occupies it."

"But that is a considerable number."

"Which we must quickly narrow down."

"How do you propose we accomplish that feat?"

"By following the clues we have before us," Joanna said, and hurried out into the chilly afternoon air.

"Is there one clue in particular that should draw our attention?" I called after her.

"The blanket," she called back, and disappeared into the woods.

10

A Secret Informant

Joanna excused herself before dinner and asked our forbearance, for she had been contacted by a secret informant in the village who wished to speak with her alone and specifically insisted no one else be present. She saw no danger in the encounter since the meeting was to take place at a small restaurant we had dined at previously and was not far from the inn where we stayed. However, should clues be revealed that required immediate attention, Joanna requested that my father and I join up with her later that evening at the rear entrance to the inn where we would not be noticed. Our meeting place was well away from the secret lodger's window, and thus we could not be seen nor overheard by him.

My father and I strolled about the wooded garden of the inn and smoked two pipefuls while we eagerly awaited our meeting with Joanna. We timed our walk to end near the rear entrance at the appointed hour, so as not to appear to be loitering and draw unwanted attention. But on our arrival,

Joanna was nowhere to be seen. As the minutes ticked past nine o'clock, we became concerned for her safety.

"Let us pray no harm has come to her," my father said worriedly.

"I should have demanded we escort her, for, as she mentioned on our train ride here, crimes every bit as vicious as those in London can take place in the quietest of English villages," I noted. "Nevertheless, I take some comfort in knowing that she is quite capable of looking after herself. Were you aware she took instructions in the Japanese sport of jujitsu?"

"That does not surprise," my father said. "For Sherlock Holmes was likewise keen on the martial arts, and in fact excelled at bare-knuckle boxing. That skill, like the art of deduction, must run in the genes."

"Indeed."

"Have you actually seen her perform?"

"I have not. But she has been awarded a purple belt at the school she attends, which indicates a fair degree of proficiency in the Japanese craft of self-defense."

"That may hold true in the classroom, but not in real-life experience."

"Father, I have learned over the past year not to underestimate Joanna, for you do so at your own peril."

We heard footsteps approaching as a shadow came out of the darkness.

"At last!" I breathed a sign of relief.

To our disappointment it was not Joanna, but an old, bespectacled woman, wearing a tattered dress, with unkempt gray hair that looked unwashed and poorly cut. Her eyebrows were equally gray and untrimmed, and there was a smudge of dust on her forehead. As she came nearer, we could not help but notice her limp and bandaged left ankle.

"Are you the gentlemen who called for a proper cleaning woman?" she asked in a raspy voice while dropping a large cloth sack to the ground.

"We are not," my father answered impatiently. "Now, move on unless you wish to become entangled in official police business."

"Then I'd better leave, but I wonder, guv'nor, if you could spare a shilling for a worker who has come on hard times?"

"Move on," my father demanded. "And I will not say it again."

"Even if I bring news from Joanna?"

"What!" I grabbed the woman by the arm and drew her closer. "Tell us all at once!"

"I will when I am good and ready," she said, and jerked her arm away.

"Do you realize that withholding information of a crime is a crime itself?" I threatened.

"And who says I am withholding it?"

"I do," my father growled. "Perhaps you would be more talkative if we called in an inspector from Scotland Yard."

"Lestrade would only bungle things." The old woman's voice changed to Joanna's. "It is best we exclude him for now."

My father and I were stunned with amazement as we watched Joanna remove her spectacles, then her wig and fake eyebrows, and finally the thick bandage from her ankle. She then straightened her posture and, with a damp handkerchief, dabbed away the smudge on her forehead.

"So much like Sherlock Holmes," my father said in a whisper. "One never knew what was to come next."

"How did you arrange such a disguise?" I wondered, still amazed by the remarkable transformation.

"A simple matter," Joanna replied. "You will recall the

thrift shop we passed on our way to question the tobacconist. Such stores hold a variety of clothes, often including used costumes. I had no problem collecting this getup, and the shopkeeper was good enough to allow me to use a back room to dress, for I told him I was on my way to a costume ball and wanted to surprise my husband. Even he did not recognize me when I reappeared from the dressing room."

"But why the disguise?" I asked.

"To go places and talk with people who would instantly clam up when questioned by the police or by people of higher rank," Joanna explained. "The working class fear these types and either hide from them or, if questioned, lie and deceive and then make every effort to disappear. So, with my disguise firmly in place, I went to an inexpensive drinking establishment on the edge of the village where I was welcomed by all, including workers from the Halifax estate and from the Hampshire Inn. They form a clique, you see, and love to share secret stories about their superiors, which they would never divulge to an outsider, much less the police."

"Sharing a sense of loyalty, I would guess," my father opined.

"No, my dear Watson," Joanna said. "They are showing the good sense that, if caught doing so, they could lose their positions."

"So you had to be careful and not appear to be prying."

"All I had to do was sip beer and keep my ears open."

"Ah! The stories they could tell," my father said knowingly.

"And did tell," Joanna said, then hooked her arms into ours as we strolled away. "I gathered more from them in an hour than Scotland Yard could learn in a month. Let us begin with the workers at the inn where the most valuable clues lay. I am referring to the chambermaid and waiter who provided the services to the inn's most secretive lodger. Please recall that the chambermaid was only called upon to clean the room twice a week, on Monday and Thursday between the hours of 6 and 6:30 P.M. She never laid eyes on him, but did note his peculiar demands and ways. In particular, the window was to remain open at all times and, if closed because of rain, was never to be locked. The explanation given for this practice was the lodger's frequent asthmatic attacks that required immediate fresh air."

"Sensible enough," my father said. "Inhaling fresh air can at times abate an attack."

"Yet the maid told us that the ashtrays in the room were filled with ashes and the ends of cigarettes, and the air contained the heavy odor of stale tobacco smoke," Joanna countered.

"That does not fit," my father said at once. "Asthmatics never smoke, for it is a certain way to set off an attack."

"Thus we can conclude that the occupant of the room did not suffer from asthma."

"We can indeed."

"And we can also conclude that he was not a writer," Joanna continued on. "The chambermaid, who thoroughly cleaned the room, saw pen and ink and stacks of white paper, yet none of the sheets had been written upon. The chambermaid looked for such pages, for she is a reader and was interested in what the lodger might be writing about. Furthermore, there was no trash on the floor, and the trash can held no crushed or discarded papers. As a previous writer yourself, Watson, and one who chronicled the adventures of Sherlock Holmes, what do you make of these findings?"

"All writers have their throwaway pages that are poorly done in their opinion and are thus discarded or pitched into a glowing fireplace," my father replied. "On many days the floor around my desk was littered with unwanted, crushed sheets of paper."

"Which leads you to what deduction?"

"That the occupant of that room was not a writer."

"And what if I told you the chambermaid saw neither books nor reference volumes that any historian would surely depend on when writing about Elizabethan England?"

"It would confirm my suspicion beyond any question."

"Thus he is neither an asthmatic nor a writer, both of which he claimed to be, so he would be left alone in seclusion and have an open window that looked out onto the forest. Why were these requirements so important to him?"

"The seclusion offers protection that he would not be seen or recognized," I reasoned. "It also explains why he had a London agent book the room at the inn, rather than doing it himself."

"Excellent, John! You are indeed coming along wonderfully well," Joanna said. "Now please tell us the necessity of having an open, never locked window close by the forest."

"The answer to that is quite obvious," I replied. "He used the window as an entrance and exit, so he could leave and return unnoticed whenever he wished."

"Bravo!" Joanna said, and smiled over at my father. "I must say, Watson, there are times when I wonder if John had missed his true calling as a detective."

"He does have his moments," my father praised.

"Indeed," Joanna said as the smile faded from her face. "And it is the window that brings us to the young waiter and the most intriguing clue of all. On his third beer, he told a story that captured the attention of the entire pub. Again recall that the waiter was instructed to serve dinner by leaving the tray outside the lodger's room at precisely 7 P.M., and to return an hour later to collect the dishes. He performed these duties the night before last, but before returning for the dishes, he stole away for a cigarette break at the rear of the inn. During this time he stayed in the shadows, for the innkeeper does not like to see his employees idling about. As he was finishing his cigarette, the waiter saw the strange lodger alight from the window of his room and dash to the edge of the forest where a woman awaited him. The moon was full that night, so he was able to see the couple, but only for a moment because a passing cloud dimmed the moonlight. Although he cannot swear to it, he believes the man strongly resembled Roger Bennett."

"The stable boy?" my father cried out in disbelief. "There is no way in the world a stable boy could afford even a meal at the Hampshire Inn, much less a two-week stay."

"Which was the opinion of all those present in the tavern," Joanna said. "So they quickly dismissed the idea."

"But you appear not to have."

"One should never discard an important clue simply because it does not fit your preconceived notion."

"But everything argues against the boy being a guest at the inn."

"It is most unlikely," Joanna agreed. "Nevertheless, we should not reject the sighting altogether until we have proof to the contrary."

"But what if it is the boy?" my father mused.

"Yes. What if it is?"

"Then the pieces of the puzzle begin to come together."

"But wait, Watson," Joanna said. "There is yet another shoe to drop. Would you care to guess who the woman was?"

"I have no idea."

"None other than Elizabeth Halifax."

My father's jaw opened. "I say!"

"Again the light was less than good, but the waiter firmly believes it was her," Joanna said. "And I take him at his word."

"Was it a romantic assignation?" I asked.

"That was not possible to tell, for although they were close together the waiter could not determine if they were touching," Joanna replied. "But the encounter was brief, lasting no more than a minute or two, so I would be of the opinion that the meeting was a business matter rather than one of romantic attachment."

My father shook his head sadly. "I simply cannot fathom Elizabeth Halifax, a lady of high standing, being involved in a traitorous act."

Joanna reached into the large cloth sack for her coat and put it on to cover her tattered dress. She took a final glance at the dark forest before saying, "There are more than a few knots here that need to be untied, for all is not what it appears to be."

11

The Halifaxes

"It is a close match," said I, comparing the sketch of the foot-print in the clearing to that present on the attic floor. "Very close indeed."

Joanna shone her torch directly on the footprint and asked, "Does it reveal an uneven left heel?"

"It is impossible to tell, for the dust is not deep enough to allow for such details."

"Most unfortunate," Joanna said, helping me to my feet. "A perfect match would have been of great significance."

"Yet the similarity of the two footprints must be taken into account."

"It must indeed, for they may well connect the thief in the attic to the secret lodger at the inn. Both are obviously important in this regard, but it is the footprint in the clearing that continues to arouse my curiosity."

"Is that because it most likely belongs to the mysterious lodger?"

"There is yet a more intriguing reason," Joanna eluci-dated. "Assuming the footprint in the mud did in fact belong to the secret lodger, why would he find it necessary to slip out to the clearing in the darkness of night?"

I gave the matter thought before saying, "As I recall there were no clues to indicate his purpose nor do we know on which night he made the footprint."

"Perhaps Walter, the waiter, gave us that information, while regaling his audience at the local pub," Joanna hinted.

The waiter's late-evening sighting of the secret lodger immediately came to mind. "To meet Elizabeth Halifax! He may have made the footprint on his way to meet Eliz-abeth."

"That is a distinct possibility. Also, you will recall that there was rain that afternoon, but none since. Thus the foot-print was made the night the secret lodger crept out to join up with Elizabeth."

"But can we trust the waiter's story?"

"Do you doubt he saw the secret lodger leave through his window in the darkness?"

"I do not."

"Thus, Walter must have watched the lodger exit, which strongly indicates he was in a position to view the meeting that took place in the clearing."

I nodded at Joanna's conclusion. "And Walter mentioned he only had a clear view when the moon peeked through the clouds."

Joanna nodded back. "So for now we must assume that Walter's account of that evening is accurate and that the se-cret lodger did in fact meet with Elizabeth Halifax."

"But why would she bother to meet with the secret lodger who may well be our thief?"

"Has it crossed your mind that she may be acting on behalf of the Halifax family?"

I was stunned by the possibility, to say the least. "In a plan to obtain the missing document."

"At a price, of course."

"Unbelievable!"

"We shall see."

We walked along the attic passageway back to the trapdoor above the closet, looking for areas where the dust might have settled deeper and allowed for more distinct footprints, but found none. On reaching the area of the library, we could hear the voices of the Halifaxes below.

"Were they the least bit suspicious?" I asked quietly.

"None whatsoever," Joanna replied in a soft voice. "They expect a progress report."

"Will you give them one?"

"Yes, but not the one they expect."

"Surely you will not confront Elizabeth Halifax in the presence of the family."

"That would prove unproductive. She would simply deny it and we have no way of proving otherwise, save for Walter's sighting in the night that no one would take seriously, for it would be his word against hers."

"Then how should we go about proving the meeting took place?"

"With guile," Joanna said, then warned, "and make no mention whatsoever of the secret lodger."

"What if they bring his name into the conversation?" I asked, as I lifted the trapdoor.

"They won't."

"And if they inquire about my father's absence?"

"Say only that he is resting at the inn, which he will be

doing shortly. We should not breathe a word that he is at this moment interviewing the local doctor to determine if there have been any recent cases of drug-induced mania in the village."

"I was particularly pleased that it was my father's idea to do so," I remarked. "His mind seems to be returning nicely to its former self."

"Let us hope his muscles are not far behind."

As we entered the library, the Duke of Winchester stepped forward and asked anxiously, "Has any progress been made?"

"There is now evidence to indicate the missing document has not yet left the estate grounds," Joanna reported.

I watched the collective expressions on the faces of the Halifaxes. His Grace appeared the most relieved, Harry and Elizabeth much less so.

"May we know the particulars?" the elder statesman requested.

"At this point of the investigation, I think it best we not go into details," Joanna said evasively.

"Can you say there is a chance for imminent recovery of the document?"

"I cannot be that optimistic, but we are now in the process of further narrowing down the list of suspects," said Joanna. "I believe Your Grace's family may be of particular help in this regard."

"We shall assist you in every way possible," the Duke pledged. "But Scotland Yard has informed us that a prime suspect has been named and is currently on the run."

"The stable boy, Roger Bennett," Harry said disgustedly. "And he may have done in his own father as well."

Since there was no real proof to back up either assertion, I wanted to interject, but held my tongue.

The Duke shook his head sadly. "Roger is such a kind and gentle boy, which makes it difficult for me to believe he could commit so dastardly an act."

"He has always been sweet and helpful," Elizabeth added in a soft voice.

"Those features may have only been on the surface," Harry pointed out. "Who knows what evil lurks below the outward appearance?"

"Indeed, one has to be careful not to read a book by its cover," Joanna agreed. "But at this stage of the investigation, Roger Bennett must only be listed as one of the suspects. To focus our attention on him alone might distract us from other suspects who also warrant our scrutiny."

"But who are these other suspects?" His Grace asked.

"That is to be determined," Joanna replied. "And that is the purpose of my request for the three of you to be present at this meeting. You are certainly aware that the thief had to have knowledge of the manor and in particular the attic space. Such an individual would have visited and stayed over at the manor, perhaps for an entire weekend. I need to know all who might fall into that category. Leave out no one, regardless of rank or social standing."

"How far back shall we go?"

"A year, but you can exclude the prime minister and other high-level ministers, as well as women and children."

"There have not been that many," Elizabeth volunteered. "For the past year we have spent most of our time in London, with only occasional visits to the estate."

"How many exactly?" Joanna asked.

"No more than five."

"Who was in attendance?"

Elizabeth thought back at length. "Only the Halifax immediate family, which included my father-in-law, my husband and I, along with our twin sons. On a single occasion we had a grand dinner, with the prime minister and several members of his cabinet being present. They stayed the night and were gone in the morning."

"What of the Stanhope immediate family?" Joanna asked without inflection. "I am referring to your father and brother."

The expressions on the faces of both His Grace and Harry tightened at the mention of the Stanhope name. Their displeasure was no doubt related to the role the Stanhope brokerage firm played in the current financial misery of the Halifaxes.

"My father is ill and infirm, and thus does not travel these days," Elizabeth said in a sad voice. "My brother Ian now resides in Edinburgh and rarely visits."

"When he comes to London, does he ever stay here?" Joanna inquired.

"Never," Elizabeth said curtly.

Joanna watched Elizabeth's expression suddenly harden and wisely decided not to pursue further information on the Stanhope family. "Let us turn to disgruntled employees who may have left under unpleasant circumstances."

"There have been none," the Duke said without hesitation. "All of our in-house employees have been with us for years and years, with Charles, God rest his soul, having been in service for over forty."

"Which of your current employees have complete run of the manor?"

"Several of the chambermaids, a housekeeper who is somewhat elderly, and of course Charles, the butler, up until his death."

"Did Roger Bennett ever accompany his father into the manor?"

"Never," the elder statesman replied, then wrinkled his brow in thought. "But when he was a young lad we caught Roger sliding down the bannister of the main staircase. He had somehow crept into the manor without being seen."

"On how many occasions did that occur?"

"At least twice that I recall, but of course we always chased him out with a stern warning."

"Perhaps that is when he learned about the attic space," Harry said with a firm nod.

"Quite possibly," the Duke assented.

"Was he ever seen in the manor as an adult?" Joanna inquired.

The three Halifaxes answered with a shake of their collective heads.

"Is the groundskeeper ever allowed in?" asked Joanna.

"Never," Harry replied.

"Or the chauffeur?"

"Only to help with packages or luggage," Elizabeth said.

"But Ned is also quite a handyman," His Grace added. "On occasion he does some painting or woodwork about the manor. Nevertheless his visits are short and limited to a single room or area."

"Is he the sole driver on the estate?" Joanna asked.

"He is indeed," the Duke answered. "He is responsible for the carriages and motorcar and all the trips they make."

"Is it the motorcar or carriage that is used most frequently for journeys into the village?"

"That depends on the weather," Elizabeth said. "But most often we take the carriage."

"So, on a cloudless day like today, I assume Ned would know to bring around the carriage without being instructed."

"He would indeed," said Elizabeth, and gestured to the library window. "As you can see, Ned and the carriage await me now at the front entrance, for I must journey into the village shortly."

"Then I shan't keep you longer," Joanna said. "Allow me to thank all of you for the information you have provided. It may prove to be quite helpful."

Once the Halifaxes had departed, Joanna hurried over to the window and gazed out at the front entrance where Ned and the carriage were waiting. She continued to stare, for something had caught and continued to hold her interest. I came to her side to study the driver and carriage and saw nothing unusual except for the extraordinarily handsome appearance of the driver. He was a large man, broad-shouldered, with thick, black hair and rugged good looks.

"What so draws your attention?" I asked.

"Ned's possible involvement in this sordid affair," Joanna said, as the driver helped Elizabeth into the carriage.

"I do not follow your reasoning here," I admitted. "What makes you believe the carriage driver is involved?"

"Simple logic," Joanna replied. "Assuming Elizabeth did meet the secret lodger—and there is evidence to back up this assumption—she would not have traveled through the woods at night to reach the clearing. Not only would it have been dangerous, she would have surely been seen by the security guards now stationed about the estate. With that in mind, pray tell how did she reach the clearing?"

The only explanation came quickly to me. "She had to arrive by carriage."

"Driven by whom?"

"Ned, of course. And he, being a large, rugged man,

would have served as protection should matters have gotten out of hand."

"And thus all the pieces come together."

"Are you saying Ned, the driver, is definitely involved?"

"I am saying that our circle of suspects grows."

12

The Chambermaid

"Did you learn anything of interest from the local physician regarding drug-induced mania?" asked Joanna.

"There have been no recent cases," my father replied. "He did recall that some years back a visiting artist took the hallucinogen peyote because it enhanced his vision of colors. Unfortunately he ingested a large dose for an even brighter effect, which resulted in hallucinations that lasted for nearly a day."

"Was the stable boy ever a patient?"

"Years ago he saw the lad for some skin affliction that was successfully treated with zinc oxide. He also mentioned that the boy was a kind, gentle soul who would be incapable of harming his father."

We continued our postprandial stroll on the half-mile stretch of road that led from the inn to the main thoroughfare. The night was brisk and clear, with a full moon that gave us a splendid view of the tree-lined surroundings. My father's endurance appeared somewhat improved in that he now showed only a slight limp. I found this encouraging but thought it best not to push too far, for fear of overtaxing his leg muscles. Ahead I saw the main thoroughfare, as did Joanna and my father, so we turned back for the inn.

"Did you glean any new information at your meeting with the Halifaxes?" my father inquired.

"Only that the bad blood between the Halifaxes and the Stanhopes persists to this day," Joanna responded.

"Can we thus conclude that none of the Stanhopes have visited the Halifax estate in recent years?" my father asked further. "I am of course referring primarily to that scoundrel, Ian Stanhope."

"That was promptly denied by Elizabeth," Joanna answered. "She stated that her brother now resided in Edinburgh and to her knowledge rarely visited London and never the Halifax estate."

"I do not know if I would trust her word," my father said frankly.

"I did not," said Joanna. "That is why I spoke with the innkeeper prior to dinner. He recalls no such guest, but to be certain he reviewed his rather extensive files. You see, Trevor MacGregor, being the excellent innkeeper he is, keeps a record of all visitors dating back years. He does this in the event the guest may have particular needs or wants. There was no Stanhope listed."

"But a scoundrel like Ian Stanhope might have crept his way back to Hampshire unseen," I interjected. "He could have come and gone via a hidden bridle path or registered at the inn under a false name."

"Or have an agent register for him and keep himself secluded at the inn so as not to be recognized," my father suggested.

Joanna nodded at the possibilities. "The black sheep of a family have an uncanny habit of showing up unexpectedly and causing real mischief."

Up ahead the inn was brightly lighted, with all its windows aglow. My gaze went to the right side of the inn where the lighting was quite good and I again wondered about the depth of Elizabeth Halifax's involvement in this traitorous affair. As we came closer, I could make out the clearing at the edge of the woods.

"Is it fair to say that Walter, the waiter, would have viewed the meeting of Elizabeth and the secret lodger at approximately this time of evening?" I asked.

"It would be quite close to it, for he would have already removed the lodger's dinner plates," Joanna replied.

"Then he would have had a clear sighting of the couple."

"So it would appear."

"But why would she take the very real chance of being discovered?" I pondered. "Here she was, standing in a lighted area where anyone working at the inn could have been and recognized her."

"It almost certainly had to do with the missing document," Joanna said. "There can be no other reason."

"Can you exclude a romantic assignation?" my father asked.

Joanna shook her head at the notion. "There would be too great a risk of being seen, with so little to gain. Would she chance everything for a momentary embrace and quick kiss? I think not. Far more likely, she was there at the insistence of the secret lodger who wishes not to venture away from the inn."

"For fear of being recognized," I mused aloud. "Which tells us his face must be known to those who work at the inn."

"That is the most plausible explanation," Joanna concurred. "But there are others."

"All the answers lie with Elizabeth Halifax who sooner or later must be confronted."

"But for the present, we must allow this hand to play itself out," said Joanna. "If we act precipitously, it may well frighten off the secret lodger and it is he, not Elizabeth, who holds or knows the whereabouts of the missing document."

"It sounds as if you wish us to concentrate on the lodger and ignore Elizabeth altogether."

"For now."

"But the lodger stays confined to his room."

"Not at night."

"But we cannot keep a watch on his window through the entire night hours."

"I know those who can," Joanna said as we reached the front entrance of the inn. Turning to my father, she asked, "Watson, would you care to join us at the bar for a nightcap?"

"Perhaps on another occasion," my father replied wearily. "I believe my day has been long enough and tomorrow will be an even longer one."

"Indeed," Joanna agreed. "Then a pleasant good night to you, Watson."

From outside the inn we watched my father stroll across the lobby, showing only the slightest of limps. But, as he ascended the stairs, he began to favor his right leg. The weakness had obviously returned, to my disappointment.

"He is limping once more," I said in a whisper to Joanna. "And I was so encouraged by how well he performed on our evening stroll."

"You should continue to be encouraged, for that evening

stroll was nearly a mile in length, and his gait was quite normal to the casual observer."

"But he limped noticeably going up the stairs."

"That is because his muscles have tired from the long walk and now he faces a steep incline that brings out the fatigue in his legs."

"So you truly believe my father is progressing on schedule?"

"I am certain of it," Joanna assured. "As with the stroke victim I cared for at St. Bart's, a steep incline is the last major hurdle such patients must overcome."

"I wish I could be as patient as you."

"Patience is difficult when the afflicted is someone you happen to love," Joanna said with a gentle smile, then turned for the door. In an instant the smile left her face and she quickly came back to me. "Kiss me on the right cheek, John, and in doing so, glance at the individual walking past the clearing. Only glimpse and do not allow your gaze to linger."

I brought Joanna in closer and pecked her cheek, all the while focusing my eyes on the attractive chambermaid who was responsible for cleaning the secret lodger's room. She had a shawl wrapped around her shoulders and walked at a rapid pace.

"Where do you think she goes?" Joanna asked in a whisper.

"Certainly not on a casual stroll at this time of evening," I whispered back.

"Nor would she venture into the woods in the darkness," Joanna said, slowly shifting her head on my shoulder for a better view. "Notice how she continues to glance around."

"She obviously does not wish to be seen," I noted. "Perhaps she is meeting her secret lover."

"Or perhaps she is carrying a message to a person waiting

in the shadows," Joanna suggested. "Remember, she is one of only two individuals who have had contact with the secret lodger."

"Or she may be carrying an object under her shawl that she wishes to keep hidden."

"Capital, John! When guessing, it is important to list all possibilities. I must say your detective skills are coming along nicely. So tell me, how do you propose we discover what she is truly up to?"

"Following her is out of the question, for we would easily be seen or heard."

"What then?"

"We could obtain a fine view from the window in our room that faces the woods."

"My thoughts exactly! Now we must move quickly, but not appear to be hurrying."

At a quick yet even pace we strode across the lobby and up the steep stairs to the second floor, where we saw my father dressed in a robe, with a thick towel draped over his arm.

"I thought a nice, warm bath would be of benefit to my aching muscles," my father explained.

"It would indeed," Joanna agreed. "But you may wish to join us and put your bath on hold for a few moments."

We picked up the pace as we hurried to our room, with Joanna recounting our observations outside the inn and the need to keep our room dark. She also hastily spoke of Ned, the carriage driver's possible involvement, and how it might be he whom the chambermaid was rushing to see.

My father's eyes twinkled as he noted, "Ah! The plot thickens."

"More than you will ever imagine," said Joanna.

"Will the light outside be sufficient to allow for an accurate identification?"

"Let us hope so."

"If not, perhaps they will stroll back to the clearing."

"I think not, Watson. There is a reason they chose to meet in the shadows."

We entered our room and dashed to the window overlooking the woods. The lights from the inn gave us a fine view of the clearing, but the forest itself remained dark. To our far right we could see the outline of two figures, one male, one female, but the dimness made it impossible to see the details of their faces. The figures were very close together in what appeared to be an embrace, but it was uncertain whether or not they were kissing.

"Can you determine if there was an exchange of some sort?" my father asked.

"It is not possible to say in the darkness," Joanna replied, as a cloud passed by the moon, making the scene even darker. "But now they seem to be parting."

"Such a momentary meeting would indicate an item was exchanged," I ventured.

"Or perhaps the words of a brief message," Joanna proposed.

We backed away from the window as the chambermaid began her return to the inn. Now, rather than acting furtively, she walked in a nonchalant fashion, as if on a leisurely evening stroll. Her hands could be clearly seen and were free of any items. In the distance we heard the sound of hoofbeats galloping away.

"I am afraid we have missed our chance," I said disappointedly.

"I suspect this will not be the last of their meetings," said Joanna.

"But we will still be faced with the difficulty of identifying whom the chambermaid meets and for what purpose."

"There is a way to solve that problem."

"How so?"

"By arranging for a closer look," she said, and left it at that.

13

The Baker Street Irregulars

I did not know that the Baker Street Irregulars were still in existence, but Joanna did and wasted no time calling upon them. She dispatched a wire to their leader, who carried the name Wiggins, and requested he come by rail to Hampshire at his earliest moment. He was instructed to bring along another member known as Little Alfie, but was given no reason.

As we waited at the train station just before noon, my father reminded us of the extraordinary history behind the Baker Street Irregulars. Sherlock Holmes had somehow gathered up a gang of street urchins whom he often employed to aid his causes. They consisted of a dozen or so members, all streetwise, who could go everywhere, see everything, and overhear everyone without being noticed. When put to the task, they had a remarkable success record. For their efforts each was paid a shilling a day, with a guinea to whoever found the most prized clue. Since Sherlock Holmes's death, more than a few of the original guttersnipes had either drifted away or become ill, but Wiggins remained and took in new recruits to replace those who had departed. Joanna had employed them earlier unbeknownst to me, for I was occupied at the time looking after my ill father. In that particular case, which she now recounted in detail, the irregulars tracked down a steam launch that had mysteriously disappeared. They had scoured the waterfront, day and night, until they found a recently repainted launch, with a new name lettered on its bow. It was discovered hidden away in a boathouse far upriver on the Thames where few would venture to search. Joanna considered the case to be a minor one, hardly worth mentioning, much less being chronicled.

On hearing the sound of the approaching train she quickly returned to the mystery at hand. "The irregulars are to be given only the barest facts and nothing more. Then we shall set them loose."

"To what end?" my father asked.

"Why, to track our thief of course."

Moments later the train from London pulled into the station and an oddly matched pair of lads stepped onto the platform. The older one, in his late teens I would guess, was the leader Wiggins. He was tall and quite thin, with hollow cheeks and dark eyes that seemed to dance around, as if searching for something that might be lurking in the background. By his side was a boy of no more than twelve, short for his age, with unkempt brown hair and the look of innocence about him.

"Got your message, I did, and came at my quickest," Wiggins said in a deep Cockney accent. "That will be a pound and two bob for the tickets, if you please, ma'am."

Joanna handed over some silver and got directly to the point, addressing the younger lad first. "As I recall, Little Alfie,

I was told you were born and spent your early years in Edwinstowe, on the edge of Sherwood Forest. Correct?"

"Yes, ma'am," Little Alfie said shyly.

"So you know your away around a forest and how to track the creatures within."

"I am very good at that, ma'am."

"Better than good," Wiggins interceded. "City or forest, Little Alfie can track like a cat in the night. He'll come and go without being seen or heard."

"That is what is required here, so listen carefully, for there can be no mistakes made," Joanna said gravely.

Little Alfie's eyes widened at the gravity of Joanna's voice. "What type of creature is this?"

"A man, a very clever man, so both of you must be on your toes all the time," Joanna went on. "There is a Hampshire Inn close by that sits on the edge of the forest. In the darkness of night, a lodger on the first floor of the inn will leave via the window in his room and disappear into the woods. He will only do this at night when all is quiet, and will remain in the forest for varying lengths of time before he returns to his room. This man is to be followed noiselessly. I need to know where he goes, whom he meets, and where. One place I am certain he will visit is a small, red-colored shed that is located in the midst of the forest. Here you must be doubly careful, for the shed is located on the Halifax estate, which is now under the scrutiny of Scotland Yard."

If the mention of Scotland Yard bothered Wiggins, he did not show it. "How many coppers, you figure?"

"Three or four, and they patrol mainly the perimeter of the forest that faces the estate," Joanna replied.

"So they are looking for someone trying to sneak into the estate," Wiggins concluded.

"Or out of it," Joanna said. "But if they hear anything un-usual, they will not hesitate to enter the forest. In addition, they may station an officer to keep a watchful eye on the red shed."

Wiggins considered the matter briefly, then turned to his mate. "What do you think, Alfie?"

Little Alfie asked, "How many doors does this shed have?"

"One," Joanna told him. "And it is kept securely locked."

"Windows?"

"None."

"What is in this shed?"

"Farming and dredging equipment," Joanna answered. "Why is this important to know?"

Little Alfie smiled mischievously. "I might need a place to hide if you want me to listen in on what the bloke says to whoever he is meeting."

"But there is only one door in."

"Have you ever been in a forest shed for any length of time, ma'am?"

"No."

"I have."

Wiggins interjected. "What he is trying to tell you, ma'am, is that if you wish him to overhear the conversation, he will manage to crawl his way in and do so."

"An extra guinea for that conversation," Joanna pledged.

"Done," Wiggins said at once. "How long will we be in that forest?"

"Five days at the most."

Wiggins tilted his head back and counted silently to him-self, then he recounted. "We will need two pounds more for sleeping equipment, tools, food, drink, and other such things, not of course including our fare back to London."

"Fair enough."

"Now, how am I to contact you?"

"Our room at the inn is situated on the second floor at the rear and facing the forest. A small pebble thrown against the window at night will alert us that you require our presence. And if I wish to contact you, I shall switch the light in my room off and on twice at precisely 10 P.M., which signals that a meeting should occur half an hour later at the rear of the inn."

"Very good, ma'am," Wiggins said.

"There is one last task," Joanna went on. "You are also to watch for anyone, man or woman, who approaches the edge of the forest in the dark of night. Determine who they are and what they do."

"Are we to follow them as well?"

"No," Joanna said at once. "You must remain in the woods to ensure you are not discovered. Keep a sharp eye, but stay motionless."

"That doubles the difficulty, ma'am."

"An extra crown for each individual identified."

"Done," Wiggins said. "And with that I will get on with me work."

As he turned to leave, I noticed that he was by himself, with his mate nowhere to be seen. "Where is Little Alfie?"

Wiggins smiled crookedly. "Just showing you, guv'nor, that he is a magician when it comes to disappearing right before your eyes. And that is the trick of a bloody good tracker."

Lestrade and Dunn called us into conference just outside the mansion to announce the case was rapidly coming to a conclusion and that the missing treaty was now within reach. Both were brimming with confidence, seemingly certain they would soon share in the limelight of success.

"New information has come to us that tightens the noose around Henry Miller's neck," Lestrade proclaimed. "For this, I must give credit to Lieutenant Dunn and the fine staff at Naval Intelligence, and thus it is only proper that he tell you of the incriminating evidence."

Dunn cleared his throat, like a man about to render a formal presentation. "As you must be aware, intelligence agencies from different countries often share information when it is in their best interest to do so. Thus the French have provided us with all their data on Hans Stoltmann, the German attaché who was expelled from their Paris embassy for espionage activities. And what was that activity? He was attempting by bribery to learn the contents of a new treaty with England that was being carefully scrutinized before being signed by the president of France. At the very same time, Hans Stoltmann's brother Eric, the well-known German track coach, was in London as an honored guest of the Deutsche Society, where he was seen in the close company of Henry Miller. Would it interest you to know that Eric Stoltmann is married to Henry Miller's aunt, who is a stenographer for Germany's Ministry of War?"

"Do we know what department in the war ministry employs her?" inquired Joanna.

"The section on foreign affairs," Dunn replied, then added, "which is closely tied to their various intelligence agencies."

"I say!" my father exclaimed. "This is looking rather awkward for Henry Miller, who had such a vague recollection of the name Stoltmann."

"You are being too charitable with your use of the word *awkward,* Dr. Watson," Dunn said sternly.

Joanna asked, "Do you know how close Henry Miller is to the aunt you mentioned?"

"An aunt is an aunt," Dunn retorted. "And that is not a distant relative by any definition."

"I think it would be wise to look into that matter," Joanna urged.

Dunn nodded, but only begrudgingly so. "There is more damning information. This morning Henry Miller asked for permission to travel to London this weekend to attend a meeting of the recently reopened Deutsche Society, where he is to be nominated for the office of the presidency. According to our informant, this meeting was originally scheduled for a month from now, but for unknown reasons it was moved up to this weekend. It does not take a genius to understand this piece of the puzzle."

"Henry Miller is using it as an excuse to meet with Roger Bennett," Lestrade joined in. "It is the perfect cover he requires to leave the Halifax estate."

"We granted him permission of course," Dunn continued on. "He will be watched every step of his journey, for we believe he will lead us to the scoundrel Roger Bennett who remains in possession of the document."

"Very clever," Joanna praised. "But this presumes that all of your assumptions are correct."

"Oh, they are, madam," Dunn said. "They most certainly are, down to the finest point."

"You are to be congratulated, Lieutenant, for bringing all these complex clues together," Lestrade added. "It was no simple task to gather and interconnect them."

"Which could not have been accomplished without the keen minds of our Naval Intelligence group," Dunn said. "And your assistance was invaluable as well, Inspector."

"You do me too much praise," Lestrade said, suppressing a smile.

"And with that, we shall leave you," Dunn concluded. "I caution you not to question Henry Miller further or give him any indication that we are now aware of his guilt. In addition, we shall pull back our security guards somewhat and thus appear to be lessening our suspicion that he is any way involved."

We watched the detectives depart for the grand manor, then began to leisurely stroll across the wide expanse of green lawn. Ahead near the edge of the forest, we saw a changing of the security guards in the late afternoon sun.

"What do you think, Joanna?" my father asked.

"The evidence is interesting, but far from conclusive," she replied.

"Yet the finger of guilt seems to be pointing directly at Henry Miller."

"It is all too convenient," Joanna said. "Lestrade and Dunn pick up a clue here and there, and fit them into their preconceived notion. Then they go about congratulating one another on their deductive skills."

"So you have doubts?"

"I have questions."

"Is there one in particular that should draw our attention?"

An indecipherable smile crossed Joanna's face. "The one that should be the most obvious."

"Which is?"

"Why would Henry Miller journey to London to meet up with the stable boy when all he has to do is step over to the Hampshire Inn where Roger Bennett is currently residing?"

14

The Secret Lodger

Just before the stroke of midnight that same day, we heard a small pebble tap against the window of our room at the Hampshire Inn. Being light sleepers, Joanna and I awoke at once, quickly dressed and moved silently by the night manager asleep at the front desk. We did not wake my father to join us at the late hour, for earlier he had seemed quite fatigued, with heavy eyelids and frequent, stifled yawns. It was clear his physical endurance had not yet returned to its former self, so we believed it best not to disturb his much-needed rest.

Outside the sky was moonless and a dense fog had set in, which made our footing treacherous in the darkness. We stepped carefully along the side of the inn to the shadows at the rear where the Baker Street Irregulars awaited us.

"We have news for you, ma'am," Wiggins said in a low voice. "For Little Alfie here has been hard at work."

It was difficult to see Little Alfie in that he appeared to

be part of the darkness surrounding the inn. The clothes he wore were black as night, and his face and hands were covered with smears of mud. Only up close were we able to see the whites of his eyes.

"But I will first tell you of the openers," Wiggins went on. "A tick before ten, when all was bloody dark, the lodger decides to do a skip through the window. Quiet he is, mind you, as he disappears into the forest faster than you can say gone. Here is where Little Alfie latches onto the bloke."

"He moves quick and even and in no rush, like a dodger after the pinch," Little Alfie began.

"So he knows his way around the forest," Joanna said.

"That he does, ma'am. He seems to glide along and make nary a stupid step. And he's very clever at this, ma'am. He takes a path where anyone following him would make noise. At intervals he stops and listens, just as hunted animals often do."

"But you remained undetected. Correct?"

"Correct, ma'am. I kept my distance and followed him more by sound than sight. He was suspicious, that's for sure, because he didn't go directly to the red shed, but circled it several times."

"What did you make of that?"

"He was testing to see if he was being followed or watched, of which he could find no evidence."

"How can you be so certain he had not detected your presence?"

"Because after the third circling, he entered the red shed."

I now became aware that I had underestimated Little Alfie's age because of his short stature and innocent looks. His manner and speech indicated he was into his mid-teens and was obviously smarter than most street urchins his age. In addition, his vocabulary suggested he had at least some education.

"Were you able to follow him into the shed?" Joanna asked.

"No, ma'am. 'Cause it had but a single door," Little Alfie replied. "But I saw everything he did."

"How did you manage that?"

"Most forest sheds are tightly closed and this causes the smell inside to get bloody bad. And if an animal happens to die in there, well—" Little Alfie made a face as his voice trailed off. "Terrible, it is. But a way to move the air inside about is to leave a narrow gap between the side walls and the overhanging roof. That is what was done here. So I climbed a nearby tree and was able to peek in."

"Was it not dark within?"

"It was until he turned on a small torch."

"Describe this man," Joanna urged.

"The small torch he carried gave off only a narrow stream of light, but from what I could see he was tall, about the height of Wiggins, but a good few years older. His hair was cut short except for a lock that hung down over his forehead. I couldn't make out his face all that well." Little Alfie paused to think back, then nodded to himself and continued on. "And there was one other thing. He had big shoulders that kind of glistened with sweat after he did his push-ups."

"Push-ups, you say?" Joanna asked in wonderment.

"Yes, ma'am. He did a hundred or so, fast too, like he was accustomed to it."

"As if he were an athlete?"

"Which was my thought as well. But then he lit a cigarette and smoked it, then another and another, lighting each from the end of the last. Athletes do not do that, ma'am."

"They most certainly do not," Joanna agreed, and gave me a knowing glance.

I nodded my understanding, for it now seemed even more likely that the thief in the attic space of the mansion and the secretive lodger at the inn were one and the same. A man capable of performing a hundred push-ups rapidly could easily climb up and down a length of hanging rope. And both were obviously addicted to tobacco, for the man in the shed had to smoke one cigarette after another, while the individual in the attic space was driven to smoke a cigar as he waited for his chance to slip into the library and steal the document. Yet here again was the striking contradiction surrounding Roger Bennett upon whom all suspicion fell. How could an aspiring long-distance runner be so addicted to tobacco?

"After his exercise," Joanna said, picking up the conversation, "did the man sit and wait?"

"He did not, ma'am, for he was the jumpy type who moved about even when he was smoking," Little Alfie replied. "And then the sound in the forest really set him off."

Joanna's brow went up. "What kind of sound?"

"A big animal, I would guess, like maybe a deer or wild boar," Little Alfie said casually. "It sniffed around a bit, then was on its way. As soon as he heard the sound, he went for a pickax and swung it about, as if it were to be used as a weapon. Then, when all was quiet for a while, he cracked open the door and whispered out, "Madam, is that you?""

"Are you certain he called 'madam'?" Joanna asked at once.

"I couldn't swear to it, but that is how it sounded," Little Alfie answered. "But nobody was there, so I guess the bloke got tired and returned to the inn."

"During your watch, did he leave the shed on any occasion?" Joanna asked. "This is very important."

Little Alfie gave the question thought before saying, "He

did take off to have a pee, I think. He walked a fair distance away, according to the sound he made."

"Strange he would move so far from the shed for that purpose."

Little Alfie shrugged. "Maybe he believed the woman he called after was near and he didn't want to cause an embarrassment."

"Was he carrying anything when he returned?"

"Not that I could make out."

I could now follow Joanna's line of questioning about the lodger entering and leaving the shed. Perhaps he had hidden the document deep in the woods and had gone to fetch it.

"Did the man do any digging while out in the woods?" I asked.

"Not to my ears."

"By chance, did he happen to leave anything behind when he left the shed a final time?" I asked.

"No, sir."

"Did he search about while inside the shed?"

"No, sir. He showed no interest, other than to make certain the door was well locked when he left."

"And he came directly back to the inn?"

"Straight on," Little Alfie said. "I followed him right up to the edge of the forest where Wiggins took over."

"Slipped through the window of his room, neatly as you please, but did not bother to turn on the lights." Wiggins continued with the story. "That was a bit unusual, yet what happened next was even more unusual. Quicker than a cat in the night, he comes through the window once again and stares around, like he believes something is amiss. He looks left and right, then concentrates on the forest, but sees nothing because

Little Alfie and I are well concealed. Satisfied then, he climbs back into his room and retires for the night."

"Is it possible he spotted Little Alfie earlier?" Joanna asked at once.

"Not a chance," Wiggins said confidently. "We were still and quiet for a good five minutes before he came out a second time."

"I am still concerned," Joanna said.

"I say again, ma'am, he neither heard nor saw us," Wiggins insisted. "Nevertheless, some of the best snatchers are said to have an inner sense that tells them they are being watched. It is like a warning bell that goes off inside them. They know something is not right."

Little Alfie nodded. "Like Sarah, the Gypsy, who we use as a lookout before the nab."

Wiggins nodded back. "Sarah can sniff out a copper three blocks away. Says her skin begins to itch when they get too close. She saved our arses more than once, she has. And lucky for us, Little Alfie has a bit of this talent in him as well."

"He may well need it," Joanna said. "For the man you are up against is most clever and difficult to outwit. You should also be aware that the man you are tracking is a cold-blooded murderer."

Wiggins swallowed audibly. "A cold-blooded murderer, you say?"

"Right down to his marrow."

The rain began to pour down with large drops, so we all dashed away, Joanna and I for the front entrance to the inn, Wiggins and Little Alfie into the darkness of the forest.

15

Another Unexpected Death

A loud bang on the door awakened us at seven the following morning. We then heard the shrill voice of the local constable who had earlier alerted us to the butler's death.

"There has been another murder!" he cried out.

Joanna and I gazed at each other through sleep-filled eyes and shivered at the thought that the secret lodger had discovered and killed Little Alfie. Donning my robe, I hurried to the door.

"Who is the victim?" I asked.

"Henry Miller, the groundskeeper," the constable replied. "Please come along quickly."

As Joanna and I dressed, I could not help but think the unexpected death would cause everyone to recalibrate their suspicions, for the waters surrounding the missing document seemed to be growing murkier by the day. My head was spinning with possible explanations as we dashed through the vacant lobby and into a waiting hansom. My father was already seated within, neatly dressed and not showing a hint of sleepiness. But then, I reminded myself, he was a retired physician with some thirty years of practice behind him. He was accustomed to being awakened early and suddenly and clearing his mind soon thereafter.

"Nasty business, eh?" my father commented.

"And most confusing," I noted.

"Or perhaps illuminating," Joanna said, as the hansom moved along.

"Would you care to give us particulars?" my father asked.

"Only when I have the facts to prove or disprove my assumptions."

Joanna rested her chin onto her steepled fingers and stared out into the misty morning air. Her brow became furrowed, which was the sign that her finely tuned brain was assembling and rearranging all the preceding clues into a recognizable pattern. I have seen her in this state of concentration for hours upon hours until she either reached a conclusion or decided the data was not sufficient to do so. There was never anger or frustration associated with the process, only cold reasoning devoid of any emotion.

With our carriage approaching the Halifax estate, Joanna turned to my father and asked, "What do you think, Watson?"

"The evidence at hand seems to point at Roger Bennett," he replied.

"Are you convinced of his guilt?"

"Not entirely, but at this juncture it is difficult to conceive of a more likely suspect."

"Then please explain how Roger Bennett carried out this feat while under the watchful eyes of the Baker Street Irregulars the entire night."

"They have no recollection of him leaving the inn?"

"Oh, he left, but only once and only to enter the forest and the shed. He never set foot upon the Halifax estate."

"There must be another involved," my father concluded.

"That is one possibility," Joanna said as the carriage came to a stop at the entrance to the estate.

We could clearly see a dozen or more constables and detectives scouring the area surrounding the narrow stone bridge. Workers were dredging the stream with hooks and ropes, and tossing various items found up to the muddy banks. Drawing closer to the murder scene, we saw Lestrade and Dunn standing over a draped body.

"What we have here is a violent dispute among thieves." Dunn greeted us with his conclusion.

"Based on what?" Joanna asked.

"The fact that one of them, Mr. Henry Miller, is dead and the other, Roger Bennett, is on the loose."

"But why the killing?"

"Over money," Lestrade answered. "With thieves, it is always over money."

"It all fits together," Dunn went on. "As soon as we gave Miller permission to travel to London, he somehow contacted Roger Bennett and arranged for a secret meeting to discuss their future plans for the missing document. The stable boy was here to tell the groundskeeper where the document was hidden, so Miller could retrieve it and bring it to London for sale."

"And that is when the dispute broke out," Lestrade joined in. "Most likely the fight was over who would receive the majority of the money. We believe the stable boy demanded he take the larger share, for he had actually stolen the document and assumed the greater risk. It all ties together in a very neat package."

"So it would seem," Joanna said. "The only things missing are the facts to back up your assertion."

"Oh, I believe the facts are plain enough to see," Dunn insisted.

"Then perhaps your vision is superior to mine," Joanna said, and pointed to the covered corpse of Henry Miller. "Please be good enough to remove the covering."

Dunn lifted the bloodied sheet and exposed the groundskeeper's body. Henry Miller lay on his back, his blue eyes open and staring into emptiness. Rigor mortis had set in about his face, jaw, and neck, with the remainder of the corpse thus far spared. The most striking feature, however, was the hideous head wound. Virtually the entire left portion of his skull was caved in, with gelatinous brain tissue oozing out. Joanna briefly studied the disfiguring gash.

"No doubt the cause of death," she remarked.

"No doubt," I agreed.

"Please employ your expertise in pathology and inform us of any peculiarities about the wound."

"Give me a moment," I replied, then knelt and leaned in closer for a better view. The parietal bone, which comprises the left side of the skull, was smashed into splinters and pieces, leaving an opening that the edge of a hand could easily pass through. Yet the upper border of the wound was smooth, with spicules of grit embedded in it. The clotted blood surrounding it was dark, almost black, indicating that the coagulation had taken place hours earlier.

Rising up, I said, "The death blow was struck with incredible force. The relatively smooth upper portion of the wound indicates the weapon had a sharp, thick side made of metal. There is also evidence that it has been used previously."

"For murder?" Joanna asked at once.

"For work," I said. "There are spicules of dirt and rust about the bone fragments that tell us the weapon was not new and had been soiled."

"Very good, John," Joanna praised. "Your findings are most helpful. Tell us, would it be fair to say that the murderer was approximately the same height as the victim?"

"I believe that to be the case, for the blow was delivered on a level plane—not from below or above—and most likely from behind."

"Which makes our murderer left-handed since the left side of the victim's skull received the lethal blow," Joanna said, and returned her gaze to the corpse's sleeved arms. "Were you able to detect any defensive wounds?"

"None were apparent, but I did not examine the arms or shoulders, for fear of disturbing other evidence atop the clothing," I explained.

"Inspector, do you have any objections to such an examination?" Joanna asked.

"None whatsoever, in that the body has been searched and all items secured," Lestrade said, and motioned to two nearby constables who promptly removed the corpse's shirt. His arms had a few minor scratches and well-healed scars, but no defensive wounds.

"Clean," I pronounced.

"Which indicates he was surprised," Joanna reasoned. "For he had the opportunity to neither duck nor raise his arms as the blow was delivered."

"As would be expected, in that Henry Miller and Roger Bennett knew each other well and were partners in crime," Lestrade concurred. "Their partnership ended in the middle of the night when one killed the other."

"How do you know the event transpired in the middle of the night?" Joanna asked.

Lestrade hesitated briefly before answering, "Because he was found just after dawn by one of the guards, and the corpse was quite cold even then."

"So was the weather," Joanna said, and looked to me. "Can you give us a better time, John?"

I pondered the matter at some length, for although rigor mortis usually sets in four to five hours after death, there are other factors that can alter its onset. "I would approximate death occurred eight to ten hours ago. The start of rigor mortis in this case was no doubt delayed because of the cold weather. Since we are only seeing the beginning of it now, I believe an eight- to ten-hour estimate would be in order."

Joanna turned her attention to Lestrade. "Are we correct in assuming the guards saw nothing unusual at say ten or eleven last night?"

"Nothing out of the ordinary," Lestrade said. "But you must remember that both Lieutenant Dunn and myself agreed to pull back security somewhat to allow Miller more free rein and give the impression we had lessened our suspicion of his involvement."

"Are you telling us they did not notice Henry Miller on a late-night stroll?" Joanna asked skeptically.

"They saw him when he approached the bridge, and a minute or two later they saw him returning to the grounds, so they thought little of his walkabout."

"The sighting was at a distance, of course?"

Lestrade nodded. "At a distance."

"In the fog."

Lestrade had no response, and glanced over to Dunn who now had an uncomfortable expression on his face. He appeared about to speak, but thought better of it and instead stared out into the morning mist.

"You mentioned items that were taken from the corpse." Joanna broke the protracted silence. "May we have a look at them?"

Lestrade reached into a small satchel and retrieved Henry Miller's belongings. "There were just a few—a small pocket-knife, two shillings, a well-used pipe, and several strike-anywhere matches. For what it is worth, we also found clip-on reading glasses in his shirt and beneath the glasses a shred of torn paper, with the word *BACH* written on it. Perhaps he cared for classical music."

"B-A-C-H?" Joanna spelled it out.

"Yes," Dunn answered, then carefully reiterated, "B-A-C-H, as in Johann Sebastian Bach, of whom I am a strong devotee, particularly his Brandenburg Concertos."

"Henry Miller did not impress me as the Johann Bach type," Joanna remarked.

"His devotees come in all shapes, forms, and classes, madam," Dunn retorted.

"I am certain they do," said Joanna. "May I see the note, please?"

Lestrade handed over the sliver of paper for us to examine. The word *BACH* was capitalized as was the letter *U* which followed it. At this point the paper was torn off and it was not possible to determine if the *U* was a single letter or part of a word. Whatever it was, the note was indecipherable.

"We should look into whether any of Bach's works begin with the letter *U*," Dunn proposed. "It may offer a clue that the groundskeeper was withholding."

"Such as?" Joanna asked.

"The location of the missing document," Dunn replied.

"Perhaps it was hidden within a holder for a musical instrument or behind a cabinet that contained books on the great composer."

"I do not recall seeing these items in the groundskeeper's sitting room."

"Nor I," Dunn said. "But they may have been situated elsewhere on the estate."

"Hmm," Joanna murmured, obviously not convinced. "Do let us know of your findings."

Lestrade peered at Joanna's expression and asked, "You appear to be concerned over something, madam. May I inquire what it is?"

Joanna nodded ever so slowly. "We need to know what the note actually said, for that I believe holds the most important clue of all."

"And on what do you base that assertion?"

"The fact that the murderer went to the trouble of retrieving it from a dead man."

Our conversation was abruptly cut short by a cry from the nearby forest. "Sir! I believe we have discovered new evidence!"

Lestrade led the way over the stone bridge and into the thick woods, his shoes splashing in muddy puddles from the previous night's rain. Standing beside a stout tree was a constable in high boots, pointing down to the ground.

"There are several cigarette stubs here, sir, as well as a crushed, empty package that once held them," the constable reported.

"This is where he hid and waited for his victim," Lestrade surmised.

"So it appears that it wasn't a sudden fight that occurred, but a planned murder," Dunn said.

"Premeditated murder for certain," Lestrade concluded.

"No honor among thieves," Dunn added.

"Or among murderers."

Joanna reached down for the two cigarette stubs and examined their paper portions, then sniffed at them. "There are no markings on the paper and the aroma of the cigarettes is difficult to discern because the tobacco has been wetted by the rain. However, the crushed package next to the cigarette stubs clearly indicates they were of Turkish origin."

"A common enough brand," Dunn said with a shrug.

"But not inexpensive," Joanna said to herself more than to the others. Her gaze drifted over to some leaves at the base of the tree that were oddly colored. Some were green, some brown, a few spotted with red. She picked up a spotted leaf and rubbed her finger over it, then held the finger up for us to see. "Blood!"

Lestrade's eyes flew open. "So the body was here."

"More likely the weapon rather than the body rested here, for there are no drag marks to be seen nor is the corpse's shirt soiled with dirt and mud."

"But why not take the body into the forest where its discovery will be delayed?" Lestrade asked.

"Sometimes it is in the murderer's best interest to have the victim found earlier rather than later."

"I cannot envision why this would ever be so," Lestrade said.

"I refer you to the von Peltz case in Berlin last year that was widely reported. Did you read about it?"

"I must admit I did not."

"Then you should, you really should," Joanna went on. "It was most instructive. A banker was found stabbed to death early one morning. His drunken son was asleep in an adjoining bedroom, with a bloody knife in his hand. The two did not get along well, for the son was a layabout only interested in eventually inheriting the family's fortune. The son was thus charged with murder."

"And rightly so," Lestrade said.

"Wrongly so," Joanna said. "It was the secret lover of the banker's wife who did the deed, and placed the knife in the hand of the son who was deeply asleep from drink. The wife made sure the body was discovered early while the son was still asleep, so he would have no chance to clear his mind and immediately profess his innocence. Thus, you see, in that instance the earlier the corpse was found, the better. Which makes me wonder if our murderer had a reason to leave Henry Miller's body out in the open."

"Do you believe our murderer is that clever?"

"And some."

A constable dressed in a dredging outfit and dripping water ran up to us. He had a sharp-edged brick in his grip. "Sir, we brought this up from the bottom of the stream, along with several others, any of which could be the murder weapon."

"Well done," Lestrade said. "Let us have a look."

As Lestrade and Dunn rushed away, Joanna held us back with an open hand. When they were completely out of sight, she said, "We must go quickly to the shed."

"For what purpose?" I asked.

"To examine the real evidence."

"But surely the bricks are worth examining," my father argued mildly.

"That wound was not caused by a brick, for a brick at close range does not take off half a man's head."

We hurried along the winding path until we came to the red shed that had its door locked. Joanna found the key in its usual hiding place and, as we entered, cautioned us to remain off to the side, so as not to disturb any evidence. The ground was littered with cigarette stubs and cold gray ashes, which accounted for the heavy smell of stale tobacco smoke.

"Little Alfie has a keen eye," I remarked.

"Indeed, for there must be a dozen or more well-smoked cigarette stubs about," Joanna said, and began examining each and their ashes by sight and smell. "All are Turkish. You will also note there are no spent matches on the ground. Like our thief in the attic, he does not mind sprinkling ashes carelessly, but pockets every used match."

"But why?"

"Habit is the only explanation." Joanna strolled over to a nicely folded blanket near the side wall and remarked, "He plans to return."

"Which means he did not receive the missing document from Henry Miller," my father deduced.

"That is the key point here, Watson. The document remains somewhere on the Halifax estate, and only our thief knows its whereabouts." Joanna's gaze went to the rear of the shed, which was now clearly visible since all the dredging equipment had been removed and was now in use. Standing up against the rotted back wall was a sturdy pickax. She hurried over and swiped a finger against its metal head, which was stained with dried blood. "Ah! The weapon!"

"This is what Little Alfie saw the lodger swinging about, for he was planning on using it as a murder weapon," my father said.

"And a powerful blow from the chiseled end of the pickax could easily inflict the killing wound," I noted. "It would also account for the smooth edge at the upper edge of the skull fracture."

Joanna nodded in agreement. "Just imagine the force generated by a pickax that is being swung by a heavily muscled man."

"Death had to be instantaneous," I said.

"Is it not surprising that Little Alfie neither heard nor saw the deed being done?" my father asked.

Joanna gave the matter thought before answering, "Remember that Little Alfie remained in place when the secret lodger left the shed and walked some distance away to relieve himself. That is when, I believe, the killing occurred."

"And Little Alfie's reasoning that the lodger strolled far into the woods to avoid exposing himself to the woman is quite lame," I concurred. "To meet that end, all he needed to do was step behind the shed."

Joanna's attention was next drawn to the muddied handle of the pickax. On it was stuck a sliver of paper that she carefully detached and read. She nodded once more as a knowing smile crossed her face. "Now the note in Henry Miller's pocket becomes clear."

"Pray tell, what does it say?" I asked.

"You will recall the torn piece of paper found in the victim's pocket read '*BACH U*,' which Dunn interpreted as an inference to Johann Sebastian Bach. It was not and this torn-off shred of the message proves it. The shred reads '*M ZEHN*.' Thus, if you put the pieces of the note together, the message says '*BACH UM ZEHN*,' which translated from the German means 'the stream at ten.' You see, *Bach* is the German word for *stream*."

"Brilliant!" my father complimented. "This tells us he was lured to his death by the note."

"So it would seem."

"However, it does seem strange that the perpetrator was fluent in German, does it not?"

"He may not have been," Joanna replied. "He could have looked up the phrase in a German-English dictionary or simply asked someone at the Deutsche Society how to say it."

"But why bother to write the note in German?"

"So it could not be deciphered if intercepted or, as in this case, found by the police."

"It is most fortunate for us that you have a grasp of the language," my father remarked. "Did you know my dear friend and your father, Sherlock Holmes, was also fluent in German?"

"I was unaware."

"He was indeed and employed it to great advantage in several of our cases. This was particularly so in *A Study in Scarlet* in which the word *Rach* was written on the wall in blood. Lestrade's father, who was an inspector at the time, thought *Rach* indicated a woman named Rachel was involved. Holmes was later to inform him that *Rach* is the German word for *revenge*."

Joanna smiled gently, pleased with the story. "Perhaps the ability to acquire foreign language runs in the genes."

"Oh, come now," I said. "Surely you did not inherit your knowledge of German."

"Not the language per se, but the knack to learn," Joanna elucidated, as a tone of melancholy came to her voice. "My deceased former husband, John Blalock, was a fine surgeon who spent a six-month sabbatical in Berlin learning new procedures for tendon and ligament repair. I accompanied him and worked there as a surgical nurse where I picked up the language over time." She quickly flicked her wrist, as if dismissing the memory, and returned to the matter at hand. "But all the evidence we have gathered still leaves us with one major unanswered question—why would the thief kill the one man he needed?"

"Perhaps Lestrade was correct in his belief that he was killed in a dispute over money," my father suggested.

"Pshaw!" Joanna said at once. "Thieves decide that sort of business in advance. And if the thief wished to kill Henry Miller, why not commit the deed after the groundskeeper had been used and the money collected? It simply does not fit or follow."

"Do you have any idea then why the groundskeeper was murdered?"

"Only one that stands out."

"Which is?"

"Henry Miller was not the man we thought him to be," Joanna said, and headed back to the crime scene.

16

The Game Is Afoot

The butler's funeral was scheduled for 2 P.M., but a sudden downpour forced it to be delayed until 3:30 P.M. that dreary Wednesday. Despite the inclement weather there was a large turnout, for most of the villagers, along with the Halifax family and staff, had gathered to say a final good-bye.

As dirt was being cast upon the casket, the priest's voice was partially drowned out by thunder in the background.

". . . and so we commit his body to the ground: earth to earth, ashes to ashes, dust to dust."

While most of those present had their eyes on the grave, Joanna's were glancing about, but always coming back to Lestrade and Dunn who stood well off to the side. Just behind them were a number of constables partially hidden among the tombstones.

"Why are Lestrade and Dunn and all the constables in attendance?" I asked in a whisper.

"In the event Roger Bennett is drawn to the funeral of his father," Joanna whispered back.

"Surely he would not be so bold, particularly since it was he who murdered the old man."

"Blood sometimes runs thicker than you would think."

"If he were to show up, his capture would be imminent."

"Do not underestimate him, John. Thus far he has outwitted all of us, including the best that Scotland Yard has to offer."

Suddenly a commotion started at the rear of the cemetery, which was nestled up against the forest. A dozen or more constables broke into a run, with Lestrade and Dunn close behind.

"Ah! The game is afoot!" Joanna said, and joined the pursuit.

We dashed after her, but not too rapidly, for I did not wish to place too much stress on my father's endurance. Fortunately the pace slowed as the pursuers entered the thick woods. For the first time I noticed that some of the constables held the leashes of tracking dogs who howled in the delight of the chase. I could detect no sign of the stable boy, but the hounds were close on his scent and had to be restrained. Up ahead, just past a clearing, was the red shed.

I came up alongside Joanna and waited to catch my breath. Even in the late afternoon light I could see the door to the shed was unlocked and cracked open. The tracking dogs were barking loudly and being held back from entering.

"They have him!" I cried out.

"So it would seem," Joanna said without enthusiasm.

"You have doubts?"

"I have doubts."

"Why, pray tell?"

"The open door."

Lestrade drew his revolver and, after checking its rounds, moved in closer to the door of the shed. He stood well aside and called out, "Mr. Roger Bennett, you are surrounded with no hope of escape. You must surrender immediately or you will be taken by force. You have one minute to reach a decision."

The seconds slowly ticked off. All was silent except for the dogs, and even their barking seemed muted now. Constables were stationed on both sides of the shed and one had climbed a nearby tree to view any possible escape through the roof. Dunn stood next to Lestrade, with his revolver at the ready as well. There was no sound or motion from within the shed.

"You have thirty seconds remaining," Lestrade warned in a loud voice.

All remained still as more seconds passed by. The air was not moving as a dense mist began to descend upon the forest, which gave it a most eerie feeling. Suddenly one of the dogs broke loose from its leash and dashed into the shed, howling at the top of its lungs. Lestrade and Dunn crouched and held their revolvers in the firing position.

The dog within the shed let out several loud barks, followed by a few feeble yelps, then came back to its master.

Lestrade and Dunn, with constables behind them, rushed to the shed and smashed the door wide open. They were shaking their heads when moments later we followed them in. The shed was empty, with no trace of Roger Bennett. His escape route was obvious. Several wide planks of rotted wood had been kicked out from the rear wall of the structure.

"Clever devil," Dunn grumbled.

"He is a stable boy who has spent most of his life on this

estate," Joanna reminded. "He knows every trail and structure like the back of his hand, which gives him the advantage."

"But how did he manage to outsmart the dogs?" Lestrade asked.

"That was simple," Joanna replied. "Roger Bennett was aware his scent would be strongest within the shed, so he left the door open to draw all of the dogs' attention as well as that of the police. This gave him ample time to remove the planks at the rear and disappear into the woods."

"*Disappear* is the correct word, madam," Lestrade said gloomily. "Dusk will soon be upon us and, with the falling mist, he will be impossible to follow."

"Perhaps the dogs can pick up his scent again," Dunn suggested.

"I do not think that will be possible, sir," a constable said, and pointed to several dogs that were vigorously rubbing their noses with their paws. "Our man has laid down some strong substance that the dogs have sniffed. It appears to be a powerful irritant that throws off their sense of smell."

"What type of substance does that?"

"Pepper is the one used by most criminals, sir. And its effect can last for an hour or more."

"So we have lost him again," Dunn said unhappily.

"He cannot go far," Lestrade said. "And wherever he chooses to make an exit, we shall be. Constables will keep an all-night vigil on the village, and all sides of the forest will be placed under close surveillance. Eventually he will have to come out. Meanwhile, I shall have our men scour the forest to see if the scoundrel left other clues behind."

"If agreeable, Inspector, could we follow your officers to the far side of the forest?" Joanna requested. "It will give us security as we return to the inn. And we too shall search for evidence that could assist in Roger Bennett's apprehension."

"All help is welcome, madam," Lestrade said, and motioned to a nearby constable.

As we moved through the mist and deeper into the forest, I whispered to Joanna, "I doubt there will be any clues to be found in this dim light."

"That is not our purpose," Joanna replied in a barely audible voice. "I wish to make enough sound with our feet and voices to warn the Barker Street Irregulars that a group is approaching and they should seek even deeper cover. Their discovery would place us at a distinct disadvantage."

"But surely with the close scrutiny of the forest now under way, our need for them will end."

"To the contrary, dear John, it is only beginning."

17

The Telegram

The tobacco shop was quite busy at noon the next day, with only the owner and not his son behind the counter. So we waited patiently to speak further with Brendon Hughes, who waved genially to us and held up a finger indicating he would be with us momentarily. Joanna busied herself studying a display of fine cigars under glass. Her focus seemed to be directed to a brand labeled Dutch Masters. There were several varieties, but all contained the same rich, brown tobacco and bore no distinguishing features.

"Is there something unusual about the Dutch Masters?" I inquired.

"They have an interesting background," Joanna replied. "The tobacco is grown in the tropics of the Dutch East Indies and is beautifully rolled to give it a width almost that of a corona, but less than that of a cigarillo. The particular cigar under my hand is called a blunt and gives off a rich but mellow smoke that accounts for its popularity."

"But why is it called a blunt?"

"Note the thickness at its ends, John."

The tobacconist had apparently overheard our conversation and happily joined in as he approached. "It is a pleasure to see you again," he greeted. "I was delighted to hear your words on the Dutch Masters. There are more than a few cigar connoisseurs who do not carry the knowledge you do."

"I make it my business to know what others do not," Joanna said. "It is most helpful in my line of work."

"Ah, yes," Hughes recalled. "You are associated with Scotland Yard and the terrible circumstances surrounding Roger Bennett."

"Precisely," Joanna said. "Which brings us to the purpose of our visit. As you no doubt know, the stable boy remains on the loose and is believed to be in the vicinity."

Hughes shook his head wistfully. "What a sad world it is when a boy not only kills his father, but returns to the man's funeral. And then only to cause a ruckus while those of us who knew and liked Charles Bennett prayed for his soul."

"Terrible," Joanna agreed in a monotone. "And of course all efforts are being made to apprehend him. In that regard, we have learned he was a heavy smoker of Turkish cigarettes and wondered if by chance he purchased those here."

"I do not remember him doing so," Hughes said. "It is possible my son Lawrence made such a sale, but unfortunately he is ill at home with fever and bronchitis."

"When you see him next, please inquire for us," Joanna requested.

"But surely the stable boy would not be so bold as to return to the village where he would easily be recognized."

"He may have no choice. By all evidence he is a habitual smoker and is addicted to Turkish cigarettes. Since they

are somewhat expensive and sold only here, he may be forced
to visit your fine shop."

"And if he does?"

"For now, I would like you to remove all Turkish cigarettes from your display," Joanna directed. "If he or anyone
associated with him enters to make a large purchase, inform
him that the brand is recently out of stock, but that a new
shipment is due tomorrow. Then notify the police."

"I shall do so immed—" Hughes stopped abruptly in mid-
sentence and nodded to himself. "Now that you mention it,
I do recall an unusually large purchase of Turkish cigarettes
the other day. Walter, a waiter at the local inn, came in to
buy half a dozen packages of Turkish cigarettes for a lodger
who was confined to his room. But of course the lodger at
the inn could in no way be associated with the stable boy, now
could he?"

"One would think not," Joanna said. "Well, thank you
for your time and your kind offer to assist us."

How remarkable, I thought, and how clever. If you know
a man's habits, you should be able to predict his actions. We
were all aware of the thief's addiction to tobacco, but only
Joanna was astute enough to use it to track his movements.

We strolled away and were almost to the door when
Joanna abruptly stopped. "We must back away quickly!"

"What is it?" I asked.

"Gaze across the street to your right," Joanna replied as
we retreated from the large glass window. "And focus on the
limousine in front of the telegraph office."

It was the limousine within which the body of Charles
Bennett had been found, and from which Elizabeth Halifax
was now alighting. She glanced furtively over her shoulders
in all directions, then motioned for the chauffeur to drive on.

Only after another series of rapid looks about the street did she hurry into the telegraph office.

"What do you make of that, Watson?" Joanna asked, lowering her voice so we could not be overheard.

"She is in a rush to dispatch a secret telegram," my father replied quietly.

"Excellent, Watson!" Joanna said, her eyes fixed on the office. "Note the extremes she went to in order to remain unseen entering the telegraph office—the continuous glances about, sending the Halifaxes' recognizable limousine away, and then the hurried entrance. She is hiding something of delicate importance."

"But what?" I asked.

"That is what we must discover," Joanna said, furrowing her brow, which indicated her finely tuned brain was shifting into a higher gear. A glassy-eyed stare came to her face for a moment, then vanished. "From my earlier visit to the telegraph office, I recall a clerk behind the counter and a desk off to the side for one to write down the telegram to be dispatched. You should immediately cross the street, John, and stroll by the office, with a hand by your face so as not to be recognized. Glance in the window and determine if she is in fact sending a telegram, which I believe is the case. Please note whether she is at the clerk's counter or at the writing desk. Now go! Be quick, but do not rush."

I stepped out into bright sunlight and crossed the street, stopping briefly for a passing carriage. The sidewalk held a dozen or so pedestrians, which helped conceal my presence. Raising a handkerchief to my nose, I glimpsed into the telegraph office and saw Elizabeth Halifax at the writing desk, intently jotting down her message. Once more she glanced over her shoulders, as if sensing she was being watched, then moved to the clerk's desk where she was second in line. I turned away, having seen enough.

Before crossing the street to the tobacco shop, I had to delay, for the Halifax limousine was passing by. It slowed but did not stop and drove on. The chauffeur had returned too soon, I thought. The very last thing Elizabeth Halifax would want was for the family's limousine to be parked, motor running, in front of the telegraph office.

I reentered the shop and found Joanna and my father still studying the display of fine cigars, no doubt as a pretext for their continued presence. The tobacconist was serving another customer near the curtain at the rear of the store.

"Well?" Joanna asked at once.

"She is sending a telegram," I reported.

"Was she at the writing desk or the clerk's counter?"

"The writing desk."

"Good," Joanna approved. "Did you happen to notice her behavior when she wrote? In particular, was she agitated or harried?"

"She glanced about several times, but when she came back to the message she seemed quite intent on the writing itself."

"And finally, was anyone else at or waiting to use the writing desk?"

I shook my head. "There was only one other in the office and he was at the clerk's counter."

"Excellent!" Joanna said, rubbing her hands gleefully together. "That increases our chance for success."

"Of what?"

"Of following the trail Elizabeth Halifax is about to leave behind," Joanna said, and positioned herself so she could keep a close eye on the telegraph office.

"I wonder if she is truly involved." My father asked the

question we were all pondering. "It would explain why she lied to Joanna during the interview."

"And her behavior is most suspicious," I added. "She is hiding everything about the telegram. Perhaps she is wiring a coded message to an accomplice."

"Guesses, all guesses," Joanna said dismissively. "They do not advance our case a tenth of a millimeter. We must learn the contents of the telegram, for that will tell us why it was sent under such secrecy and to whom."

"That will be no easy matter," my father advised. "The telegraph clerk will not utter a syllable of information because he is aware that could cost him his position. And from my past experience with Sherlock Holmes, I can assure you that even Lestrade, with a search warrant, would not suffice in this situation. It will require a court order to reveal the telegram and that would be most difficult to obtain without the strongest evidence, which we do not possess."

"If we are fortunate, we will need neither a court order nor information from the clerk to gain our end," Joanna said.

"You do realize it is against the law to steal a telegram," my father cautioned.

"My plan is to read it, not steal it," Joanna said, then abruptly craned her neck forward. "Ah! She makes her move!"

Our attention was drawn across the way to the telegraph office. The Halifax limousine pulled up to the curb and, as soon as it stopped, Elizabeth Halifax hurried out of the office and entered the rear compartment, keeping her bonneted head down the entire time.

"Notice the chauffeur did not leave the wheel to open the car door for Elizabeth Halifax," Joanna observed. "She is doing everything possible to conceal her presence."

"Why did she not instruct a servant to carry the message

to the telegraph office in a sealed envelope?" I wondered. "That would have accomplished the task without her being seen in public."

"Too much could go amiss," Joanna said. "Suppose after sending the telegram, the clerk innocently returned the message in an open envelope to the servant. I can guarantee you it would have been read and become the next topic of gossip in the village."

"You always seem to see the unpleasant side of people," I remarked.

"Because that is the side I must do business with," Joanna said, her gaze following the limousine as it disappeared from sight. "We shall give them a minute or two to make sure they are well gone, then take to the stage."

"As in a play?" I asked.

"Yes, but with few words," Joanna replied, then turned to my father. "Watson, you are to remain behind in the event Elizabeth Halifax returns here to purchase Turkish cigarettes. If she does, take no notice, other than a brief nod."

"Why would she do so?" my father asked. "Her husband would not allow her to smoke, for his asthma makes him most sensitive to it."

"Nor did I detect the smell of stale tobacco smoke on her dress while interviewing her," Joanna said. "Thus the cigarettes would not be for her."

My father's eyes twinkled. "Perhaps for Roger Bennett who we think she met at the edge of the forest in the dead of night."

"Do you believe they are a couple?" I asked.

"Stranger things have happened," Joanna said without inflection. "A lonely, lovely woman married to an overworked, inattentive husband can lead to the oddest of matches."

"But surely she would not be so bold as to bring the cigarettes to him, with the forest being so closely guarded," I argued.

"She could have them delivered by a secret, circuitous route," Joanna countered. "And that would tie the two of them together beyond any question."

"But who would follow such a circuitous route?" I asked.

"Why, the Baker Street Irregulars of course."

My father shook his head in disbelief. "It is difficult to envision a woman of such standing in the arms of a stable boy."

"As I have stated on a number of occasions, nothing in fiction can begin to rival that which occurs in real life," Joanna told him. "In any event, Watson, busy yourself in the shop so as not to make your presence appear to be idle. I suggest you purchase a new supply of Arcadia Mixture which you have come back to."

My father looked at her oddly. "How could you possibly be aware of that?"

"Because you had been smoking black shag, Sherlock Holmes's favorite, while recuperating at 221b Baker Street. Since our arrival in Hampshire, you have returned to the Arcadia blend, which leaves a fluffy, white residue behind. Thus, your change in tobacco was very recent." Joanna moved closer to the window and gazed at length both ways down the street. "We shall wait a few moments more."

"Why such a long delay?" I asked.

"At times individuals in a state of agitation dispatch a telegram that they soon regret, and hurry back to send another to make amends. It would be most unfortunate if Elizabeth Halifax should return and find us snooping about the telegraph office." Once again Joanna peered up and down the street, which was now quieting. There was little traffic and several shops were closing for lunch. "It is time to make our entrance."

"What role shall I play?" I asked.

"That of an uninformed husband," Joanna replied. "When I give you the signal, present the clerk with questions that will draw his undivided attention."

We crossed the trafficless street and found the telegraph office vacant except for the clerk, who gave us the briefest of nods, yet kept his eyes fixed on both of us. Joanna moved to the writing desk and, with her back to the clerk, reached into her purse for a dull graphite pencil.

"Go chat with the clerk," she said, and appeared to be writing a message on a blank sheet of paper that sat atop the desk.

I strolled over to the counter and made certain the clerk's view of Joanna was totally obstructed, then asked, "Might I inquire if there is an express delivery of a wire to Edinburgh?"

"Yes. It can be arranged."

"Might I know the cost?"

"Allow me a moment," the clerk said, leaning sideways for a thick catalog.

"Such special deliveries can be expensive."

"They do add to the cost, sir," the clerk said, and began turning pages.

In my peripheral vision I glanced over to Joanna who nodded subtly to the door. The expression on her face showed neither success nor failure. Waving to Joanna, I told the clerk, "I see my wife is beckoning me, for we have a luncheon date and are a bit behind our schedule. We shall have to return later to complete our business here."

"Very good, sir."

We were almost to the door when the clerk called after

us, "I beg your pardon, but would you by chance be familiar with Mrs. Elizabeth Halifax?"

Joanna turned, instantly on guard. "We are indeed. Why do you ask?"

"She has left by accident a fine linen handkerchief behind, and I have no way of returning it. Might you do so for me?"

"Most certainly," Joanna said. "We will see her at a gathering early this evening."

"Thank you for your kind assistance, madam," the clerk said, and hurried over to give us a white handkerchief with the initials *E.H.* embroidered onto it.

Reaching for the door, I whispered to Joanna, "What if she comes back for it?"

"She won't," Joanna assured, pushing the handkerchief far up her sleeve. "Dear Elizabeth will have no idea where she lost or misplaced the handkerchief and will not mount a serious search, for it is by far the least of her problems."

"You should discard it at your earliest convenience."

"But it may yet serve a purpose."

"I do not follow you," I said, mystified.

Joanna smiled knowingly. "*Follow* is the key word here."

Outside, the bright sunshine had disappeared and dark clouds were gathering, threatening more rain. But the sudden worsening of the weather did not seem to dampen Joanna's spirits, for a most pleased look came to her face.

"I know to whom the telegram was sent," she announced, and showed me the blank sheet of paper she had taken from the telegraph office. Atop it she had done a fine graphite tracing, and the words *Lloyds Bank* could clearly be seen.

"You traced the lettering on the sheet beneath the one Elizabeth Halifax had written upon," I said admiringly, now understanding why Joanna had me observe Elizabeth

Halifax so closely while the woman was in the telegraph office. "But how did you know it would show through and leave
an impression?"

"I didn't," Joanna admitted. "But, as a rule, agitated individuals tend to press forcefully on the paper as they jot down
an urgent message. This is particularly so at the beginning,
and of course the beginning is to whom the telegram is being dispatched. Unfortunately, the remainder of the note is
indecipherable. But most assuredly it is on its way to Lloyds
Bank and that in itself tells us a great deal."

"How so?" I asked.

"Because that is where her money is."

"But why telegraph the bank?"

"Think about it, John. One does not telegraph Lloyds
Bank in London for a five-pound note. We are talking serious money here." Joanna pointed a finger at the sheet and
said, "You have neglected one other finding on the tracing.
In the very middle of the message is the faint word *thou*."

"A strange word to be used in a telegram to a banker,"
I thought aloud.

"That is because most likely *thou* is not a word, but the
beginning of another, such as *thousand*."

"To be withdrawn?"

"Or transferred to a separate account. If it is the latter, we
will have no way to trace the money."

"And if it is to be withdrawn?"

"Then that will be to our advantage," Joanna said, taking my arm as we crossed the street. "I would like you to place
yourself in Elizabeth Halifax's shoes for a moment. You go
to great efforts to make secret your contact with Lloyds Bank
where you wish them to have ready a withdrawal of a large

sum of money. Now, with all this in mind, pray tell, who would you send to fetch such a princely sum?"

"I would go myself," I answered at once.

"And having secured the money, what use would she make of it?"

I gave the matter thought before bellowing out, "A payoff!"

"To whom?"

"An accomplice!" I replied too loudly, then lowered my voice. "Do you truly believe she is involved?"

"Oh, yes," Joanna said as she signaled my father in the tobacco shop to join us. "The question is to what degree."

18

The Lookouts

At precisely ten o'clock that evening Joanna switched the lights in our room off and on twice, then returned to the fireplace where she smoked a Turkish cigarette while my father and I enjoyed our pipefuls of Arcadia Mixture.

"I still find it difficult to believe Elizabeth Halifax is involved in such an act of betrayal," my father said.

"But you must admit the evidence standing against her is overwhelming," I contended. "First, she has a clandestine meeting with the secret lodger in the darkness at the edge of the forest. Then we learn that the lodger calls her name from the shed in which he is hiding. And finally there is the telegram to Lloyds Bank requesting a large sum of money. These are not the acts of an innocent woman."

"But such a fine lady from a most distinguished family . . ." My father's voice trailed off before he glanced over to Joanna. "Do you believe there is love between the lady and the secret lodger?"

"I have my doubts," Joanna replied. "When they met briefly at the edge of the forest, there was no touching or embrace, which one would expect if this was a romantic assignation. Also, love in the usual sense does not require the transfer of a large sum of money."

"But they are tied together in the theft beyond any question?" I noted.

"Yes, but to what purpose?"

Joanna lighted another cigarette from the one she was smoking and gazed into the brightly burning fire. Her eyelids began to droop, closing out the world, as she sank into deep thought. She seemed to nod at one fact, then shake her head at another, all the while trying to fit them into a cohesive picture. After a lengthy deliberation, she flicked her cigarette into the fire and reached for another.

"Really, Joanna," my father objected, "you are using entirely too much tobacco, which in the long run will be harmful."

"You are correct, Watson," Joanna said, but showed no hesitation in lighting the cigarette. "But please recall that my father was afflicted with a similar habit. When faced with a difficult case, Sherlock Holmes referred to it as a three-pipe problem. I daresay I am faced with one that will require three packs of Turkish cigarettes or more. And the answer is there, right before my eyes, but I cannot quite grasp it. There is a common link to everything, which should be obvious, yet it escapes me."

"It will come," my father said.

"No, Watson, it will not simply appear. It must be sought."

We heard a pebble tap against the window, signaling the arrival of the Baker Street Irregulars. Reaching for our coats and hats, we bundled up with shawls as well, for the weather had turned quite cold, with the ever-present threat of rain.

My father said, "I was concerned they might not show, with the forest under such close scrutiny."

"Not to worry," Joanna said. "They are a very clever bunch who could play horns in the forest and still not be discovered by the local constables. The street urchins survive by their skill to disappear, which I can assure you they are using at this very moment."

The inn was quiet and asleep except for the night manager at his desk in the lobby. He pushed a newspaper aside and rose, as if expecting a request from us.

Joanna waved him down. "We are taking a stroll to help with our sleep."

"Indeed," the manager said. "But please be careful, for there is a very thick mist in the air."

Outside the so-called mist had turned into a dense fog that rivaled anything we had ever experienced in London. We separated ourselves from the inn and, linking arms, carefully stepped to the rear of the building where the darkness was greatest. The irregulars stood in the shadows next to the wall, following us with their eyes, like cats in the night.

Drawing in closer we heard the noise of chatter coming from within the inn. Then there was quiet, which was followed by the sound of a pot or pan dropping to the floor. In the dimness we saw Wiggins bring a finger to his lips while he waited for the chatter to begin once more.

"Cleaning up the kitchen, they are, so we have to be quick," he said in a whisper.

"I have questions," Joanna said in a low voice.

"Fire away, ma'am."

"Tell us of the lodger's movements when the ruckus occurred in the forest."

"There was no movement 'cause he remained in his room the entire time," Wiggins replied. "The bloke didn't even bother to peep out his window."

"Are you certain of this?" Joanna asked quickly.

"Swear on the Holy Bible ten times over," Wiggins vowed. "We heard the dogs and the noise, and figured they were coming for him. That is when he would have to make his break, you see, but he didn't. In his room, he was, that is for sure. Right, Little Alfie?"

"In his room," Little Alfie repeated. "I actually saw him flick some burning cigarette stubs out the window. He smokes like a chimney, he does."

"Did the pursuers ever leave the forest itself?" Joanna queried.

Little Alfie shook his head. "They came near the edge, but no farther. At that point, ma'am, the dogs had stopped their howling."

"Which must have indicated that the scent had disappeared," Joanna concluded.

Little Alfie shrugged. "Or the scent had become so faint the dogs did not want to bother with it."

"But would they still not be attracted to the scent, no matter how faint?" Joanna asked.

"No, ma'am," Little Alfie responded. "It is the strength of the smell that excites them. Once it begins to fade away, the smart dogs figure they are on the wrong track."

"You appear to know a great deal about hounds," I noted.

"I do, sir," Little Alfie said quietly. "My father raised hunting dogs before he passed on."

Wiggins gave Little Alfie an affectionate pat on the shoulder and said, "Alfie, here, knows his way around hunting dogs better than most. Don't you, my man?"

Joanna abruptly turned her head toward Wiggins and asked, "What was the term you just used when referring to Little Alfie?"

"Why . . . um . . . um . . . I believe I called him 'my man,'" Wiggins stammered. "It's a name street people give to their chums. I meant no offense to Little Alfie, ma'am."

"He meant no offense, ma'am," Little Alfie repeated.

"I understand that," Joanna said, waving away their concern. "I was simply wondering if the term *my man* is commonly used among the working class."

"We all say it, ma'am," Little Alfie said. "Boys and adults alike."

"Very good," Joanna said, and began to carefully articulate her words. "Now, Alfie, I want you to think back to the evening when the secret lodger was in the red shed and called out to someone. Do you recall that?"

"Yes, ma'am."

"And you were some distance from him?"

"Twenty yards or more."

"Were there other sounds as well?"

Little Alfie scratched at his head before answering. "His footsteps, I guess, and maybe the breeze. But I heard his voice for sure."

"I am certain you did," Joanna coaxed. "And now I have a very important question for you. Could the lodger have called out, *'Is that you, my man?'* rather than *'Is that you, ma'am?'* Could you have mistaken the words *my man* for *ma'am*?"

"It is possible," Little Alfie said, with a slow nod. "But I can't say one way or the other. At a distance they sound like one another."

"Particularly when the caller was keeping his voice down, as the lodger would have done, if he thought it might be a lady visitor."

Little Alfie nodded again. "That's what any proper gentleman would do."

Our conversation was interrupted by the noise of more pots and pans rattling around in the kitchen at the rear of the inn, and this was followed by laughter and chatter.

"We'd best finish up, ma'am," Wiggins urged. "They won't be much longer now."

"There is one final piece of business," Joanna said. "And this may be the most important task you will carry out, so pay close attention. If done successfully, you will receive an extra crown in your pay."

Wiggins and Little Alfie moved in closer to catch every word.

"You can sleep tonight, for it is unlikely the lodger will leave his room this evening and you must be alert the entire day tomorrow. At dawn, Wiggins, you will go to the train station and find a position where you will not be obvious and appear to be waiting for someone to arrive. In mid-morning or thereabouts, a limousine will drive up and a most attractive lady will alight from it. Keep your distance and, if she enters the station, do not follow. I need three pieces of information, all critical, so instill these questions in your mind. First, the exact time her train departs. Secondly, the exact time it arrives in London, and thirdly, which station it is bound for."

"Easily done," Wiggins said.

"Be very careful in your watching, for she will be glancing around as will her chauffeur."

"I will be part of the scenery, ma'am, and nothing more."

"Make certain the lady's limousine is well gone before you leave to relay your report to me," Joanna instructed, handing him a slip of paper, then turned to Little Alfie. "You will remain in the forest with your eyes fixed on the lodger's window. This is particularly important in the late afternoon. If he leaves, you must track his every step in and out of the forest. If he meets someone, however briefly, see if there is an exchange of a small package or thick envelope. This is of utmost importance, but do not venture too close and put yourself at risk."

"Not to worry, ma'am," Little Alfie said, and reached in his pocket for a narrow, handheld telescope.

Joanna had to smile. "Where did you find that?"

"I bought it, ma'am."

"Which we will add to your expenses," Wiggins informed.

"Which I will gladly pay for."

The chatter within the kitchen came to a halt, then we heard the sound of cabinet doors being closed.

"They are done," Wiggins said, and without further words, he and Little Alfie disappeared like shadows into the blackness.

We strolled back to the front entrance in fog so thick it was difficult to see a hand pass before one's face. The entire inn was dark, even the secret lodger's room, but we gave it yet more space to minimize the chance of the three of us being noticed.

"And so," Joanna said quietly, "one question is answered, and another arises."

"Let us begin with the one that is answered," my father requested.

"It was our supposition that Roger Bennett called out to Elizabeth Halifax from the shed. This would have implied a secret rendezvous, perhaps a romantic assignation. It would have tied the two closely together. But such a meeting was utterly incomprehensible. Would everyone truly expect Elizabeth Halifax to sneak away in the dark of the night and cross an expansive green lawn under heavy guard, and not be seen? Pshaw! They would have spotted her in an instant, just as they did the groundskeeper, and rushed to her side to determine if she required assistance. And since Henry Miller was up and about that very night, I think it is fair to believe it was he and not Elizabeth Halifax whom Roger Bennett was expecting."

"And that explains why he went for the pickax when he heard the noise," I reasoned. "He called out *my man,* thinking it was Henry Miller, from whom he was anticipating problems."

"Precisely," Joanna agreed. "A man does not take a practice swing with a pickax for an approaching lady."

"But the two are still tied together," my father said.

"Yes," Joanna responded. "But perhaps not in the manner we had thought."

We came to the front entrance and gazed in at a now dozing night manager. A sudden gust of chilled air came at us and we turned our backs to it. Then the rain began, which seemed to be a nightly event in Hampshire.

Reaching for the door, my father asked Joanna, "You mentioned another question had arisen, and your expression told me it was bothersome. May I inquire what it was?"

"Perhaps the most important question of all."

"Which is?"

"You do recall the irregulars reported that our secret lodger neither left nor returned to his room during the entire day of the funeral?"

"They insisted so."

"Then, pray tell, how was Roger Bennett, while snugly ensconced in his room at the inn, not only able to attend his father's funeral, but to also lead Lestrade and his band on such a merry chase through the forest? A man cannot be in two places at the same time."

"Unless he is some sort of magician," my father suggested.

"Which Roger Bennett is not," Joanna said. "And that leaves us with the only possible explanation."

"Which is?"

"That either the man at the funeral or the secret lodger at the inn is not Roger Bennett."

"Hold on a moment, for I see a contradiction," I argued. "Surely it was Roger Bennett who attended the funeral, and with equal certainty it was Roger Bennett whom Walter, the waiter, identified as the secret lodger. Yet you state they are not one and the same."

A Mona Lisa smile came to Joanna's face. "Has it not crossed your mind that the secret lodger is someone impersonating Roger Bennett?"

"But would not this individual have to bear a most striking resemblance to the stable boy?"

"So it would seem," Joanna agreed. "Yet in the dimness, an approximate semblance would suffice and cause Walter to misidentify the secret lodger."

"But why would the lodger bother with such a deception?"

"When we discover the why, we shall know the who."

19

Elizabeth Halifax

Having taken the early morning train to London, we were seated comfortably in our rooms at 221b Baker Street when Wiggins phoned from Hampshire station. Elizabeth Halifax had just departed. She was in first class on the noon express bound for Victoria Station.

"Come!" Joanna urged. "We must go quickly, for she will arrive in fifty-nine minutes."

"To Victoria?" my father asked.

"Yes. But first we travel to number 3 Pinchin Lane to fetch our gentle friend Toby Two."

On our ride to Lower Lambeth we reminisced at length about Toby Two, the hound with such a remarkable nose it could track the faintest scent across half of London. She was the granddaughter of the original Toby, a dog made famous by Sherlock Holmes, who worked so brilliantly with her in *The Sign of the Four*. The current Toby was the product of a second-generation Toby and an amorous bloodhound, which endowed her with the keenest sense of smell imaginable. Joanna had employed the sweet hound in *The Daughter of Sherlock Holmes,* in which the dog not only tracked the hidden trail of a murderer, but had also detected the trace amount of poison in one victim's blood. Although Joanna and the dog were on familiar terms, my wife had never met Mr. Sherman, who boarded Toby Two in the most unusual of settings.

"Be prepared for a strange encounter," my father advised her.

"I have experienced strange before," Joanna said, unconcerned.

"You have been warned."

As on our previous visit to Pinchin Lane, my father had to knock repeatedly on the door to number 3 before a blind on the second floor opened.

"Go away!" a voice cried down.

"It is I, John Watson, the companion of Sherlock Holmes," my father announced.

"Ah, Dr. Watson! I am on my way."

Moments later the door to number 3 was unbarred and Mr. Sherman, the keeper of Toby Two, appeared. He seemed much older now, with a heavily lined face and tired eyes that squinted through blue-tinted glasses. Lean and lanky, but severely bent at the waist, he had to look up to gaze upon us.

"What a pleasure to see you once more, Dr. Watson," Sherman said. "And I see you have brought some company with you."

"I have indeed," my father said. "I trust you remember my son, Dr. John Watson Junior, from our prior visit."

"I do, sir," Sherman acknowledged, with a half bow that exaggerated his stooped posture.

"And beside him is his wife, who happens to be the daughter of Sherlock Holmes."

"Oh, yes, ma'am," Sherman cooed, obviously pleased with her presence. "I have read of your exploits and I can tell you the criminals of London are not happy to know you are following in your father's footsteps. Most unhappy, they are." He gave a long, admiring look, then flicked his wrist as his expression turned to business. "But you are not here to listen to my chatter, are you, ma'am?"

"We have come for Toby Two," Joanna said.

"And she is expecting you," Sherman said. "Her tail began wagging ten minutes ago when she first picked up your scent."

He led the way into a large room that carried the strong odor of unwashed animals. High up on the rafters one could see partially hidden birds of prey, eyeing us as if we might serve as their next meal. Off to the left was a Scottish wildcat that Sherman allowed to roam the shop freely. Larger than a house cat, it had long legs and a bushy tail, and was said to occasionally pounce on moving targets that came too near. As on our previous visit, the wildcat gave us a foreboding hiss as we passed by.

Sherman showed us down a line of metal cages that contained a variety of animals, including dogs, cats, and a pair of blood-smeared badgers that had been crowded into a single enclosure. They were noisily feasting on something they had apparently killed.

"Old Toby lives at number 15 at the very end," Sherman called out, pausing briefly to secure the lock on the badgers' cage.

"Does the smell of blood bother the other animals?" I asked.

Sherman shrugged indifferently. "To them, it's just food."

Joanna checked her watch and urged, "We must move along, Mr. Sherman, for we find ourselves on a tight schedule."

As we picked up the pace, the Scottish wildcat suddenly pounced. Out of the dimness came a loud squeal that lasted only a second. We glanced over and saw the wildcat with its jaws clamped down on the neck of a giant rat.

"Here we are," Sherman said, and opened the end cage. "Out you go, old girl."

Toby Two bounded onto the floor and let out several happy yelps, then busied herself inspecting our shoes for scents. First, she sniffed Joanna's, next my father's, and finally mine. Not quite satisfied, she came back to Joanna's shoes for another sniff, putting her nose to both heel and toe. Only then did she sit on her haunches and stare up at Joanna, as if awaiting instructions.

Joanna reached down to scratch the head of the most peculiar-appearing animal. She had many features of a long-haired spaniel, but the floppy ears, sad eyes, and snout were those of a bloodhound. The dog's attention stayed fixed on Joanna and was only drawn away when her owner reached into his pocket. Mr. Sherman handed Joanna a lump of sugar that Toby Two accepted after the briefest of hesitations. The alliance between Toby Two and Joanna being sealed, the dog eagerly followed us out and into our waiting carriage.

On our trip to Victoria Station, Toby Two kept her head entirely out of the window so she could sample the air and savor the aromas contained in it. Intermittently she would howl happily, as if detecting a scent that was particularly pleasing to her. Joanna reminded us that, according to a monograph written by German scientists, dogs had a sense of smell a thousand times greater than that of humans and could easily distinguish between a hundred different scents at the same time. Their noses were in fact one of nature's most sensitive instruments.

"But what is our current need for Toby Two?" my father asked. "We know that Elizabeth Halifax plans to visit Lloyds Bank, a major branch of which is located a scant three blocks from Victoria Station. Surely it will present no difficulty following her there."

"You are assuming she will visit the Lloyds Bank in Belgravia," Joanna said. "But that may not be the case. Remember, this is the area where the Halifax family lives when not at their country estate. She could be seen and recognized by an acquaintance. Thus, it might behoove her to transact her business at a distance, say at the larger Fleet Street office."

"Your point is well taken," my father agreed.

"And there is another point to be taken," Joanna went on. "She may choose not to hurry to the bank, but rather meet up with an intermediary who will transact this unpleasant business for her. As a rule, the aristocracy do not like to soil their hands in such matters."

"Would she actually hand the intermediary the money and allow him alone to carry out the transaction?" I asked.

Joanna shook her head. "Only a fool would do that and Elizabeth Halifax is no fool. The money and the document will change hands at the same time, but with Elizabeth watching. I can assure you that the large sum of money will either be in Elizabeth's possession or under her watchful eye at every turn."

"But would not such an arrangement place Elizabeth Halifax in danger?" I asked. "After all, she is dealing with those who are not of the best class."

"If she encounters danger, it is of her own making and

she will have to face the consequences," Joanna said without inflection. "Our concern is the missing French Treaty upon which may rest the fate of England. Thus, it is the money that we must follow, and Elizabeth Halifax is simply the carrier."

"And the money leads to the missing document, of course," I concluded.

"Which is why we will track it with the finest nose in all of London," Joanna said, and reached over to scratch Toby Two's head. "No matter where she goes, Toby's nose will follow."

"But how will Toby Two know Elizabeth's scent?" I asked.

"From the linen handkerchief she left behind in the telegraph office." Joanna opened her handbag and extracted a leather pouch that was tightly latched. "Within this pouch I have the handkerchief that contains not only her bodily scent, but the fragrance of a French perfume that she apparently douses on. I have no doubt Toby Two could follow the latter through a windstorm."

I queried, "What if Elizabeth Halifax decided to change perfume?"

"No matter," Joanna said. "She will retain a bit of fragrance from her prior perfume, and Toby Two will have no difficulty picking up its scent."

"Ah!" My father pointed to the window. "Victoria Station is just ahead."

"Excellent! Our timing is perfect," Joanna said, then turned quickly to me. "John, please hurry into the station and stroll about until the noon express from Hampshire arrives. Do not wait for Elizabeth Halifax to appear, for it is important you not be seen. Once the passengers begin to disembark, return to our carriage as rapidly as possible."

I quickly alighted from the carriage and entered Victoria Station, which was crowded with hundreds of people, all of whom seemed to be moving and talking at the same moment. Keeping my head down, I approached a porter for the information that was needed, and he pointed to a train from which passengers were disembarking. Following Joanna's instructions, I did not wait for a sighting of Elizabeth Halifax, but promptly turned and hurried back to the carriage.

"The game is afoot!" I announced.

We immediately crouched down in our seats so we could not be seen, yet still have a clear view of the station's entrance where carriages were lined up in an orderly queue. A few motorcars were there as well, but they were off to the side and not for hire. Several minutes passed as passengers continued to leave the station, but Elizabeth Halifax was not among them.

"Are there other exits to the station?" I asked.

"Of course. But they do not have waiting carriages," Joanna replied.

"Perhaps she is taking a circuitous route."

"That will not be to her advantage, for Toby Two can easily follow her scent," Joanna said, unconcerned, then abruptly craned her neck forward. "There she is!"

A bonneted Elizabeth Halifax strode out into the bright sunlight and signaled a carriage with her parasol. She kept the open parasol low in an effort to conceal her face.

"Tell me what you see, Watson," Joanna said.

"Nothing out of the ordinary," my father observed.

"Note the absence of luggage," Joanna coaxed.

My father thought for a moment before saying, "She will not be spending the night."

Joanna nodded in agreement. "Her visit will be brief,

which is to be expected when one is conducting sordid business."

The carriage holding Elizabeth Halifax pulled gently away from the curb and entered Victoria Street, then melded into a sea of other hansoms and motorcars. Joanna tapped on the roof, which was a signal to our driver to follow the carriage that had just departed. He had been instructed in the strongest terms to stay back a considerable distance, so as not to be noticed. Even if he lost sight of the carriage, it would present no problem, for Toby Two's yelps would keep us on the track of Elizabeth Halifax.

Joanna rapidly opened her handbag and reached for Elizabeth Halifax's neatly folded handkerchief. She rubbed it under Toby Two's nose for a full ten seconds, allowing the hound to register its distinctive scents, then she returned the handkerchief to its leather pouch.

Toby Two suddenly sprang to life. Sticking her head out of the window, she howled in delight as she now realized the chase was on. Her tail was upright and wagging furiously at the aromas that filled the air. But Toby Two's unique talents were not needed at this point, for Elizabeth Halifax's carriage was coming to a stop at the entrance of Lloyds Bank in Belgravia. She remained inside the hansom, and the driver did not climb down to open the door for her.

"She waits," Joanna said.

"But to what end?" my father asked. "She could be recognized by passersby if she lingers."

"Perhaps she has arranged for a banker to meet her," I suggested.

"Most unlikely," Joanna said. "Banking is a highly confidential business, and those who practice it do not greet their clients in the street. She is waiting for someone of importance."

"An intermediary?" I queried.

"Perhaps."

Another minute passed before the driver climbed down to open the carriage door for Elizabeth Halifax. She stepped out, with her parasol now open and covering most of her face. Yet she did not move to the entrance of the bank. Elizabeth Halifax looked about briefly and partially closed her parasol before allowing it to reopen. Only then did a well-built, broad-shouldered man come out of the shadows and approach her.

"She signaled him with her parasol!" I exclaimed.

"Obviously," Joanna said, and moved nearer to the window so she could better study the middle-aged man. Some feature in particular seemed to draw her attention, for she craned her neck for a closer view.

I saw nothing unusual about the man, other than his size. He was over six feet in height and, with his large frame, easily topped two hundred pounds in weight. His suit was of average quality and its coat was not well fitted.

"He is security," Joanna said, her eyes still on the man.

"How can you know this?" my father asked.

"From simple observation, Watson," Joanna said, and relaxed back in her seat. "You will note how he continually glances around and takes stock of his surroundings."

"A close confidant there to help her would do the same," my father argued mildly.

"And would this confidant carry a revolver?" Joanna asked. "Notice the unseemly bulge in his coat under his left arm. That is where a right-handed man would position his hidden weapon. And, as you can see, he is right-handed."

I glanced over to the front entrance to the bank. The man was opening the door for Elizabeth Halifax, using his right hand.

"She is being most careful," Joanna went on. "From the very moment the money touches her hand, there will be an armed guard at her side."

"But is this precaution truly needed inside a bank?" I asked.

"Particularly inside and near a bank," Joanna said. "Clever thieves at times are able to place themselves in banks where they watch for large withdrawals. They then signal an accomplice outside to perform what is referred to as *a running snatch* in their trade. The money and the thieves disappear in the blink of an eye."

The transaction within the bank was accomplished rapidly, for the couple reappeared in a matter of minutes. As Elizabeth Halifax stepped up into the carriage, the armed guard glanced around in all directions, with his right hand firmly tucked inside the front of his coat. The size of the bulge we had noticed earlier was now twice as large.

Their carriage moved away and Toby Two was instantly on the alert. With her head out the window and nose to the wind, she immediately picked up the scent and made the happiest of sounds. Joanna tapped on the roof to remind our driver to keep his distance.

"Do you have any idea of their destination?" I asked.

"I do not," Joanna replied. "But I can assure you they will take a circuitous route to reach it."

Our carriage moved along lower Knightsbridge at a steady pace, for the traffic had thinned and motorcars were less prevalent. Still, the air held the odor of used petrol and we could only hope it would not interfere with Toby Two's keen nose.

Abruptly our carriage jerked forward and increased its speed, but that lasted for only a few seconds before we slowed down once more. Then we continued on, with only gradual and intermittent increases in our rate of travel.

"Clever," Joanna remarked

"How so?" I asked.

"It is a mechanism to determine if one is being followed," Joanna said. "One speeds up and slows down several times to see if the carriage behind you does the same."

"Is our driver aware?"

"He was so informed."

We turned onto Park Lane and rode in silence past Hyde Park and into the Marble Arch area. Toby Two kept her nose to the wind, but her head was not nearly as far out the window as before. Apparently the scent of Elizabeth Halifax was so strong it required little effort to detect and follow. But the hound was not bored, for her tail was still up and wagging.

Gradually our carriage turned onto Edgware Road and Joanna sat up suddenly. She tapped on the roof and the driver slowed down. Once again she tapped and we slowed even more.

"We must be very careful here," Joanna warned. "Please sit back so your faces cannot be seen."

"Why the caution?" my father asked.

"We are now on Edgware Road."

"And?"

"This is the street where the Deutsche Society resides."

The Deutsche Society! I recollected its significance as the name echoed back and forth in my mind. It was mired in every aspect of the missing document. Here, Henry Miller had been not only a member, but the soon-to-be presiding officer. Here, Roger Bennett had come to inquire about living in Germany and how to obtain a visa to do so. And here, the brother of a known German spy had been invited to give a lecture and was seen chatting with Henry Miller.

"Perhaps we should call Scotland Yard," I suggested, unable to keep the urging out of my voice.

"Not yet," Joanna said. "Let us see how this hand plays out."

Our carriage continued on for another block, then slowed to a crawl, although traffic was noticeably light. Joanna raised her brow in concern as she reached up to tap the roof. "What is transpiring?" she called out.

"A moment, ma'am," the driver called back, then abruptly increased his voice to a shout. "Ma'am! Ma'am! They are doing a turnabout and will shortly be heading directly toward us!"

"Take a right at Portman, then another right and return to Oxford Street," Joanna directed quickly. "And do not appear to hurry."

"Will not Toby Two lose the scent?" I worried.

"Briefly," Joanna replied. "But she will pick it up again at the Marble Arch."

We performed a gradual turn onto Portman Street and continued past a large hotel, then swung right onto a narrow street that was lined with row houses. Just ahead we could see the top of the Marble Arch. Joanna tapped lightly on the roof and gave further instructions. "Go right again and down Oxford at an even pace. When you reach Bayswater, do a turnabout and return slowly to the Marble Arch. You should shortly see the lead carriage, which you again will follow at a distance."

I was not surprised by Joanna's keen knowledge of the westside of London. For most of her adult life she lived and traveled around the elegant areas of Park Lane, Knightsbridge, and Belgravia. She knew their streets like the palm of her hand.

"Elizabeth Halifax is leading us on a merry chase," I thought aloud. "I had no idea she was this clever."

"It is not Elizabeth, but rather her security man who is so clever," Joanna said. "We are observing the skills of a professional who is very adept at evasion techniques. That is the reason for the circuitous journey from the bank."

"So the trip down Edgware Road where the Deutsche Society is located was just fortuitous?"

"So it would appear."

"How long will this continue?"

"Until he is convinced no one is following them."

Our driver tapped on the roof, indicating the lead carriage was in sight once more. We moved along at a steady pace past the Marble Arch, then down fashionable Park Lane to the entrance of Knightsbridge. Traffic now became very slow, particularly in front of Harrods, the finest department store by far in all of London. Suddenly Toby Two grew excited and jumped to the side of the carriage facing Harrods. She sniffed at the air, her head turning side to side, as if trying to make up her mind.

"She is confused!" my father cried out.

"She is distracted," Joanna corrected. "Within Harrods there is a food hall filled with the most exotic delicacies, all of which give out enticing aromas. You must remember, to dogs nothing supersedes the importance of food, and Toby Two is no exception."

"How do we overcome this?"

"By reinforcement," Joanna said, and reached in her handbag for Elizabeth Halifax's handkerchief. She drew Toby Two back and rubbed the handkerchief under her nose at

length, then placed the dog on the side of the carriage away
from Harrods. Toby Two held her nose to the wind, now obviously back on the scent.

"Do you think they intentionally drove by Harrods?" I
asked.

"I would doubt that," Joanna said. "Most likely they are
on this route because it is the shortest one back to Victoria
Station."

"Do we board the same train they do?"

"We have no choice."

"But if she sees us, all is lost."

"Then we must not be seen."

"I think it too risky, Joanna," my father cautioned. "Since
her train will be the express to Hampshire, why not alert
Wiggins who can follow her once she disembarks?"

"I have no way to contact Wiggins at his current position," Joanna said. "And even if I could, it might not work to
our advantage. The express train to Hampshire, you see,
makes a stop at Basingstoke and we have no assurance they
will not leave at that station."

"Why would they depart at Basingstoke?"

"For the same reason they drove to Edgware Road."

At Victoria Station we followed Elizabeth Halifax and the
security man at a discreet distance and watched them board
the express train to Hampshire. She wore her bonnet pulled
down securely so it covered most of her face, while the guard's
large frame provided a shield that obscured a clear view of
her. After purchasing our tickets, we waited until the last moment to climb aboard, making certain we were well away
from the car where Elizabeth Halifax and the security man
were seated. Toby Two was happily preoccupied with a dog
biscuit provided by Joanna.

Drawing the curtain across the window, she asked, "What do you make of it, Watson?"

"Elizabeth came to London for the money, and now that she has it she will return to Hampshire for the transaction."

"So it would seem," Joanna said. "But pray tell, why not complete the transaction in London? She has the money and the security man at her side, and thus it could have easily been done here."

"But we believe the document is still on the Halifax estate," my father pointed out.

"An exchange of money for the missing document could have been accomplished by third parties using the telephone to communicate with the principals."

"Then perhaps she was fearful of being followed into and about the city."

"Unlikely," Joanna said. "She hired an expert at evasion to remove that threat."

"But you followed her."

"I am not most people, and most people do not have available the services of Toby Two."

My father rubbed his chin pensively. "Am I overlooking something here?"

Joanna nodded slowly. "It reaffirms my belief that the choice of location for the transaction is not hers, but the thief's."

"Does it matter?"

"Oh, yes. For it will be held in darkness at an isolated spot in Hampshire, and no doubt Elizabeth Halifax has been instructed to come alone, which will double the danger for her."

"Are you suggesting her life will be at stake?"

"A man who has killed twice will not hesitate to kill

again. Such an act would allow him to take the money and still retain the document."

"This goes beyond sinister."

"Indeed, Watson, for we are looking at pure evil and nothing less."

As we traveled through the bucolic beauty of the English countryside, I was once more struck by its peace and tranquility. But I also recalled Joanna's warning that beneath its calm and warmth could reside crimes every bit as vicious as those that occurred in the slums of London. Already in Hampshire we had witnessed two murders, one brutal, the other more subtle, and those were mixed in with traitorous acts, lies, and deceit. And now, Elizabeth Halifax was about to endanger her own life without knowing it.

The train stopped briefly at Basingstoke and an elderly couple came aboard, but no one departed. We continued on without interruption until we reached our destination just before sundown. Peeping out our window we watched Elizabeth Halifax walk briskly to her waiting limousine without glancing back at her security man who was now reboarding the train. He entered two cars in front of us just as the conductor blew his final whistle.

"Quickly," Joanna urged, and led us off the train and down the platform away from the car that held the security guard. "Keep your heads lowered until the train has left. And John, lean over to tie your shoe and make certain the Halifax limousine is well gone."

Tying imaginary shoestrings, I reported, "Out of sight."

We waited until the train was a speck in the distance, then strolled over to the side of the station where Wiggins and, unexpectedly, Little Alfie stood in the shadows.

"Alfie, you were told to keep an eye on the lodger's window at all times," Joanna admonished.

"It could not be done, ma'am, not with all that going on in the woods," Little Alfie explained. "A dozen coppers, with a new set of dogs, were on the chase, they were. You could tell it by the way the dogs barked. They were really excited, like they were closing in."

"Did the lodger make it back to his window?" Joanna asked.

"He never left, ma'am," Little Alfie replied. "Stayed in his room, as far as I could see."

Joanna looked at the boy skeptically. "Did you fall asleep at any time during your watch?"

"No, ma'am," Little Alfie said, and crossed his heart to demonstrate he was telling the truth. "Wide awake I was, the whole time."

"Are you absolutely certain he did not leave the room?"

"I didn't say that, ma'am. I said he never came out of his window." Little Alfie scratched at an armpit as he gave the matter more thought. "I guess he could have slipped out the rear, but you told me to watch the window, and that I did, ma'am."

"Were you able to determine if the man was in fact captured?" Joanna asked.

"No, ma'am. They were so bloody close to my hiding place I had to skip out of there or be collared myself. But I can tell you those dogs were quite excited, which is the way they get when they pick up the scent and the fright of the game they're after."

"Ma'am," Wiggins broke in. "According to Little Alfie, there are coppers and dogs everywhere and they mean to stay. It's probably best we not go back into those woods."

"There is no need for you to do so," Joanna said. "You both have done well and there will be an additional half crown in your pay to perform one last task."

Joanna paid the irregulars, with an extra half crown added to return Toby Two to number 3 Pinchin Lane. On our stroll to a waiting carriage, Joanna appeared to have a second thought and turned to the boys, who were walking down the platform. She hurried over to Little Alfie and asked, "Did you actually see the lodger move about in his room?"

"No, ma'am," Little Alfie replied. "For once, he kept the window closed and it could not be seen through."

As we walked away, Joanna said in a quiet voice, "There are strange occurrences, one after another, happening here and they do not fit the facts."

"Do you not believe their story?" my father asked.

"They have no reason to lie," Joanna replied.

"Then it truly complicates matters for us."

"And even more so for Elizabeth Halifax."

"Is the danger she faces now greater?"

"By leaps and bounds."

20

Footprints

The following afternoon, Joanna and I returned yet again to the attic space of the manor in an effort to match the footprint of the secret lodger with those made by the thief. But on this occasion we brought the ingredients for a special mixture to produce a mold of the attic footprint and thus determine if its left heel had a worn-down feature.

"How did you come by this special formula to make a mold?" I asked, shining my torch on the floor as we searched for the deepest imprints.

"I recalled it from a most excellent monogram on the subject by Sir Robert Trent-Smith," Joanna replied. "But I must admit I have never made a mold of any sort. So, to be certain I had all the details at my disposal, I ordered a copy of *The Science of Footprints,* which was just delivered."

"But I do not see how it would work to our advantage here. Certainly you cannot hope to produce a distinct mold from an impression in a thin layer of dust."

"It is not one in the dust we seek, but rather one that is encased in claylike mud from the thief's shoes."

"How do you know the latter exists?"

"I can offer no guarantee, but he did track mud into the attic space and thus it is logical to assume he left the signature of his shoes behind. Furthermore, since he wished to be silent and not alert the nearby kitchen workers, he no doubt tip-toed across the floor after entering through the window, and in the process his heels did not touch the surface and leave their marks, which would have surely been noticed by others. He would have also tiptoed up the narrow staircase. If my assumptions are correct, he finally rested his entire muddy shoes on the floor once he was in the attic." Joanna pointed to an area near the ashes from the thief's cigar. "Please direct your torch on that print."

I followed her request and moved in for a closer inspection. The toe of the thief's shoe had pressed down on the cigar ashes, but the heel showed only a blurred outline in the dust. "No luck."

"We should proceed to the space encircling the trapdoor above the secluded office," Joanna advised. "For it is there he would have stood after gaining entrance, and thus it is there where he would have brought in enough mud to leave a discernible footprint."

We continued down the attic, which still held the aroma of bleach, and carefully searched for prints that could be of value. But none were to be found. All were either indistinct or too shallow for a mold to be made. Nevertheless we persisted in our quest, for it was of the utmost importance to clearly establish that the secret lodger was indeed the thief who visited the attic space.

"Should we find a matching footprint, would it not be best to alert Scotland Yard?" I wondered.

"To what end?" Joanna replied. "Knowing Lestrade, he would barge into the secret lodger's room with a hastily obtained warrant, which would not work to our advantage."

"But it would reveal the identity of the secret lodger," I argued. "And that, my dear Joanna, may well be the key to the entire mystery."

"Yet it, in all likelihood, would not turn up the missing document, which is secretly hidden elsewhere. The lodger would simply deny any guilt or misdeeds, for there is no crime in secluding oneself in an inn nor in closely resembling Roger Bennett. Furthermore, a footprint showing a somewhat uneven heel is hardly the compelling evidence required to convict a man of treason. At this juncture, I am afraid we have no choice but to wait for yet another piece of the puzzle to fall into place."

"And while we wait our traitor continues to enjoy the comforts of the Hampshire Inn," I grumbled.

"His time will come," Joanna assured me. "For he has already made mistakes that will seal his fate."

We approached the end of the dark corridor and stepped around the length of rope the thief had used to climb in and out of the attic space. Streaks of light shone up through the edges of the badly fitted trapdoor, but it was not nearly enough to give us a clear view.

"We shall remain in place here and use the torch to discover deeper footprints," Joanna said. "In particular, look for tracks of caked mud."

I carefully scanned the top surface of the trapdoor and the area immediately adjacent to it. But no mud or prints were to be seen. Off to the side, spiders were busily spinning new webs across splintered wood, and above them insects of another species were crawling about. I next directed my torch to the space between the trapdoor and length of rope, and saw a pair of distinct footprints. "There!" I cried out. "There is where the thief stood."

"Most excellent, John," Joanna exclaimed and, with magnifying glass in hand, knelt down to examine the imprints. "Here he remained stationary to pull up the rope, and while doing so left behind a muddy signature of his left shoe."

"Is it deep enough to produce a mold?" I asked, shining the torch closer to the vital clue.

"It is impossible to tell, for the heel is less than a centimeter in depth," Joanna replied, now moving her magnifying glass up and down to bring out the details. "But let us give it our best try."

I watched as Joanna reached into a cloth satchel for the ingredients and utensils required to make a mold. "Are you certain of the proportions to be used?"

"They are simple enough," Joanna answered. She placed a glass bowl on the floor, then opened several packets of a white powdery substance before removing the top from a small bottle of water. "According to Sir Robert, one mixes a half cup of flour with a half cup of salt, then adds a fourth cup of water. Once this is done, one kneads the mixture until it reaches a doughlike consistency."

The entire preparation took only a few minutes, and, when the dough was firm enough, Joanna pressed it firmly into the footprint that had been made by a left shoe. She quickly removed her hands and stared down at the forming mold.

"Is something amiss?" I asked.

Joanna shook her head as she wiped the dough from her palms. "We must wait for a distinct imprint to be produced."

Moments later she reached for a small metal ladle and carefully pried up the mold before placing it onto a round dish. "Now, to the kitchen!"

We hurried down the attic space and exited through the trapdoor into the vacant library. On we went along the main corridor of the manor until we came to the kitchen where the head cook awaited us.

"Is your oven now heated to approximately two hundred degrees?" Joanna asked.

The cook nodded briefly. "As you requested, madam."

"Then please bake this dough for exactly two hours," Joanna instructed. "It is not to be touched or disturbed in any way while being baked."

"Understood, madam."

We returned to the library and, while we waited, Joanna placed a telephone call to her father-in-law, Lord Blalock, to learn of any current news regarding the financial woes of the Halifaxes and Stanhopes. Their conversation was prolonged, with Joanna being most interested in the Stanhopes and, in particular, the wayward son Ian, whose misdeeds had brought the family's prestigious brokerage firm to its knees. At length, Joanna placed the phone down, then peered out into space, lost in thought for the moment.

"Important news?" I inquired.

"Perhaps, but not unexpected," Joanna replied. "The Halifaxes have been forced to sell off yet more of the family's ever-shrinking estate, which should keep their heads above water for the immediate future. Nevertheless, their modest relief will be short-lived, for they have considerable back taxes that are once again coming due. The Stanhopes find themselves in an even more dreadful situation. They have no assets to sell and what land they own is heavily mortgaged. Their father is bedridden and dying of heart failure, while the family is facing another lawsuit being brought by South Africans over the Stanhope brokerage debacle."

"What of the scoundrel son, Ian?"

"He stays away and rarely visits, and when he does it is to scrounge for what little money there is."

"Elizabeth is no doubt aware of her brother's unseemly behavior," I noted. "You will recall the hardened expression that came to her face when his name was mentioned."

"The greed Ian Stanhope exhibits has no bounds," said Joanna. "Apparently he convinced Elizabeth to sell the land she inherited from a loving uncle and invest much of the proceeds in the New England Holding Company, knowing full well that it was fraud and that he alone would benefit from the commissions of the sale. I suspect the thousand pounds she withdrew from Lloyd's Bank was the last of those proceeds."

"There must be something sinister behind such pathological greed," said I.

"There is," Joanna revealed. "Ian Stanhope is a compulsive gambler whose debts remain to this day."

"With the dislike between them, I think it most unlikely the pair colluded to steal the missing document."

"But that would not exclude each from acting on their own."

I checked my timepiece. Just over an hour had passed since the dough mold was placed in the oven, so it was now only half baked. We smoked Turkish cigarettes and helped ourselves to a fine sherry while sitting by a wide fireplace, with its logs blazing nicely. Outside, the weather had turned cold and wet, which brought worry to my mind.

"Would you care to tell me of your concern?" Joanna asked.

"I do wish you would stop reading my thoughts," said I, wondering as always how she managed to do it.

"And now you want to know how I performed this magical feat?"

"Please do not tell me it is in my facial expressions."

"But it is, and in your movements as well. When you worry, the lines in your lower brow suddenly wrinkle and deepen, and your jaw tightens. This is accompanied by rapid puffs on your pipe, but in this instance on your cigarette. And when you are impressed by one of my deductions and try to discover how I reasoned it, your mouth tends to open while you stare at me." Joanna crushed out her cigarette and asked, "Now, what is it that bothers you so?"

"My father," I replied. "On a number of occasions since our arrival, he seems to have disappeared. He is not to be found in his room or the lobby or bar of the inn. Then he reappears and I inquire about his recent whereabouts. He hesitates for a moment before smiling and saying he was just out and around. With this strange behavior, I immediately wonder if he cannot recall where he has been."

"Surely you are not suggesting he has early dementia."

"That thought crossed my mind."

"But he has been sharp in his deductive skills, and his medical knowledge remains quite impressive."

"I keep telling myself those very same things, yet I realize that, with advancing years, dementia may make itself known in uncommon ways while sparing other parts of the brain."

"Have you considered the possibility that he is pursuing clues in hopes he can help us solve this mystery?"

"By himself?"

"Why not? Perhaps he has recalled some clue from his glory days with Sherlock Holmes and wishes to pursue it on his own."

"I still worry," said I. "And with this cold, damp weather, I fear for his health should he be wandering around in the woods or God knows where."

"I see your point," Joanna had to admit, then quickly arose from her chair. "Let us go examine our baked mold, then we can hurry back to the inn and locate our dear Watson."

We walked down the main corridor at a brisk pace, saying little, but I could tell Joanna shared my concern about my father. It was simply so unlike him to vanish without explanation. I now regretted not bringing him along on our journey to again inspect the attic space. He would have been content to sit in the library and smoke his cherrywood pipe while awaiting the results of our search.

As we approached the kitchen, Joanna cautioned, "Do not mention the particulars of the baked dough while we are in the cooking area. The staff will be gathered about the stove, with ears pricked for any hint of juicy gossip."

"But they will clearly see it is the mold of a footprint."

"It is the details that will be of interest to them."

Joanna was correct regarding the staff's curiosity. The cook and three of his aides were awaiting us, all standing back from the giant stove, but still within hearing distance. The baking dough–mold gave off a most pleasant aroma which belied its origin.

"You may now remove the dough from the oven and place it upon the table to cool," Joanna directed.

Carefully the cook performed the task, then stepped back while others in the kitchen involuntarily inched forward. The mold was well baked, with a thick brownish crust around its edges. Its center contained a clearly defined footprint, but with a most shallow depth. Nevertheless, the heel could be distinguished from the sole.

"Did you bring along your sketch?" Joanna asked in a whisper.

With a nod I reached into my inner coat pocket for the sketch I had made of the muddy footprint in the picnic area beside the Hampshire Inn. Using my moustache-trimming scissors, I had earlier cut away the extraneous edges of the sheet so that only the outline of the shoeprint itself was left behind. I slowly placed the cutout atop the impression in the doughy mold. It was a perfect match.

"Spot on," Joanna said and, with tweezers, removed the cutout. She then carefully studied the mold with her magnifying glass, beginning with the toe of the imprint and gradually working her way to its heel. Over and over again she examined the heel before announcing, "There is an unevenness."

With that brief statement she scooped up the freshly baked mold and, placing it in her cloth satchel, thanked the cook for his assistance. The cook and his staff followed us out with their eyes, their curiosity now even more piqued.

Halfway down the corridor I asked, "Is the heel on the mold worn down in a fashion identical to that of the footprint in the mud?"

"That is difficult to say because of the shallowness of the mold imprint," Joanna answered. "Nevertheless, there is unevenness on the outer edge in both instances."

"But do we have a match?"

"Not one that will stand up before an official inquiry, but the heel prints resemble each other so closely I cannot help but believe that they came from the same shoe."

"Thus the secret lodger must in fact be our thief in the attic."

"So it would seem."

"And we draw closer to a conclusion."

"But we must play our hand even more carefully now, for catching the thief without obtaining the missing document is not the victory we seek."

We ran for Lestrade's waiting carriage, which earlier had been placed at our disposal, for the weather was deteriorating rapidly. Sheets of rain poured down in torrents so dense they obscured our view of the countryside. And it magnified my worry. I dreaded the thought of my father wandering about or lost in the chilly downpour, for it would make him an ideal candidate to develop pneumonia.

I could not contain my anxiety further. "Let us hope he is not traipsing through the woods attempting to retrace the track of the secret lodger and find more clues."

"Indeed, let us hope that is not the case, for we are dealing with a cold-blooded murderer and it would not be wise to come too close to him, particularly in the secluded woods."

On our arrival at the inn, we raced up the stairs to my father's room and found it vacant except for the chambermaid who was fluffing pillows. She reported the room empty when she entered an hour earlier. We noted with concern that my father's topcoat and shawl were missing. Dashing downstairs to the lobby, we found ourselves surrounded by a crowd of French tourists complaining about the foul weather. At the reception desk we spotted the innkeeper and hurried over.

"Have you seen my father?" I asked worriedly.

"I saw him an hour or so ago," MacGregor replied. "He requested some bones to take to the dog in the stable."

"For what purpose?"

MacGregor shrugged. "I did not ask. But as you know, there are some people who simply enjoy feeding animals. I could see no harm in that."

"Indeed not," I said, taking Joanna's arm as we moved quickly through the crowd of guests and headed for the front entrance. "My father obviously wishes to befriend the border collie, but why? Surely he would not consider taking the dog-cart out in this weather."

Joanna shook her head at the possibility. "The horse is lame, so the dogcart would be of no use."

We rushed out into the rain, which had mercifully begun to slacken, and entered the stable. And came upon the most unexpected sight I had ever encountered. There was my father sitting atop the partially restored bicycle, which was placed off the ground on wooden blocks and missing its front wheel. His topcoat and shawl were on a wall hook off to the side, and he was pedaling the bike at a most vigorous rate.

"Exercise!" my father called over to us. "I thought the stationary bike to be an excellent vehicle to strengthen my leg muscles. What say you, Joanna?"

"I consider it a superb idea," she replied happily. "When did this first come to mind?"

"On our initial visit to the stable," he answered. "But I wished to try it out on my own rather than take the chance of failing miserably before the two of you."

"So that is why you chose to do it in secret," said I, thinking how foolish my earlier notions of his disappearance had been. "Do you find it working?"

"Quite so," my father said, climbing off the bike and walking past the border collie who was busily chewing on a lamb bone. "On my first go, I was somewhat disappointed because my legs ached and felt weak afterward. I nonetheless persevered in my endeavors and my legs are now coming along nicely. With each outing I feel that more and more of my muscle strength is returning. This is evidenced by the fact that I am currently capable of rapid pedaling for bursts of several minutes."

"Well done, Father!" I cried out. "Well done indeed."

The dog suddenly looked up as Walter, the waiter, entered and waved to my father. "Ahoy, Dr. Watson. How goes today's workout?"

"Splendidly," my father responded. "And thank you again for your assistance."

Walter motioned away the gratitude. "It was nothing at all, Dr. Watson."

"Oh, but it was," my father insisted, then turned to us. "I asked Walter's permission to use the bike, for he has a partial ownership in it."

"But I thought it was Roger Bennett who possessed a partnership in the bicycle," Joanna queried.

"Walter and Roger own it together," my father said. "It is an interesting partnership that you should be aware of. Please explain it to my colleagues, Walter."

"Well, me and Roger are close chums, you see," Walter began. "So after the terrible transport crash, it was me who found the wrecked bike in the high grass off the thoroughfare. I brought it to Roger's attention, knowing how good he was with his hands at repairing things. So we came to an agreement on the ownership, with me scavenging about for spare parts from the wreck, while Roger did the hard work of restoring it."

"But you thought it best not to tell Mr. MacGregor about your partnership with Roger Bennett," Joanna interjected.

"Indeed I did, madam, for I am a full-time worker at the

inn and did not wish to appear I was not attending to my duties as a waiter. Mr. MacGregor, you see, does not put up with slackers. If he knew the time and trouble I went to for spare parts, he would not be happy." Walter walked over to the far end of the stable and pulled an old woolen blanket away from a stack of bike parts. Most prominent was a wheel and somewhat rusted fender. "I bought the wheel from some lads who found it by the roadside and were using it as a toy to spin around and run after."

"What was the cost?"

"A cherry pie baked by Mr. Felder, the chef at the inn," Walter replied. "And for a bag of cookies they gave up the fender. So now Roger and I had all the necessary parts and, with a bit more work, our bike would be ready for renting. Things were progressing so well, they were. Then the trouble started, and now all the blithering idiots are trying to place the blame on poor Roger."

"Do you believe him to be innocent?" Joanna asked.

"Beyond any doubt, madam," Walter replied at once. "Honest as the day is long, he is. Are you aware he would not accept the damaged bike until he checked with the authorities to make certain it was within the law? He is the kindest, most gentle fellow I ever met, and goes out of his way to help people and even injured animals. Once we found a hurt squirrel and I thought we should put it out of its misery. But Roger refused and built a small cage for the animal and fed it until it recovered. That's the kind of chap he is."

"Yet the police say there is evidence he killed his own father," I argued.

"Then they say wrong, because Roger loved his old dad more than the sun and the moon and all the stars put together.

Do you know what he planned to do with his earnings from the rental of the bike? Want to take a guess?"

"Buy his father a gift," I surmised.

"Right you are, sir. But it was to be a very special gift. He would take his father on a holiday to Scotland where they would attend the rugby championships, for it's a sport the old fellow held dear to his heart. Roger told me he had already saved up five pounds and with the bike rentals he could add another fiver, which would make for a splendid holiday. Now, does that sound like a lad who would kill his own sweet dad?"

"Hardly," I agreed.

"So let us hope they catch the real killer and put all this foolishness to rest." Walter turned to the border collie and beckoned to her. "Come on, Sally, and do your business outside, so I can return to mine."

As the pair departed, my father said, "I would dearly love for Lestrade and Dunn to hear Walter's story, but I doubt it would make a dent in their convictions."

"It might not, but we now have other evidence that surely will," Joanna reported. "Perhaps it would best be told over an early dinner."

"An excellent suggestion," my father said, walking away with a lively step to fetch his topcoat and shawl. "Nothing works up the appetite like good exercise."

In a quiet voice, I asked Joanna, "Are you referring to the footprint mold as the other evidence?"

"That, along with the bike," said she.

"The bike? How so?"

"To be used as an ideal escape vehicle," Joanna elucidated. "Roger Bennett could have easily placed on the wheel and fender, making a complete bicycle, and pedaled away on it unseen."

"But the main roads would have been under surveillance."

"Not at night, and he could have traveled the bridle paths by day. And when he reached his destination, he could have easily sold the Military Humber for ten pounds or more. The bike provided Roger Bennett with the perfect escape, yet he chose to remain here in Hampshire."

My father approached us, wrapping on his shawl, and asked, "What are you two whispering about?"

"The man who is not our thief," said Joanna.

21

The Arrest

On our return to the lobby we decided to celebrate my father's excellent progress with drinks at the inn's bar. Over glasses of a fine, rich Madeira, my father showed great interest in the matching heel print we had uncovered, then took some delight in recounting a case in which Sherlock Holmes had made a mold of a hand that revealed a missing fingertip. It proved to be a decisive clue, but Holmes thought the case to be of minor importance and thus it was not chronicled.

Joanna asked, "Do you recall if he used the technique of Sir Robert Trent-Smith to produce the mold?"

My father thought for a moment before shaking his head. "I believe he came up with his very own method, for he was quite good at such things. You may recollect that it was he who discovered the test to detect human blood that we used so well in *The Daughter of Sherlock Holmes*."

"How ingenious he was," I remarked.

"Indeed," my father agreed. "When Holmes needed a

particular instrument to solve a crime and it was not available, he simply invented one."

"Did he record the ingredients he used to make a mold?" Joanna asked.

"Not to my knowledge, but we should consult his volume on *The Whole Art of Deduction* to be certain," my father replied.

"I wonder if his method was superior to that of Trent-Smith's."

"I would not be surprised if it were."

Joanna sighed softly, then mused aloud, "I am afraid we shall never see the likes of Sherlock Holmes again."

"Oh, I am not so certain of that," my father said, with a twinkle in his eye.

We decided against a second round of drinks for the dinner hour was approaching and a change of attire was in order. As we reentered the lobby, Lestrade suddenly appeared at the front entrance and hurried over to us. He was barely able to contain himself as he announced with pride, "We have him!"

"Who?" Joanna asked, feigning ignorance.

"Why, Roger Bennett, the thief," Lestrade went on. "He is now handcuffed to his bed in the butler's cottage and under most careful guard. But even if he were to wiggle free he could not go far, not with his badly broken leg. That is where you come in, Dr. Watson. The leg requires medical attention and the local doctor is off in the corner of the county attending to a difficult delivery. We would be grateful for your services to give him some relief, which even a traitorous thief deserves, you will agree."

"Has the fractured bone penetrated the skin?" my father asked.

"Not as yet, but it appears bound to do so," Lestrade replied.

"Then we must hurry."

We boarded a waiting carriage and galloped back to the Halifax estate in the fading afternoon light. Along the way Lestrade provided us with the details on the capture of Roger Bennett. The thief had ventured out of his hiding place, which was a small cave, to search for food and water. The hounds quickly picked up his scent and gave chase, but he easily outdistanced them, for he is a well-trained runner. But he had the misfortune to trip and fall, and in the process badly fractured his leg. He offered no resistance when apprehended.

"Has he confessed to the crime?" Joanna asked.

"Of course not," Lestrade answered. "Like all thieves worth their salt, he loudly professed his innocence."

"So I take it you do not have the document."

"That is correct," Lestrade said. "But I have every confidence we shall shortly."

"The dogs should be of great assistance in locating it, for his scent will be on the document." My father stated the obvious.

"Under ordinary circumstances you would be spot on, Dr. Watson. But I am afraid the dogs will be of no help in our search, for Roger Bennett had sprinkled the cave and all about it with a heavy dose of cayenne pepper. Once the dogs sniff the strong pepper, their sense of smell disappears, so they learn to avoid it at all costs. That is why we have had such difficulty finding the thief's hiding place."

"Stable boys born and raised in the countryside have all the advantages," my father noted.

"Until they break their leg."

We entered the Halifax estate and found its expansive

lawn near the forest now swarming with police. A dozen or more constables and detectives carrying brightly lighted torches roamed the area, calling out instructions above the howling dogs. The grand manor had all of its lights on and the road leading up to it was heavily guarded by men at close quarters.

"In the event Roger Bennett has an accomplice who decides to make a grab for the document, he would certainly be dissuaded by the added security," I remarked, then added, "Assuming of course that the boy is guilty."

"The boy is most certainly guilty," Lestrade said, with conviction. "And an accomplice would not dare show his face, for if he did it would be the end of him."

We left the carriage and strolled over to the butler's cottage, which was under close guard, with two constables at the door and one at every window. Inside, the sitting room was a cluttered mess, with chairs and sofa overturned and their cushions ripped open. The framed photographs on the wall were hanging askew, so their backs could be searched for hidden items. At the door to Bennett's bedroom stood Lieutenant Dunn, with an expression upon his face that told us he was not pleased with our presence.

"Be quick," he ordered. "For we are planning to shortly move the prisoner to London."

Roger Bennett had the appearance of a very frightened young man. Tall and lanky, with tousled blond hair, he took up every inch of the mattress and then some. His eyes were wide open, his pupils markedly dilated, and the hand that was handcuffed to the bed was shaking with fear.

"Are you in a great deal of pain?" my father asked.

"Yes, sir." Bennett grimaced in a quivering voice. "I can barely stand it."

"Let us have a look."

Using a pocketknife, my father gently cut away the stable boy's trousers to expose a misshapen right leg. Just below the knee the extremity was bowed, with the head of the fibula pressing so firmly against the skin it appeared ready to break through. My father wisely decided not to check the leg's range of motion, for it would serve no purpose other than to make a bad situation worse.

"Splint it and get on with it," Dunn barked.

"We must be very careful here, for the wrong move could turn a simple fracture into a compound one, and cost the boy his leg," my father advised.

"One-legged men swing from the gallows just as well as those with two," Dunn said harshly.

"Prisoners, no matter their crime, deserve humane treatment and he shall receive it," my father said, standing up to the intelligence officer. "And you will not interfere. Do I make myself clear?"

Dunn glared back at my father, but made no response.

"Tell us what is required, Dr. Watson," Lestrade interceded.

"I will splint the leg firmly to prevent the fractured end of bone from piercing the skin. Once the swelling has begun to recede, we can decide how much realignment is necessary and apply a suitable cast."

"How long will it take for the swelling to subside?" Lestrade asked.

"At least a day or two, I would think."

"That is too long!" Dunn said, raising his voice. "My orders are to have him in London tomorrow, and I plan to carry them out. He will be on that train, with or without a cast."

"Then you risk the boy's leg," my father said.

"My concern is not the boy's leg, but the document," Dunn retorted.

"My leg!" Bennett screamed through his pain. "Please do not let me lose my leg. I cannot run without it!"

"Where you are going, boy, running will be the least of your worries," Dunn said, then came back to my father. "Are you saying a tight splint will not do?"

"It will be risky," my father replied. "Better to wait a few days and be safe."

"Please!" Bennett pleaded as tears came to his eyes.

"Tell us where the document is and we will see to it you are seen by a proper specialist in London," Dunn offered.

"But I did not take the document," Bennett said, grimacing as a bolt of pain shot through his leg. "I swear it on my father's grave!"

"The same father you murdered!" Dunn snapped.

"I did not, sir! I loved my father with all my heart!" Bennett attempted to sit up against the handcuff, and this heightened the pain even more. "Oh! Ohhh!"

My father eased him down and, using two slats from the bed, splinted the stable boy's misformed leg. He secured the splint with two ties from the butler's closet, then made suggestions. "I think it wise to remove the boy's handcuff."

"Never!" Dunn shouted.

My father waved away the officer's objection. "Really, Lieutenant, do you believe the boy will run away on a leg so painful he could not take a half step without collapsing in agony?"

"It will be done," Lestrade said firmly. "What else?"

"Please have one of the constables hurry to the village chemist for a dozen doses of laudanum, which will ease the boy's pain. He may use my name as the prescribing physician."

"The chemist may have closed his shop for the night."

"Then have him reopen it."

We rode back to the inn in silence, the three of us now feeling the fatigue that comes from a very long and busy workday. After all, we had started off at dawn to again inspect the red shed and surrounding area, looking for additional clues but finding none. The remainder of the morning was spent in the village requestioning the tobacconist and his son, both of whom were certain they had seen Roger Bennett. None of the other shopkeepers could confirm the sighting. Finding the ingredients and utensils to produce a mold and making the mold of the footprint itself took up most of the afternoon, which ended with the search for my father whose endurance now seemed to match ours. His spirits were also quite high and I believe he was rejuvenated by the opportunity to once more practice his beloved medicine.

Approaching the inn, I asked him, "Do you think the boy may yet be found guilty?"

"On the surface it would appear so," my father said. "But there are too many contradictions that cannot be ignored. The thief and the secret lodger are heavy smokers, yet the stable boy avoids tobacco like it was the plague. We assume the boy acted under the influence of an hallucinogen, but we cannot explain where he obtained it or how he could have afforded such an expensive drug. And then there are the matching footprints, which I must admit would not stand the test before an official inquiry. Nonetheless, the closeness of the match weighs heavily in the boy's favor."

"So you have real doubts as to his guilt, then," said I.

"Don't you?" he replied.

"What say you, Joanna?"

"I will have my say once the document is recovered," she answered.

After freshening up, we retired to the inn's dining room and ordered seasoned lamb chops. The chablis from an obscure village in France was nicely chilled and tasty enough to require a second filling of our wineglasses. My father and I discussed the case of the missing document at length, going over each fact and each occurrence, and even attempted to explain away the contradictions. Joanna listened to our words and conclusions, but made no comment although her interest was obvious. On several occasions I watched her eyes twinkle, followed by a hint of a smile, but I could attach no meaning to these expressions. Our conversation was interrupted by the approach of the inn's owner.

"Good evening," he greeted. "And thank you for dining with us. I feel certain you will find the lamb to your liking."

"We shall look forward to it," Joanna said.

"And now that the ruckus in the woods has died down, I am of the opinion that all can enjoy a comfortable night's sleep."

"Were there complaints from the guests?" Joanna asked.

"Only from the French, but they complain about everything."

"None from the mysterious lodger on the ground floor?"

"Not a peep."

"I am surprised it did not disturb his writing."

"Apparently not, for he went about his business as usual," the innkeeper said. "And his appetite remains good, for he cleaned his plate of lamb chops that was served promptly at 7 P.M. sharp. It would seem he is content and only wishes to be left alone."

"So it would seem."

"Well then, enjoy your dinner which should be coming shortly."

Joanna waited until the innkeeper was out of earshot, then turned to us and said in a low voice, "And so we are again faced with the same contradiction, the solution to which will unravel the puzzle of the missing French treaty."

I quickly leaned forward. "What is this contradiction?"

"How could Roger Bennett be dining in his room at the very same time he is handcuffed to a bed in the butler's cottage?"

My father nodded at the undeniable conclusion. "It is not possible, which indicates that Roger Bennett is not the secret lodger."

"Obviously."

"But who then is this secret lodger?" I asked.

"The thief, who must bear close resemblance to Roger Bennett," said Joanna.

My father lowered his voice to a whisper and asked, "Should we not alert Scotland Yard?"

"We shall," Joanna said. "But not until we have the proof and the document in hand."

22

The Evidence

The swelling around the fracture site had not diminished. Both my father and the kindly country doctor, Joseph Bell, agreed that another day or two would be required before a cast could be placed on Roger Bennett's leg.

"I do not believe any adjustment of the fracture will be needed," Bell said in a low voice at the entrance to the butler's cottage. "I have encountered these injuries before and once the swelling subsides the ends of the bone tend to fall into place."

"I of course will bow to your expertise on this matter," my father said graciously. "But what if this does not occur?"

"Then it will have to be set by better hands than mine or the fractured ends will never unite, and the boy will be left with a permanent, painful limp."

"That is not the greatest of his concerns at the moment."

The elderly country physician nodded sadly. "So I have been told."

My father watched the country physician walk to his waiting carriage, then turned to us and lowered his voice further. "I did not wish to contradict my colleague's opinion, but I can assure you the swelling about the fracture will persist into the weekend. No one would dare cast it until then."

"Lieutenant Dunn will not stand for it," I said.

"He will have no choice, for Dr. Bell's vote and mine far outweigh his authority, and thus young Bennett will be treated as any other patient."

"I would not put it past Dunn to withhold the stable boy's pain medication to persuade the lad to give up the information," I opined. "I am afraid he has that ruthless look about him."

"We shall see that it does not happen."

We entered the butler's cottage, with Joanna a half step in front of us. Using her foot, she cleared away the cluttered items on the floor of the sitting room. The torn-up cushions and pillows were of particular concern, and she made certain they were neatly stacked against the wall.

"It is foolish to leave a room in such disarray," Joanna remarked. "Any obscure or hidden clue will be covered by the shambles Lestrade's men left behind."

"What do you expect to find?" I asked.

"Proof," Joanna said, picking up a dictionary and flipping through its pages.

"The document could not possibly be tucked away in a book, no matter how large," I said.

"But it might contain a clue as to the document's whereabouts." Joanna reached for a second and third book, and found them empty as well. "We must leave no stone unturned."

"If only Roger Bennett would speak," I said, with a sigh.

"Perhaps he already has."

My father led the way into the bedroom, which now carried a stale body odor. Roger Bennett was no longer handcuffed to his bed and was now propped up on several pillows, which gave us a better view of him. He had boyish good looks, with a straight nose and thin lips, and his eyes were blue as the sea but still filled with fright.

"How is your pain this morning?" my father asked.

"It will not let up, sir," Bennett said. "It is like a pounding in my leg that increases with every beat of my heart."

"That is a good sign, for it indicates blood is rushing to the fracture site and this will promote the healing process."

"But please, sir, might I have more of the pain medicine while it is healing?" Bennett requested.

"How many times have you received it?"

"Only twice, sir."

My father gave Lieutenant Dunn a stern look and said, "As I prescribed last night, he is to have laudanum every four hours unless he is asleep. Are we clear on this matter?"

Dunn only stared back, but Lestrade nodded.

"You do realize what is at stake?" Dunn said.

"Yes. Our civility, which we will not relinquish whatever the circumstances." My father turned to Joanna and asked, "Do you have any questions for Mr. Bennett?"

Joanna moved in closer to the bed and studied the stable boy's face for a moment before saying, "You must tell the truth in every detail, for not to do so will weigh heavily against you."

"I do not lie, madam, for my dear father taught me never to do so," Bennett said in earnest.

Dunn made a derogatory utterance, which Joanna ignored.

"While in the forest, did you happen to see anyone?" she asked.

"No, madam," Bennett said.

"Think hard," Joanna pressed.

Bennett furrowed his brow in thought, then clenched his jaw against a bolt of pain that came and went. Taking a deep breath, he went back to the question. "I saw no one within the forest itself, but I did spot two young lads near the edge closest to the inn."

"What was their purpose?"

"I could not be sure, but they were not far from the inn's kitchen and sometimes little beggars wait there for discarded food."

"Can you describe them?"

"No, madam. Except one was tall and the other quite short."

Joanna nodded at the honest response. "So there was no one else, man or woman?"

"No one else, madam."

"It struck me as odd that you would remain in the forest while it was under such close scrutiny," Joanna continued. "Why not slip away in the dark of night and head for London where you could lose yourself?"

"I had no money except for a few farthings that would not take me very far. But in my room I had hidden away a five-pound note, which was my life's savings. My plan was to fetch it and then flee."

"Here you are being less than truthful," said Joanna. "Despite your lack of funds, you attempted to escape from Hampshire on one occasion, did you not?"

"I did," the stable boy affirmed. "For I was desperate, you see, and could not hide in the woods forever."

"So you decided to steal away in the darkness on Trevor MacGregor's dogcart, but the mare went lame and you were forced to turn about and come back to the stable."

Bennett's eyes widened in astonishment. "How could you know this? It was well past midnight and all the lights were out."

"I make it my business to know what others don't," Joanna said. "But again, you had no funds save for a few farthings. Surely you could not survive on such a meager amount."

The stable boy hesitated before admitting ashamedly, "I planned to sell the dogcart and somehow arrange for the mare to be returned to the good Mr. MacGregor."

Dunn scoffed, "How thoughtful."

Joanna ignored the remark and went on with her questioning. "Why not stay and profess your innocence?"

"Because everything was against me, just as before, and I had no way of defending myself."

"Your father could have helped."

"But he was murdered, madam! The kind old man was killed for no reason at all," Bennett said, his voice choking with emotion.

"Oh, there was a reason all right," Dunn interrupted. "He discovered your guilt and was about to turn you in, so you murdered him."

"I did not!" Bennett cried out.

"And you hoped the evidence he had against you would die with him," Dunn shouted back.

"I would not kill my dear father, for he was so kind and so—"

"Give it up, boy!" Dunn demanded. "Give it up and perhaps the court will reconsider your punishment."

"But I am not guilty!" Bennett pleaded.

"Tell that to Henry Miller whose skull you destroyed with a pickax."

"But Henry was my friend."

"And Charles Bennett your father," Dunn said angrily, then shook his head in disgust. "Have you no conscience, boy?"

Joanna held up her hand for silence between the two and waited for the air to calm. "I have only a few more questions, but answer them carefully, for your guilt may hang in the balance."

Bennett pricked his ears, all of his attention now focused on Joanna and her words. "I will tell you only the truth, madam."

"Why did you not use the bicycle in the stable to escape?" Joanna asked. "There was a spare wheel hidden beneath a woolen blanket and all you needed to do was attach it. Then you could have been gone."

"But there was an important bolt missing that was required to secure the wheel," Roger Bennett explained. "Only Walter could have obtained it and I was not about to bring my troubles onto my dear friend and ruin his life forever. I know the penalty for just helping a thief all too well. Such an untrue charge once cost me a year in prison."

Joanna nodded at the stable boy's believable explanation, then asked, "Why did you not hide in the shed where there was some warmth and protection against the elements?"

"Because the dogs would have found me quicker than you can whistle."

"You could have covered your scent with cayenne pepper, just as you did with the cave."

"I beg your pardon, madam, but that is not so. The cave

had a small entrance, no more than three feet across, and thus the pepper could be sprinkled at its mouth and the surrounding area. The shed is much, much larger and there was not nearly enough pepper to cover it and the ground around it. And one good rain would have washed it away anyhow."

"Surely you must have sought shelter in the shed at some time."

"No, madam. I stayed well clear of it, for I knew the police would be watching."

"But in the wetness and cold of a cave, you must have become ill."

"No, madam. I was never sick."

"Not even a bad cold?"

"My health remained good," Bennett insisted, and reached up to scratch his tousled blond hair. "That is probably the result of my vigorous training."

"I see you are right-handed."

"Yes, madam."

"I have one final question. When you bale hay with a pitchfork, which hand do you place on the end of the handle?"

"The right, madam, for that is by far my strongest."

As Joanna stepped out of the bedroom, she beckoned to Lestrade and Dunn to follow her. In the middle of the sitting room, she turned and, after giving them a long, serious look, proclaimed, "The boy is innocent."

"What!" Lestrade cried out.

"Innocent," Joanna repeated.

"But all the evidence is against him."

"To the contrary, Lestrade, all the facts say otherwise. Shall I list them for you?"

"Please do."

"One," Joanna said, holding up an index finger. "Do you

truly believe a poorly educated stable boy has the wits to kill his father with cyanide and cover his crime with the pretext that his father committed suicide by carbon monoxide poisoning?"

"Hardly evidence of innocence," Dunn scoffed.

"There is more," Joanna said, as she raised a second finger. "If he murdered his father, why would he risk everything to honor the man by coming to his funeral in broad daylight? That is the act of either a fool, which the boy is not, or someone who is mentally disturbed, which he shows no evidence of."

"I wondered about that myself," Lestrade said. "And the boy clearly loved his dad."

"Clearly," Joanna agreed, and held up a third finger. "Now you must also consider this. The suspected killer was seen up close by the village tobacconist and appeared to be quite ill, with a very sallow complexion. Yet Roger Bennett shows no sign of chronic illness and has the facial color of a trained athlete. How can we explain that away?"

"Perhaps he was lying about being ill and has since recovered," Dunn proposed.

Joanna turned to my father. "Watson, as a physician with many years' experience, could someone so complected revert back to normal in a matter of days?"

"Never," my father replied. "Such a pale, sallow color often remains for a week or more after the illness has passed."

Dunn sneered at the finding. "I do not believe a change in complexion lessens the boy's guilt."

"But it does raise doubt," Joanna contended. "It has been my experience that one doubt leads to another and yet another, and when all are placed together the end result is innocence."

An expression of concern crossed Lestrade's face. "Are there other matters that should be brought to my attention?"

"There is a most important clue you have overlooked," Joanna said.

"Which is?" Lestrade asked at once.

"The abundance of evidence that shows our thief is addicted to tobacco."

"Addicted, you say?"

"Deeply so. Do you not recall the cigar ash in the attic space and the numerous cigarette stubs left behind in the shed?"

"I do indeed."

"Then you are facing a difficult dilemma, Inspector," Joanna said. "On the one hand you have a thief who smokes continuously, and on the other a stable boy who avoids tobacco at all costs, yet you declare the two of them to be one and the same person. How do you account for this discrepancy?"

Lestrade remained mute as he searched for an answer. With a shrug, he glanced over to Lieutenant Dunn who could offer no assistance.

"Thus the doubts mount, do they not?"

"They do indeed," Lestrade concurred, with a slow nod. "Moreover, it is clear that the lad is not addicted, for never once during his arrest has he requested tobacco. It has been my experience that when heavy smokers are placed under stress, their urge for nicotine increases even further." The inspector turned to Dunn and asked, "Have you witnessed this as well?"

"I have on a number of occasions," Dunn replied. "They crave tobacco to the point of mania."

Lestrade turned back to Joanna. "Is there other evidence that points to the boy's innocence?"

"There is one final observation that I believe is most important," Joanna answered. "Roger Bennett is right-handed."

"So?" Dunn asked.

"Henry Miller was killed by someone wielding a pickax from the left side, which indicates the murderer was left-handed."

"Maybe the boy is ambidextrous," Dunn said.

"It would not matter, for the dominant hand always dominates, particularly in acts of violence," Joanna elucidated. "I would advise, Lestrade, that you rethink our case, for the evidence you have will not hold up in my court."

"This does cast a different light on the case," Lestrade had to admit. "What say you, Lieutenant?"

"The lady's arguments do raise doubt," Dunn conceded. "Yet I am not totally convinced of the stable boy's innocence."

"Dwell on the doubts and you soon will be," said Joanna.

"My superiors in London will demand more substantive evidence than that which you have presented," Dunn called after us as we headed for the door.

Joanna turned to respond, but her foot caught on a torn cushion and she tripped. Quickly she reached for the wall to steady herself and, in the process, dislodged a large, framed photograph that fell to the floor and came to rest atop the cushion. As Joanna picked up the photograph to rehang it, she studied it briefly, then jerked her head forward. Hurriedly she took a magnifying glass from her handbag and examined the family photograph once again.

"What is it that so draws your attention?" I asked.

"The missing link," Joanna breathed.

"Which is?"

"The evil one," Joanna said, then called out to Lestrade, "Inspector, please come immediately and bring Lieutenant Dunn with you."

The men rushed out, both sensing the urgency in Joanna's voice. They rapidly glanced around, as if expecting some danger. Dunn had his hand inside his coat next to his weapon.

"Do you require assistance?" Lestrade asked.

"Only if you wish me to solve this case before the sun rises tomorrow."

"I do, madam. I most certainly do."

"Then you must follow my instructions. First, I will require the name and phone number of Scotland Yard's most experienced officer when it comes to investigating criminal records. He must have immediate access for all of England."

"Easily done."

"The second request will not be so easy for you. I must insist that you withdraw most of your security forces from the Halifax estate immediately."

"Impossible!" Lestrade said at once.

"There is no other way and failure to do so will guarantee failure," Joanna went on. "To explain such an abrupt withdrawal, you must spread the rumor that the document has been traced to Surrey and all efforts must therefore be concentrated there. See to it that everyone on the estate is made aware."

"But, madam," Lestrade argued, "we believe the document is here and we still do not have it."

"Follow my instructions and you shortly will."

23

The Bait

As Joanna predicted, it was 6:45 P.M. when the chamber-maid strode out of the rear entrance to the inn and gave the impression she was taking a moment to stretch her back.

"Ah! The message carrier!" Joanna said.

We moved away from the window in our room and watched the chambermaid casually walk to the front of the inn. Glancing briefly over her shoulder, she veered off to a riding path where a rider and his horse awaited.

Joanna quickly reached for the handheld telescope that Little Alfie had purchased, and focused in on the meeting. She adjusted the telescope in the fading light before an-nouncing, "It is the Halifax chauffeur who serves as the relay."

"To Elizabeth Halifax," I noted.

"And so the play begins."

"And what do we do now?"

"Wait for the next act." Joanna stepped forward and again adjusted the telescope. "Hello, there!"

"What?"

"Now they kiss, which indicates they are lovers and not simply acquaintances," Joanna said, nodding to herself. "In all likelihood, the faithful chauffeur has demanded his woman not utter a word of their attachment. That is why I did not hear of it the night I visited the local pub."

"I will wage you a guinea she is being paid as well," Lestrade commented.

"That too can ensure silence."

The horse and rider galloped away and disappeared in the dimness. The chambermaid gave her back a final stretch and returned to the inn.

"Do you think she is involved?" Lestrade asked.

"No," Joanna replied. "They are only using her as a carrier."

There was a brief rap on the door and my father entered, with a bounce to his step. He hurried over to us and said, "The word is out. The entire village is speaking of the sudden withdrawal of security from the Halifax estate."

"Do they know the reason?" Joanna asked.

"Oh, yes," my father answered. "They believe the missing document is in Surrey and will soon be in the hands of the authorities."

"Well done, Watson," Joanna praised.

Lestrade let forth a worried sigh. "You do realize that if your plan does not work and the document slips away, my head will be on the chopping block."

"And if it does succeed, you no doubt will be invited to the queen's birthday party," Joanna said. "Now I trust you left behind a few guards at the butler's cottage, for not to do so would raise suspicions that something was amiss."

"Not to worry," Lestrade said. "Two constables were posted at the door and they are the only visible security."

"Excellent," Joanna said. "Then our trap is set."

"How can you be so convinced the thief will show?" Lestrade asked.

"Because, with no apparent security, we have given him an open avenue to sell the document and be on his way," Joanna replied. "He will find the opening irresistible."

"And we grab him at the exchange," Lestrade concluded.

"But this villain is most clever," my father warned. "If he detects even a hint there is a trap, I fear he will kill Elizabeth Halifax and escape with both the document and the money."

"That is the risk we take when playing this dangerous game," Joanna said.

"But the greatest risk is for Elizabeth Halifax," my father noted concernedly. "I am afraid she is not aware of the danger she faces."

"She cannot be that blind."

We waited in silence, with one eye on the riding path and the other on the space between the inn and the forest. Not a word was spoken, but our worries were all the same. Would the plan work as designed? Would harm come to Elizabeth Halifax? Would the clever thief see the trap and back away from it? And most importantly, I thought with my emotions stirring, would the document, on which so much depended, fall into the enemy's hands and seal the fate of England?

"How much longer?" I asked impatiently.

"Shortly," Joanna said. "For the lodger's demands must be answered quickly."

"I would think he will be giving instructions."

"When one has absolute power, instructions become demands."

"But why the rush?"

"Because he does not want to give her time to think or change her mind and alert the authorities."

Once again our attention was drawn to the window. Below, a solitary figure strolled by and headed for the riding path. Although the light was fading rapidly, we could recognize the figure's face. It was the waiter who served the lodger dinner in his room every night.

"Yes!" Joanna said under her breath. "He comes for the return message."

"Which states?" Lestrade asked.

"Elizabeth Halifax's acquiescence."

"I have a bad feeling here," I admitted.

"I do as well," Lestrade said. "He is such a clever devil to use the chambermaid and the waiter as messengers."

"Which I anticipated," Joanna said.

A quizzical look crossed Lestrade's face. "How could you possibly have known that?"

"Think about it, Inspector," Joanna coaxed. "Here we have a secret lodger who spends the entire day in his room and avoids all contact with the outside world. The only two people who come near him, but never see his face, are the chambermaid and the waiter. Thus they are the only ones who could serve as his messengers."

"And they no doubt are handsomely paid for their services."

"And for their silence as well."

In the distance we heard the sound of approaching hoofbeats, drawing nearer and nearer.

"Are your men ready?" Joanna asked Lestrade.

"Ready and armed, with Lieutenant Dunn taking the lead," Lestrade replied. "Dunn is not a bad sort, you know, and is only intent on carrying out his orders, which come from the highest level."

Joanna shrugged indifferently. "Nevertheless, he is a professional soldier who is not very imaginative and at times gets in the way. But I will say this for him. In a fight to the death, he is the one you want on your side."

"Do you anticipate such a fight?"

"We are dealing with a traitor who has already killed two innocent people. He will not hesitate to kill more rather than face the certain fate of a hangman's noose."

"I had best stress that point to my men."

"A wise decision."

As Lestrade departed, the sound of hoofbeats grew louder and louder and were almost upon us. My heart began to race in anticipation of what was to come next and I had to strain to hold myself still. But Joanna showed no emotion whatsoever. She seemed to care little for the people involved and even less for the consequences they might face. Her only focus was on the chase and a successful conclusion. My father had once commented that Sherlock Holmes was the very same, for untangling a difficult case was all that mattered to him, with everything else being insignificant. Thus it would seem Joanna had inherited that trait from her father as well.

The hoofbeats stopped abruptly, so we crept closer to the window. To our surprise, it was not the horseman we had seen earlier, but the Halifax carriage itself. The driver remained in place; the door did not open.

"Things will now move along quickly," Joanna said. "Watson, do you have your service revolver?"

"At the ready and fully loaded," my father responded.

"If you must shoot, aim for the leg."

"Which would ensure he lives and gives us the pleasure of watching him hang."

"True. But more importantly, we do not want him dead in the event he did not bring the document with him."

The carriage remained in place, with its passenger inside and motionless. The driver glanced around continually, obviously on the alert, but we could not tell if he was armed. My gaze went back to Elizabeth Halifax and I again wondered if she had any idea of the danger she was about to face.

"It seems so unfair to use her as bait," I said quietly.

"Fair has nothing to do with it," Joanna replied without inflection. "For there are no gentlemen's rules here. She has chosen to play in the game of treachery and she must assume the risk."

"But she takes on such a great personal risk."

"It is not for herself alone that she does it."

"For England, then?"

"And for her husband."

We heard the sound of noisy clatter coming from the first floor of the inn. It was the group of French tourists who were either entering the inn for dinner or leaving for an evening stroll. I hoped it was not the latter, for if it was, they were about to find themselves in the midst of a terrible danger. Now there was laughter and the booming voice of the innkeeper.

Joanna nudged me quietly with her elbow. "The carriage door opens."

Elizabeth Halifax stepped out into the dimness, clutching only an envelope in both hands. She remained stationary, close to her carriage.

"No purse," I noted.

"No purse, no weapon," Joanna said. "That too was no doubt part of her instructions."

"Careful devil, isn't he?"

Joanna nodded. "That is why he has stayed free so long."

Elizabeth Halifax was gazing around nervously, as if waiting for someone or a signal to appear. Then, ever so slowly, she began to walk to the side of the inn, with each step measured. As she reached the edge of the forest, a shadow suddenly came up behind her.

"Come quickly!" Joanna urged, sprinting for the door. "There is not a second to lose!"

We hurried along the corridor and down a flight of wooden stairs, only to find our passage blocked by the group of French tourists standing in front of the dining room.

"Make way!" Joanna shouted.

But the French tourists did not move and only gave us puzzled looks of not understanding.

"*Écartez-vous, je vous en prie!*" my father cried out.

As they stepped aside, the innkeeper rushed out of the dining room.

"There is great danger outside!" Joanna warned. "You must lock the door and let no one in or out!"

We dashed through the front entrance and turned for the side of the inn. As we passed the Halifax carriage, we saw the driver slumped over in his seat, bleeding profusely from a head wound. It immediately became clear what had transpired. The secret lodger had somehow managed to slip out of his room unnoticed and gotten to a hiding place where he waited for the Halifax carriage to arrive. Once Elizabeth Halifax had stepped away, he silently dispatched the driver. Surely she would be next.

"There!" Joanna pointed through the misty drizzle. The

secret lodger was holding a torch that allowed Elizabeth Halifax to see the document and make certain it was genuine. "Notice the weapon he is grasping behind his back."

I focused in on the figure's left hand, but saw only a small sack in his grip. "I see only a sack."

"That is not a simple sack, but a sap that can crack open a skull noiselessly."

"Which he used on the driver."

"And plans to use on Elizabeth Halifax."

"Perhaps we should rush him now," I pressed.

"Wait until she produces the money, for that will distract him," Joanna instructed.

Suddenly the horse behind us whinnied nervously, which caused the secret lodger to glance over and spot us. In an instant, he grabbed Elizabeth Halifax by the throat and spun her around, using the woman as a shield. "Who goes there?" he yelled.

"The daughter of Sherlock Holmes," Joanna answered calmly. "You are surrounded, with no hope of escape. It would be in your best interest to surrender and bring no harm to the Halifax woman."

The lodger, holding Elizabeth Halifax tightly, began to back his way into the forest. He was far taller than her, so most of his head remained exposed.

"Watson, is there enough of his head showing to give you a clear shot?" Joanna asked quietly.

"More than enough," my father said.

"Then I would like you to fire a warning shot when I give the signal," Joanna said, then raised her voice to the secret lodger. "Making it to the forest will do you no good, for Scotland Yard is there waiting for you."

The lodger hesitated.

My father was crouched in the firing position and taking his aim. On first thought, I had no doubts about his skill as a marksman, which he had honed during his days in the Second Afghan War and had maintained resolutely over the years. But then I recalled he had not visited the practice range since his stroke months ago.

The lodger appeared to be raising his hand that held the sap.

"Now!" Joanna cried out.

The shot came so close to the lodger's ear that it unnerved him. The sap dropped from his grip and, releasing Elizabeth Halifax, he sprinted for the forest. But rather than enter the woods, he turned for a large tree that had thick limbs that drooped toward the tin roof of the inn. Up the tree he went, hand over hand, like an animal with claws, and disappeared into thick foliage.

"He is treed!" I exclaimed.

"Keep your revolver at the ready, Watson," Joanna directed. "And now you may shoot to kill, if necessary."

Lestrade and Dunn ran to us, with revolvers drawn. There were two constables behind them and a third was attending to the badly shaken Elizabeth Halifax. All had bright torches that they pointed at the high, dark area of the tree.

"We shall just wait him out, then," Lestrade said, catching his breath.

"He did not climb the tree to be caught," Joanna said. "The thief has skills you do not know of."

"Is he a magician?" Lestrade scoffed.

Above in the high shadows of the tree, we heard the noise of branches moving. The sound grew louder as the torches went to a figure, with his arms fully extended, who was swinging back and forth on a thick limb. Each swing took him closer and closer to the inn until he was a mere five feet away. On the final swing he released himself and, seeming to fly through the air, landed feetfirst on the tin roof of the Hampshire Inn.

"We cannot allow him to reach the other side where there is a stable and hidden riding paths!" Joanna cried out.

More constables came out of the woods and raced for the far side of the inn, but the secret lodger was already at the peak of the roof and climbing over, using a chimney stack as a hold.

Joanna turned to my father. "Another shot, Watson, but preferably to the shoulder."

My father crouched and fired, but this time his aim was a fraction off. The bullet missed the lodger's shoulder, but caught his arm just above the elbow. As he screamed and grabbed for the wound, he lost his grip on the brick chimney and fell backward, tumbling head over heels off the wet roof. He landed headfirst, with a loud thump, not more than ten feet away from us.

We rushed over to the secret lodger who was obviously dead with a badly broken neck. His opened eyes did not blink as rain splashed into them. To be certain of death, my father checked for a carotid pulse, then shook his head, showing no regret.

Lestrade shined his torch at the corpse's face and jumped back. "Holy God in Heaven! It is Roger Bennett!"

"No," Joanna said. "It is Roger Bennett's twin brother, Richard."

"Blimey!" Lestrade leaned over for an even closer look. "Did you know this all the while, madam?"

"Like the rest of you, I had no inkling at the start," Joanna admitted. "But the thought crossed my mind when Roger

Bennett began to appear in different places at the same time. Of course, it could have been someone else who just happened to resemble the stable boy, which I considered the more likely possibility. But then this morning, I accidentally dislodged a framed family photograph as I was leaving the butler's cottage. While replacing it on the wall, I saw two young boys, arm in arm, with identical faces. That is when I knew there was a twin. But to put the pieces of the puzzle together and make certain all the facts fit, I required the twin's entire history. Only his biological father and his stepfather could have provided that, but both were dead."

Lestrade nodded knowingly. "That is why you asked for the name of Scotland Yard's most experienced detective when it came to old records."

"And he is to be commended, Lestrade, for he was most helpful," Joanna continued on. "I believe you will find the history fascinating, as I did. Charles Bennett and his wife, now long dead, had identical twins that they could ill afford to raise. The youngest by five minutes, Richard, was given to Charles's brother, a dockworker in Liverpool. As a juvenile, the boy was in continuous trouble, with fights and vandalism and torture of small animals. He even fought with his father, whose death from a fall was called accidental, although the police had a suspicion the boy had precipitated it."

"Bad to the core," Lestrade commented.

"It becomes worse. He was arrested numerous times for drunkenness and brawling, and spent some time in a local jail. He eventually ran away from home at age twelve to join a circus. That is where he learned to become an acrobat, which he so aptly demonstrated tonight. But trouble followed him and he was arrested for fights and petty larceny and unfortunately was shown leniency because of his age. However, when he progressed to armed robbery, he was given a ten-year sentence at Pentonville where he became the meanest of the mean, and seemed to enjoy killing other inmates when the guards were absent. In that dreadful place, murder meant nothing except it provided an empty cell that could be used promptly for an incoming inmate. After several failed attempts, the twin managed to finally escape using his circus skills. He made metal spikes for his shoes and several for his hands, which allowed him to climb over the stone walls of Pentonville."

"So it was the lack of sunlight in prison that gave him the sallow complexion," I remarked.

"Which the tobacconist took for being the result of illness."

"But why return to Hampshire?"

"For several reasons, I should think," Joanna replied. "First, you must recall that he spent summers here when his family came to visit. He and his twin brother no doubt explored every inch of the estate, so he knew it well and believed he could find the perfect hiding place. During those visits, he in all likelihood became acquainted with the surrounding villages and the valuables they might hold. As you mentioned earlier, Inspector, there has been a recent rash of burglaries and break-ins at these locales that have gone unsolved. Beyond a doubt, it was Richard Bennett who committed these crimes which provided him with the funds to buy expensive cigars and pay for lodging at the Hampshire Inn. But the most compelling reason for his return to the Halifax estate would be that he dreamed of even more money and planned to rob the grand manor of something that could fetch a handsome price on the black market. That is why he was in the attic space searching about when he learned of the very important French Treaty. He managed to steal it, but could not escape with the document because the estate was placed on immediate shutdown. Thus he had to hide it and intended to return for it later. But the tight security made this impossible, so he tried to enlist the assistance of Henry Miller, believing the German-born groundskeeper would delight in doing something for the fatherland. When Miller refused, the twin killed him. And of course he killed his father as well. I suspect the twin hid the document in the garage and when he came back to retrieve it, he encountered his father who met the same fate as Henry Miller."

"What a sordid story," Lestrade said, shaking his head in disgust. "What kind of person kills their own father?"

"One without a conscience," Joanna said. "He is the exact opposite of Roger, who is a kind, gentle boy and who, by the way, should be exonerated from his previous crime. It seems that the theft of artworks from the adjoining estate was orchestrated by the greedy owner of the estate. The nasty fellow was recently discovered selling the missing, insured items to a European buyer, and he is now serving a most deserved sentence at Newgate. See to clearing the boy's name, will you, Lestrade?"

"I shall," Lestrade replied. "And because of the trouble we put the boy through, I shall see to it he receives proper care for that leg."

"A nice touch," Joanna praised. "My husband will give you the name of a specialist at St. Bartholomew's."

Gazing down at the lifeless body of Richard Bennett as the rain splattered upon it, Lestrade mused, "Is it not strange that identical twins could turn out so differently, with one being a gentle soul and the other a cold-blooded murderer?"

"That contradiction crossed my mind as well," Joanna

said. "But an Oxford expert was most helpful in that regard. According to scientific studies, twins separated early in life and raised apart often have remarkably different personalities. Thus it is believed that it is environment rather than heredity that in large measure determines the nature of a given individual."

"Whatever the explanation," Lestrade said, stepping aside to allow a constable to cover the corpse with a blanket, "in all my years, I have never encountered a more unusual case."

"It does have its peculiarities."

"I do have a question, madam," Dunn said, as he flipped through the pages of the document to be certain it was intact. "But first, allow me to apologize for underestimating you."

"Apology accepted," Joanna said graciously. "Now, to your question."

"We know that identical twins share identical features, yet Roger Bennett is right-handed while all the evidence indicates that Richard was left-handed. Despite this obvious difference, you persisted in your belief that they were in fact twins. How were you able to reconcile this discrepancy?"

"By consulting with the specialist in twins I just mentioned," Joanna explained. "It also bothered me that the identical twins were not same-handed. But the authority at Oxford told me that this phenomenon occurs in twenty percent of all twins, thus removing the problem."

"But one other problem remains," Lestrade said.

"Which is?"

"Elizabeth Halifax. You see, she knowingly conspired with a traitor, without notifying us."

"But she only did so in an effort to recover the stolen document," Joanna argued. "There is nothing illegal on her part."

"The courts will have to decide that."

Joanna pondered the dilemma for a moment, then said, "I think it prudent we protect her innocence. To do so, I suggest we simply say that she provided information that proved invaluable in catching the thief and regaining possession of the document."

"But that is not the entire story," Lestrade said.

"I am not interested in the entire story, but only in justice being served. We gain nothing by dragging the distinguished Halifax name through the mud."

After the briefest of hesitations, Lestrade pledged his agreement with a nod and an "Amen."

Dunn remained silent, his expression grim and fixed.

Joanna gave him a long, patient look before saying, "I would very much like your amen, Lieutenant."

"Madam, this places me in a most difficult position, for my report becomes an official document of His Majesty's navy," Dunn said. "I cannot in all good conscience sign a document that twists the truth."

"There is no twisting here, for it is a fact that she provided assistance of great importance in recovering the stolen document," Joanna argued. "Perhaps unknowingly, but nevertheless she did."

"And therein lies the problem, madam," Dunn persisted. "There is no certainty her intention was to aid us."

"Her intentions were to place her life on the line to regain the missing document and restore her family's good name. Can you name me intentions better than those?'

"You make a very convincing argument, madam."

"Then say what we have decided and omit any mention of intention. Thus, you will have signed your name to a factual document. I can assure you that once the missing document is in the First Sea Lord's hand, he will not press the issue of Elizabeth Halifax's intentions."

Dunn thought for a long moment, then slowly nodded. "You have my amen, madam."

"A wise choice," Joanna said, then turned to Lestrade. "Please tell Elizabeth Halifax how much you appreciate her cooperation in bringing this case to a successful conclusion. Stress that it was the *confidential* information she provided me at the telegraph office that allowed us to track the thief and gain possession of the missing document. Let her know she has done England a great service."

Lestrade fidgeted in place. "Can you be certain she will understand?"

"I am certain of it, but you must insist on her silence, which she will be bound to once she signs the Official Secrets Act," Joanna went on. "And end your conversation by uttering the word *ikebana*."

"Ikebana?"

"It is the Japanese way of saying that everything is now perfectly arranged."

"Very good, madam."

"Then all is settled."

Joanna linked her arms into mine and my father's as we strolled in the mist back to the front entrance of the inn. In a low voice I asked, "Are you convinced Dunn will keep his word?"

"Absolutely," Joanna replied.

"May I ask why?"

"Because he values his naval career so highly and knows we are close to the First Sea Lord. And that, dear John, is a line he will not dare cross."

"But we are not that close to the First Sea Lord."

"We will be once he has the missing French Treaty in his hands," Joanna said, and turned to my father. "I must say, Watson, your aim was a bit off tonight, particularly with the second shot."

"The dimness played a role, you see," my father asserted.

"Nonetheless, you may wish to return to the shooting range to sharpen your marksmanship," Joanna proposed.

My father's face lighted up with joy. Just the thought of returning to his beloved target practice brought a bounce to his step. He had done it so diligently over the years until his stroke caused him to stop. But now, with his near complete recovery, there was nothing holding him back. At length he said, "I think that would be entirely in order."

"Every fortnight, then?" Joanna suggested.

"If John would be available to accompany me, as he has done in the past," my father replied.

"It would be my pleasure," I said.

"Jolly good." My father beamed, his step even more lively now. "Jolly good."

Joanna gave me a sweet, subtle smile, which I returned, for the very same thought had crossed our minds.

We had our Watson back.

Home

On our return to London, we settled in for a peaceful week-end at 221b Baker Street. I busied myself with the morning *Daily Telegraph* while Joanna and my father went back to their mind-sharpening game, in which they gazed down at the passersby below and noted characteristics that were hidden to even the practiced eye.

"Look, Watson." Joanna beckoned to my father and tapped on the window. "What do you make of the man coming our way?"

My father gave the figure a quick look and replied, "His posture is ramrod straight and he has a military bearing about him."

"Yes, indeed. You will also note that his shoes are well shined and his pants neatly creased."

"As would be expected of a man who spent most of his adult years in His Majesty's army."

"And the color of his skin?"

"Brown, obviously."

"Is it natural or deeply tanned?"

"Impossible to tell."

"Hold on, Watson! He is now raising his hand to signal for a carriage. Note that his wrist is pale, while his face is brown. Thus he is tanned, which I believe is a consequence of his service in India."

"Recently, then?"

"Quite."

"He is out of uniform but continues to wear his ammunition boots, which tells us he is on leave or just retired."

"If it is the latter, he may be recalled," Joanna said gravely. "Events on the Continent grow more dire by the day."

That worrisome comment brought my attention back to the *Daily Telegraph*. Every article on the front page told of the winds of war spreading across Europe, with each side arming themselves to the teeth. Military analysts were predicting that Germany would first invade Belgium, which would draw in France, and then Great Britain. It was to be a conflict like no others before it and would be called a "world war." The dreadful specter of thousands upon thousands of killed and many more wounded weighed heavily on everyone's mind. And to what end? Like most wars, it served the purposes of the powerful at the expense of the weak. It was all insanity and the cost to Britain would be enormous.

"Do not worry, John," Joanna called over. "England will prevail."

"I do wish you would stop reading my mind," I said, putting the newspaper down.

"I am not reading your mind, but your actions," Joanna said. "You are intently reading and rereading the front page of the *Daily Telegraph,* which tells only of the coming war. All

the while you grip the newspaper tightly, which shows us your
anxiety over the matter. And you bite down repeatedly on
the stem of your pipe because you worry over the outcome.
Thus your concern for our country is quite obvious."

"Do you truly believe we shall prevail?"

"I do indeed," Joanna affirmed. "Although the battle will
be long and hard, we should take some comfort in knowing
we have done our small part by recovering the missing French
Treaty."

"Do you think we will ever be allowed to disclose this
case to the public?" I asked.

"In time," Joanna said, and went back to window gazing.
"Ah, Watson! See the middle-aged woman limping our way?"

I returned to my newspaper and scanned the next page.
At the bottom was a brief article stating that a prisoner who
had escaped from Pentonville was killed while being apprehended by police in Hampshire. No details were given,
other than he was being buried in a potter's field. My mind
drifted back to the exciting role we played in bringing Richard
Bennett to justice.

I could only hope that Joanna was correct and that someday the tale of our adventure could be told, for what a tale it
was. But I was having difficulty coming up with a suitable
title. Several came to mind, but none seemed a good fit. So I
turned to my father, the most excellent chronicler of the Sherlock Holmes stories. "Father, were our most recent case ever
to be published, how would you entitle it?"

"Surely you have thought of appropriate titles," he said.

"I keep thinking *The Evil Twin*."

"That gives away too much."

"*The Missing Document*?"

"Too bland."

"What then?"

"*A Study in Treason,* I would think," he replied, and went back to window gazing.

A Study in Treason, I thought to myself. Perfect! So be it. But were I ever to chronicle our remarkable adventure, there remained one question that needed to be answered. "Joanna, during the course of our investigation, you mentioned that the blanket in the shed would narrow down the list of suspects. In my mind, it only told us that the thief would return to the shed and nothing more."

Joanna gave me a warm smile and replied, "Had you studied the blanket more closely, you would have seen its significance."

I shrugged. "It was a fine wool blanket."

"It was much more than that. The blanket was identical to the one in our room at the Hampshire Inn and had some unique features. In particular it had the characteristics of a Harris tweed, which is currently in vogue and in great demand. So I inquired of the innkeeper about the origin of the blanket under the pretext I planned to purchase one during my stay in Hampshire. He informed me that the blankets in the inn were special-ordered from the Outer Hebrides in the north of Scotland where they had been woven into a most excellent tweed. He assured me they were not to be found in any other inn or in any other store in all of Hampshire. Thus, the fine tweed blanket in the shed told me that its possessor had to be a guest at the inn. Since the French tourists, the old woman in the wheelchair, the three of us, and the secret lodger were the only guests, by simple deduction the blanket had to come from the secret lodger's room. All of which made him the thief who would eventually lead us to the missing document."

I sighed quietly to myself. "I must learn to observe more carefully."

"Yes, you must," Joanna said, with another endearing smile.

"I have a final question in the event our adventure ever finds its way into print," I requested. "It is one readers will demand to have answered."

"Which is?"

"How did Richard Bennett go about enticing Elizabeth Halifax into such a duplicitous arrangement?"

"The enticement was straightforward," Joanna said. "Richard Bennett gave Elizabeth Halifax the opportunity to spare her family public disgrace and humiliation. Neither the British government nor the Duke of Winchester nor his son would have paid the ransom, which left Elizabeth as the one to prey upon."

"By what means did they communicate?"

"Of that I cannot be certain," Joanna said. "But keep in mind there was a fair amount of contact between the workers on the Halifax estate and those employed at the Hampshire Inn."

"They all frequented the same pub that you entered while disguised," I recollected. "But who among them would be the messengers?"

"The most likely candidates would be the chambermaid and Elizabeth's driver who were lovers and met secretly at night by the side of the inn," Joanna replied. "Richard Bennett could have paid the chambermaid handsomely to deliver sealed messages to the driver, who would leave them in the carriage to be discovered by Elizabeth. Then the messages could have been exchanged back and forth without anyone noticing."

"So they too could be considered complicit."

"But proving it would be another matter, and it does not merit pursuing, for it would only stir a pot not worthy of being stirred. Let us be satisfied and follow Shakespeare's wise words that all's well that ends well."

"Then my lips are sealed."

"As they should be," Joanna said, then returned her attention to the slow-moving passerby on the street below. "See how the woman limps, Watson. She keeps her leg straight, so as not to bend her knee."

"She does that to avoid placing weight on the joint, for it is her knee and not her hip that is afflicted," my father noted.

"From generalized rheumatism, for you will observe that her hand is gnarled and barely able to hold her cane."

"And it is a chronic disorder, in that her neck is bent down and fixed, which indicates that her cervical spine is fused from long-term inflammation."

I had to interrupt with a question. "If her joints are so diseased, why does she not take a carriage?"

"Because she is a woman of some character and inner strength," Joanna replied. "She perseveres despite her pain and disability."

"Perhaps she cannot afford the usual forms of transport," I suggested.

Joanna shook her head. "The fine cut of her attire tells us she is a woman of means and could easily hire a hansom, if she so wished."

"The elegant jewelry she wears attests to that as well," my father added.

"Particularly the gold necklace that glitters in the sunlight," Joanna said. "Notice she has a bracelet to match."

As I listened to the interchange between my father and

Joanna, I could not help but believe that he and Sherlock Holmes must have engaged in the same mental exercise so many years ago. How strange it was then, I thought on, that the mind of the now dead Sherlock Holmes still resided at 221b Baker Street. And at this moment in history, how fortunate it was for all England.